PENGUIN CLASSIC CRIME



# BECAUSE OF THE CATS

Born in London of English parents, Nicolas Freeling has spent his life in Europe. Since 1964 he has lived in Strasbourg, handily between France and West Germany. In his own words, 'This has made for the intricate problems of the expatriate writer. There are privileges and also handicaps.'

Nicholas Freeling has a world-wide readership and has received every honour known to crime writers. His books have all been published by Penguin, including the 'van der Valk' series set in Holland and the more recent 'Castang' books, which have a French background.

Nicolas Freeling

# *Because of the Cats*

Penguin Books

PENGUIN BOOKS

Published by the Penguin Group
Penguin Books Ltd, 27 Wrights Lane, London W8 5TZ, England
Viking Penguin, a division of Penguin Books USA Inc.
375 Hudson Street, New York, New York 10014, USA
Penguin Books Australia Ltd, Ringwood, Victoria, Australia
Penguin Books Canada Ltd, 2801 John Street, Markham, Ontario, Canada L3R 1B4
Penguin Books (NZ) Ltd, 182–190 Wairau Road, Auckland 10, New Zealand

Penguin Books Ltd, Registered Offices: Harmondsworth, Middlesex, England

First published in the United States by Harper & Row
Publishers, Inc., New York, 1963
Published by Penguin Books Inc. by arrangement with
Harper & Row Publishers, Inc.
First published in Great Britain by Victor Gollancz 1963
Published in Penguin Books 1965
10 9 8 7 6 5



Printed in England by Clays Ltd, St Ives plc
Set in Monotype Times

*All the characters and situations described in this book, without exception, are completely imaginary, as is the town of Bloemendaal aan Zee. Where, incidentally, reference is made to a person or office that in fact exists, such as the Procureur-Général in Amsterdam, or the head of the Children and Morals Department of the police in that city, no connection exists or caricature is intended*

## *Chapter One*

A seaside town in Holland; perhaps sixty thousand people. The Ministry of the Interior will have the exact figures. Brick-built houses; brick-paved streets. Plenty of glass and concrete; large, new, modern blocks, handsome for the most part, with tall, graceful lines tracing spirals and parabolas. Some, of course, really arrogant in their ugliness. The overall impression is fairly homogeneous: serious, durable, liveable, but imaginative. This is a new town, the pride of Dutch building and planning.

It was built to house the young married couples, clamouring for living space. Sited conveniently near the industrial terrains that cluster round the North Sea Kanal, the townsmen are for the most part skilled technicians or rising executives, very proud of their hustling businesses in Velsen or Beverwijk. Transport is excellent; there are half-hourly trains to Amsterdam, Zaandam, and the south, through Haarlem. Many of the girls – and even of the married women – work in light industry in the town itself: plastics, biscuits, underclothes. When all is said Bloemendaal aan Zee is a very pleasant town, perhaps a little featureless.

Characterless would not be a fair comment. The town is still so new as to be raw and self-conscious. A sunny, windy town, for the North Sea air scours through, little checked by the careful breaks and screens of pine, and drifts sand – beautiful fine sand, silvery and insidious – over the brick streets and into every house. The housewives of Bloemendaal make constant war on the sand, and the vacuum-cleaners are always buzzing angrily, but next day the sand is there again, patient and indomitable.

Very modern are the people of the new town; proud of their shining homes. They have indulged themselves in glossy toys – the flowers of the Euromarket. Every second shop seems to sell expensive electrical gadgets, and every third, cars – not just Volkswagens and 'Dauphinetjes' but Mercedes two-twentys and D.S. Citroens.

It is said, proudly, that in Bloemendaal aan Zee, too, is the highest proportion of television sets per capita in all the Netherlands.

Is it because of all this emphasis on the flossy home that the beach seems a little neglected, a little undeveloped? Are these status seekers uninterested in spending money outside their very attractive houses? One does get such an idea. The beach is after all superb. Part of the magnificent strand from Den Helder to the Hook, a strand studded with beach resorts. This strand, however, is cut in two at Ijmuiden, by the North Sea Kanal, which brings the sea to Amsterdam, but cut off, traditionally, the old province of North Holland. 'Pays perdu,' said the inhabitants, angrily. But when Bloemendaal was built the canal barrier was conquered. First the Velsen tunnel, then the Ij tunnel, and lastly a wonderful complex to replace the Hembrug, and carry road traffic as well as the railway over the canal. Engineering masterpieces: Holland's glory; the lost land rediscovered itself.

The consequence was that all the sleepy little towns doubled in size. Wijk aan Zee, Castricum, Uitgeest. But Bloemendaal is completely new; before there was only sand and dune grass. The Ministry of the Interior will not allow it to grow any larger now, and you are thought lucky to live there. Rather a badge of success. To tell the truth, Bloemendaal has no need of tourists and trippers, and is even a little toffee-nosed about them. And despite a vociferous minority in the town council, the beach has been left, deliberately, undeveloped.

Admitted there is a large and fine hotel, and here industry entertains German buyers, lavishly. There is 'Zonnehoeck' which is as near as puritan Holland permits itself to get to a casino. This has a restaurant, large and expensive if not terribly good, and an indoor as well as an open-air swimming pool. Here are held concerts and art exhibitions, jazz festivals and dances and touring stage shows. It has made its owner a rich man, and he is the most vociferous of the minority on the council that would like to see the town more gay and animated. For the younger generation say frankly that it is dull.

Amsterdam is only half an hour by train, but it would be nice to have something here too. On the sea-boulevard, between the tall blocks of flats, there are a few other attractions. The Rembrandt cinema, the Cormorant sea-food restaurant, and some small smart bars. In the town there are three Indonesian-Chinese eating houses, and several 'ice-salons' which sell Dutch snack-bar food: croquettes and loempias and fried potatoes with mayonnaise. Indeed the Admiral de Ruyter Plein, where the Zeestraat slopes down into the little sheltered valley at the town's centre, is called, locally, the 'Fritejesplein' because of its delectable smell of frying potatoes blending with the salt, corrosive beach air. And the beach is there, of course; nobody took it away. One has only to cross over the boulevard. And all the shops in the Zeestraat and the Oranjestraat sell dark glasses and suntan lotion. But the younger generation find it dead, and in the winter decidedly gloomy, and many of their elders, secretly, agree.

This agreement has meant the success of one of the few places that is always alive and gay. On the corner of the boulevard and the Oranjestraat is the 'Ange Gabriel'. The Dutch tend to call it 'Het Engeltje' – the little angel. The diminutive is affectionate; it is a long narrow building and quite large. The narrow end faces the sea; this last a slim tower, with windows on three sides. At ground level this tower is an ice-cream salon, the most popular with youths of Bloemendaal; it has a shooting gallery and the latest records. Upstairs there is billiards, and above that again the owner's flat. But the real Ange Gabriel, for adults, is the building adjoining, in the Oranjestraat.

Here is a really good bar, with a log fire in winter; here is a small restaurant where the service is deliberately very slow indeed, but where the food is French, and easily the best in Bloemendaal. Here is a very quiet nostalgic pianist, and at weekends a lively little jazz combo and a girl blues singer from Germany. The owner knows his business. It is a club really. For intimates it is open till four in the morning, but after midnight you are scrutinised through a judas, and only admitted if Hjalmar approves of you, unless you are known.

Yes, his name really is Hjalmar. Where does he come from? Nobody is quite sure. Norway perhaps? But he speaks Dutch with no accent. Maybe he is from the north, with a dash of exotic blood from some sailor in Gronigen. There is something faintly foreign about him. But he has worked in Hamburg in the night-club business; that might be it. He was one of the first in Bloemendaal. He had had a little 'boîte' on the Thorbeckeplein in Amsterdam, but the premises were cramped, and the lease in some way troublesome. Here, there is no doubt at all of his success. All the personages of the town are known in the Ange Gabriel, and next door the sons and daughters of those personages spend, likewise, much of their time and money. Hjalmar does very well. But there, all the shopkeepers of Bloemendaal do well.

People living here have incomes higher than in any town of Holland, taken on an average. The houses are attractively laid out and gaily painted, furnished in good taste, on wide, well-landscaped streets. Alert, thrusting, educated people. The schools here, too, are excellently equipped, and a surprising number of children go on from them to the professional or technical higher schools, or the universities. Here, they feel – with some self-satisfaction – in the corridors of the Ministry of the Interior, is a town, a creation, to be proud of. Many, doubtless, of our leaders of the future are finishing their education in Bloemendaal.

The police, here, fit well into this picture. They are taller, and better-looking, seemingly, than elsewhere; their uniforms are better pressed, and they speak a purer Dutch. The bureau is large and splendid, and peaceful as a nunnery, since, naturally, there is a shortage of crime here. Better to say a shortage of disturbances, for dishonest business men are known, who embezzle, and think up the most ingenious frauds. But in these quiet streets the neighbours' wives are never shrill or abusive, and all the drunks are polite. Fights in cafés are unknown, and breaking-and-entering is a rarity, though hard boys out of Mokum, that sinful city Amsterdam, have occasionally been tempted by the thought of lush pickings.

There remain, admittedly, the youths of the town. They go in for pinching ridiculous things from shops, out of sheer fantasy; saucepans, or lace brassières. And they are given to joy-riding in other people's cars. But the police shrug at all this. These are well-brought-up children, not poor or neglected. They have to blow off steam sometimes. Crime – that is for the uneducated, the deprived.

Why, then, did the Amsterdam police, of all people, develop an interest in Bloemendaal?

*

Commissaris Boersma, a fat, sedentary, intelligent personage from Friesland, is the head of the department called 'Zeden en kinder-Politie'. This is Dutch for 'Morals and Children'. He lit a match and blew it out irritably, tilting his chair backwards on two legs.

'This is making a fool out of me. Where can these blasted boys come from?'

At the corner of the desk, slouching, legs crossed and pushed comfortably out into the room, Chief Inspector van der Valk spat thoughtfully into the waste-paper basket.

'Damn it, don't do that. This isn't the Zwinderen police bureau; don't behave as though it were.'

Van der Valk did not bother to answer; he had, besides, nothing to say. Old Boersma could be pompous, and tetchy, but he was a good policeman; they got on well together. Which was lucky for him, a new boy. His promotion was recent; his transference to this branch more recent still. He had wondered about it. They were being clever again, he had decided. Good fortune; he wasn't going to complain. But it meant for him an unknown kind of work, to which he was not yet accustomed.

He had passed the exams, and now held a special diploma. But one could not take children for granted. In this branch, he was learning, there were no real rules. He had to assess every happening individually and play by ear. That suited him. And handling children took patience and calm. Friendly, very talkative, with a lazy, joking manner, good at creating confidence, he did well at this work, and enjoyed it.

But in the last six months a pattern had been emerging that worried Boersma, and was slowly crystallising into something unfamiliar. A gang, but not quite like other gangs.

The juvenile police hate gangs. Oh yes, sooner or later they walk into your arms, and that turns out to be only the beginning of your troubles. They do an incredible amount of wanton damage; they steal things and throw them away. They are senselessly brutal, and sometimes ingeniously cruel, and they seem to take unusual pleasure in being detestable to inoffensive persons. They throw knives, bottles, anything handy at you, with force and good aim – but if one of the dears gets hurt there are brutal headlines in liberal newspapers. The psychiatrists might perhaps enjoy all this, but the police did not.

The difference between this gang and other gangs, which worried Boersma, was that its behaviour might be as half-baked as any, but its tactics were remarkably professional. It specialised in flats; it observed, and when no one was at home it simply whipped in and plundered, and destroyed. It might have uncanny luck; more probably it was unusually well supplied with intelligence. And nothing about or after its passage ever gave the faintest hint where it came from.

Gangs usually have an instinct for self-destruction. They display their loot; they show off to parade their cleverness. They leave little signs about – this is the Mark. Nothing so childish about this one, which had evaded all fingers spread to hold it. A tremendous scour throughout Amsterdam was finally mounted. This had excellent results. Two notorious rowdy bands were rolled up and tied with ribbon, and all the wild boys were well damped. Good, good; congratulations.

But three days after a well-publicised trial of twenty-three delinquents, marked by a ferocious peroration from the prosecuting Officer of Justice, followed by some sharpish helpings of corrective training – peppered with acid and quotable phrases – from the Children's Judge, disillusionment arrived with a bang. Three apartments in a 'nice' street by the Beatrix Park were stood on their heads, giving a very pleasant haul; a little under a thousand gulden in money, two cameras, a diamond ring and an unusual amount of damage.

'Getting their own back on the Officer of Justice,' remarked Boersma. 'Those sentences don't catch the boat; re-educating is no substitute for educating. Split the sentence in half; make the boys serve one and the fathers the other – we might see some results then.'

Van der Valk had been there, and found it a sorry affair, even more than usual. But also unusually important. For the first time, there had been a genuine eyewitness. In fact there were two, man and wife; a handsome, pleasant, wealthy couple in the middle forties; typical target. They had been out, and come back in the middle of the evening because the man had a stomach-ache.

'One would have thought there had been a tornado; everything thrown and strewn everywhere. My wife shrieked; I ran towards the bedroom. They came out and jumped on us; seemed to be dozens of them. Weren't of course, there were five; I had an opportunity to see after we were tied up. They gagged us, by the way, with nylon stockings. Ordinary clothes; I can describe, I suppose, but it would only confuse, I think; nothing I could undertake to recognise. They had black hoods with eyeholes and a slit to breathe through. An effective disguise, and scaring, I don't mind admitting. I didn't put up much of a fight – not that I got much chance.'

The other thing that made it important – and unpleasantly serious – was that the wife had been raped. She was in a rest home with shock; Van der Valk got little impression beyond a fair, rather stupid, likeable face that had been very pretty and was even now only a little fleshy. He could guess that her body would match this. She had observed well; shock or not her account was lucid.

'They found a drawer of old stockings – you know how they accumulate – and tied us both up and pushed us on the floor. We couldn't struggle; they pulled our coats down over our elbows. They seemed very calm and unhurried. They went through everything, and took my husband's wallet, and they were ready to go, presumably, when one said – quite coolly too – "She's not bad, is she? Shall we tumble her?" Another said, "The cats won't like it," but the others simply seemed amused, as though it were a – a good joke. I don't know what he can have meant about cats. And . . . well . . . they did.'

'All of them?'

'Yes. It didn't take long; that was the only real mercy.'

'Thank you very much; I won't worry you any further.'

When he got back to the husband this was confirmed.

'The cats.'

'Yes. Said with a sort of a laugh, and yet as though it were serious.'

'That's a very sharp piece of observation.' Van der Valk was wary of witnesses who over observe. They tend to invent.

'I dare say,' said the man levelly, 'that if you were tied up on the floor while six feet away gangsters were raping your wife, you would notice details pretty sharply too.'

'Very good answer,' said Van der Valk unperturbed. 'Any other details? These are valuable.'

'Well, yes. Their voices. They talked – how shall I say? – not like gutter urchins. It sounds peculiar, I agree, but it did strike me. Well brought up, they sounded, and spoke clearly, no mumble or Amsterdam accent.'

'So. That's very good indeed.'

'But I couldn't identify or recognise anyone, I'm afraid.'

'Would be incredible if you could. At that it wouldn't do. Unsupported, a court wouldn't accept it. But it will help us, you know.'

*

Old Boersma was in a rage; he hit his pipe on the big ashtray with such a whack that it snapped, and examined the pieces with ominous self-control.

'A rape. Verdomme, it was all we needed. This demands the exclusive application of your intelligence and industry, you hear? Understand me, Van der Valk; exclusive. It means that you now take the match out of your mouth and begin.'

'Remember saying you wished this was an out-of-town mob?'

'I've checked it as far as possible. Everybody says no.'

'They say no, doesn't mean no.'

'Quite. Apart from taking their word on the matter, what do you propose that I do?'

'Lot of places they could come from; they can't all be sure.'

'Positively no indication. Haarlem, Hilversum, Zaandam – look, I've even been on to Bussum and Purmurend and bloody Bloemendaal.'

'Bloemendaal: mmm.'

'I believe it certainly is an out-of-town mob, but why hesitate over Bloemendaal? That's all a holy crowd, very toffee-nosed and how's-your-father. Child kicks a dustbin over, down there it's a crime. Marcousis says a gang there is impossible without his knowing, and unthinkable anyway. I grant Marcousis is a fool and Rademaker isn't, but I'd be more inclined to begin with Haarlem.'

'I only meant that we haven't a thing to go on that seems probable at all, so I start wondering, that's all.'

'Whole thing's improbable,' with a snort. 'Five boys, described as well brought up, rape a woman in turn, calmly, with nothing to say except that the cats won't like it. Cats. Jazzboys it sounds like.

huh? As though there were others who'd be interested to hear what they'd missed. Peculiar idea.'

'Doesn't sound at all like one of our street-corner gangs; we're agreed there.'

'And then?' irritably.

'So we look for a different type; student type, say. Just made me think of Bloemendaal; lots like that there.'

'So there are everywhere. What's the connexion?'

'Isn't any at all. Wondering whether there wasn't more to the place than meets the eye. It struck me that they're so holy over there, you just said. Bit too holy, maybe.'

Sharp china-blue eyes, across the table. A cranky old cop, perhaps, but quick on a point.

'What are you suggesting? That if a place is very holy and respectable the boys are more violent than elsewhere? You might not be so far out at that. I am thinking of a student gang, yes. But there's a funny pattern. Cold-blooded violence, there's something vicious in that. Students might be violent out of boredom, but hardly vicious.'

Van der Valk picked over his words slowly.

'I was thinking, vaguely, that boys from these so-called good families – they might be so much in conflict, uh, with the background, that they have a rage, possibly to defile, say, as well as simply to be violent. Hence the rape, maybe.'

'Mm yah, revenge rape, to humiliate; been known, perhaps.'

'Like non-combatants being the most violent and vindictive towards the enemy.'

'You've got it all wrong way round,' said Boersma with some amusement. 'You and your intuition; I'm always telling you, to be a good policeman you can't intuit – what is the goddam verb? – a goddam thing. It's too fancy.'

'Just what Captain Queeg used to say.'

'Who the hell are you talking about now? However, we have no idea where to start; may as well begin somewhere. Make a plan, start checking. But don't trip over the local police. Rademaker I can co-operate with, but Marcousis is a touchy bugger. Sent me a memorandum saying he had no – categorical no – gang trouble in Bloemendaal. The suggestion insults him, aha. Don't put yourself in the wrong. Still, one can never learn too much about the territory, or even of the neighbours.' It was one of his great maxims.

As for Van der Valk, he did not take the idea seriously. He would spend his working day in Haarlem; he had talked about Bloemendaal for lack of anything else to say. But he felt stale and stewed. An evening there, after hours, would be fresh air anyway, which might give him an idea about this business. A student gang; might be from anywhere, as Boersma had said. Why Bloemendaal? Why not Zandvoort, or Bussum?

It was a horrible March day, with a gritty wind. He sharpened a pencil that did not really need sharpening, and balanced his knife on his finger, thinking. For five minutes he played the old game of 'messie-steek' with it, which didn't do his linoleum any good. Then he made up his mind, snapped the knife shut and put it in his pocket, and reached for the telephone. Tomorrow would be time to go to Haarlem. This evening, Bloemendaal. He'd better tell his wife.

*

Riding with the rush-hour commuters in the train was not very pleasant. But a car would only be in the way tonight; a barrier to what he wanted. He was going as a tourist, to explore, conscientious.

When he arrived it was nearly dark and unencouraging. It had been raining, here. Not any more, mercifully, and the wind had dropped; be grateful for that too.

People spilled off the train and melted away with their warm voices and busy footsteps, leaving him in a deserted street, the wet pavement lit by one pool of comradely light from a cigar-shop window. The station approach, unencouraging as they always are – one post-box and three apparently dead taxi-drivers – led in a long curve down towards the centre. Rows of featureless shops; the familiar names of every Dutch town, shuttered now and dead with the depression of a closed shopping-centre on a winter's evening. He knew his way vaguely to the beach, and followed it on his feet. Nassauplein; Hofnar cigars and light up a Roxy. Haarlemmerstraat; C. & A. and Vroom and Dreesman. Raadhuisplein; that rather unsatisfactory town hall, Goldschmidt for music. Hugo de Grootstraat; the Bata, Albert Heijn and De Gruyter.

Strandweg; the Caravelle Hotel – dim lights everywhere, a

spidery script in bright blue neon, a nearly empty car park. He could smell the sea, now. Few people were about; it was the slack time when everyone was at home eating. The thought reminded him that he had not eaten, but first, it was important to find the right place to start. This town was an oyster, at which he was picking with feeble fingers. To open it he needed a knife. Journalists in strange towns have this problem and know the solution. One's own impressions are meaningless and can be misleading; it is necessary to find a person who says words unthinkingly, even frivolously, that illuminate a tangled skein and drop, suddenly, the end of the thread in the reporter's hand.

Van der Valk knew this, and also that it might not be easy to find his thread. What was he looking for? What did he wish to hear? He did not know himself.

A huge block of flats towered above him, the climbing plants in every window throwing shadows on the glowing curtains. Zeestraat; the sea was hardly more than two hundred metres further. He could hear the stealthy whisper on the cold liquid sand that is only held together by the matted roots of the tough dune-grass. There was not a soul to be seen; the lamp standards threw a harsh chilly light, and the air stole quiet and cold on his face. It would be worse still on the boulevard. He turned into a side-street, narrower, but less gloomed upon by the concrete blocks.

Duinweg Oos; God, anything to get off these streets. A garage; a cunning expensive little furnishing shop – damn marble-topped coffee-tables with a studied litter of Rosenthal porcelain on them. A radio and television engineer; a row of smaller brick houses. Duplexes; rather nice, he thought. The street was curving away, downhill again back towards the town, but he kept on stubbornly. The lights of another street marching up towards the boulevard could be seen ahead; that would be the Oranjestraat. A hundred metres from the corner was a bar. Nothing fancy, just an ordinary café with a tiny terrace, rattan chairs piled on tables. A narrow signboard saying 'Albatross': the familiar Heineken star and the crown of Dortmund. He pushed the door and went in.

A curved wooden counter. Lamps in the shape of vases of tulips, bowl and flowers alike glowing with lemony light. A good old-fashioned stove and well polished tables; a clean warm welcoming smell. The man behind the bar was tall, thin and round-shouldered. He was playing 'Go' with the only customer, a woman. As he came in she gave a whoop of laughter, seeing a sneaky move and making it. Her fair hair was bleached by sun even in March; bent over the Go board it shadowed her face. The barman looked up, nodded, and smiled.

'What'll it be?'

'You tell me.'

'Rum?'

'No.'

'Anis? Pernod or Ricard.'

'Less bad.' The woman ran a hand through her hair and pushed it back; her face was strongly tanned. She was not pretty. But a wide well-shaped mouth and intelligent eyes; laugh-lines rayed out from the corners; she was perhaps thirty-five, had a faint Slav look.

'A man with sense. Certain to be a stranger.'

'A man with sense,' said the barman, corking the bottle, 'will stay a stranger in this town.'

'Have one with me. One of these; Mademoiselle drinks that too.'

'A stranger who got almost too good manners to be Dutch.'

'Unberufen,' said Van der Valk, grinning.

'No, no, you are not German.' Her grin was as wide as his.

'But you, are – Hungarian.'

'Never. True, I come here from Hungary, but I am from Caspian. I am Tartar. Ha. You play Go? It is no fun to play with Piet, he does nothing all day but practise, practise, and now he is too good, he beat me, I who taught him this game.' She thumped her chest hollowly. 'I need something to eat first. Any chance, Piet?'

'Yes, or course. Nothing wonderful. Uitsmijtertje?'

'No, no,' cried the woman. 'Sandwich, fried egg, schrecklich. You come home with me; I fix something fit to eat.'

'Hey, hey; you are not allowed to take my business away to promote your own,' grinned Piet.

'Ah, kak niet in je broek, we come back, and drink a lot more. Anyway I am allowed everything. Business is bad. Everybody here – ashamed of themselves and their dreadful job. I not.' Her eyes crinkled at Van der Valk. 'You are frightened to come home with whore?'

'What, with food offered too? Certainly not.'

Two more men had come in.

''Lo Fé. Two Pilsies, Piet.'

Van der Valk emptied his glass. 'You two had better by God come back,' grinned Piet, skimming the froth from the beer.

*

She had a top flat, just down the street. She turned the radio on low, and got gay, silly German dance music.

'Later, we find something nice to go on gramophone. But first, food. I have not eaten either. You like farmer's pancake?'

'Very much.' He watched fascinated as she put on an enormous pan, and cut everything up deftly; onions, bacon, cooked potatoes and Spanish peppers; it all went to sizzle in a big lump of butter while she made the batter. He got plates and knives while she made two gigantic pancakes, and got two bottles of beer out of the fridge. The pancake was wonderful.

'Never met a whore that was so good a cook,' happily drinking beer.

She shook her finger, mouth full.

'You never met a whore that was so good whore, neither. My name is Feodora. What are you doing in Bloemendaal? There is nothing here of interest. Except me, maybe.'

There was a good Shiraz rug hanging on the wall. Fierce flowers; this woman suited them well.

'I am not ashamed of my dreadful job. I am a policeman.'

'Good. A policeman. Either a very good one or a very bad one, to be in such bad company as me. You knew I was in Albatross? You are after me for something?'

'No. Didn't know you existed. You don't bother my morals. I'm not here to pester you. To learn things, maybe.'

Her face closed, slightly.

'I know no things. I learn many, yes, but merci, I know how to keep them to myself.'

'All the better. Keep other people's secrets; I don't ask you for them. Keep mine too; I'll know then I'm in good hands.'

'You are here on business, then, eh? Not to go to bed. Vooruit maar, I listen.' She sat on the divan.

'Listen then. What would you think of five boys, none much over eighteen, maybe, who break into houses for fun, break what they do not take, and when interrupted by a man and his wife tie them up, and just for fun – as an afterthought – rape the woman in turn, quite calm and quiet – a woman, mark, old enough to be their mother.'

'Bah. Mean little story you tell me.'

'Happened yesterday in Amsterdam.'

'Little beasts. But I am not surprised. People are always capable, still, of such things.'

'In Bloemendaal, even.'

She finished her beer slowly.

'Now I see what you want. Well, people in this town is the same as in all others, maybe a bit more so. These boys come from here?'

'It's possible. I want to find out if it is more than just possible.'

She puffed loosely at her cigarette, thinking.

'This people here is very bourgeois, because they are very proud of their fine new town. They do not like anything to disturb the pattern. I have to be very careful in my life indeed, nearly so careful as in Russia. They like to complain of me to police, and police here – shit in big boots – you know that? Mistake for me to come here; second Russia. Here they say dirty whore, except for some nice fellows, like Piet there in the bar. Here they do their dirty tricks in the dark, because of whisper whisper. Come by me with their coat collar turned up very high, so their virtue does not get spotted.'

'Yes. I know.'

'You know; good. Well, these virtuous ones, they are very funny with their children. I got no children; I am sterile, therefore am I whore. I make these men babies again; feel nice soft warm mama in bed. But when I had children, even was I whore, I shall look good for them. Important, hein? Difficult world, complicated. But O Maria, these fathers and mothers. Work hard at good job, yes; keep the house clean, yes; and fur coat, winter-sport, new auto – all good things. But the children – they give them too much and too little. Not time to talk to them, but always money to hand out. 'Don't bother me now, child,' they say. 'Mama, how do I get a baby?' 'Don't talk about such things, girl; get away and sew your petticoat.'

'They say dirty whore; I say filthy bourgeois; worse word for worse thing. These children, they grow up; they don't fit in either world. Neither by parents, neither by me. With who will they make friends? Sometimes with bad types, who fill them with fantasies, and that causes trouble. These children have a lot of money; you got people now who make good profit out of that. Here is one fellow good at that.'

'Tell me.'

'Ach, he is a clever fellow. Owns Ange Gabriel in Oranjestraat. You should talk with him really, when you are interested in these children, because he knows them all; they make him good business. He is like me – comes from god-knows-where. I don't like him much. He tries two or three times to sleep with me, but I say no. Because for me he is too much of a hypocrite; Tartuffe, that one. To everybody he shows a different face; the one they want to see. Now I don't talk any more. You bourgeois policeman – no, no, I tease you, I like you, now I show you something different.'

*

Around ten, comfortably full of food and drink, he was watching the billiard players in the Ange Gabriel. Nobody paid him any attention. Four boys played with ritual seriousness, their eyes resting on him occasionally with indifference, as though they thought him daft but were not concerned about it. Two more were playing chess, half a dozen were gossiping over beer glasses. The girls were over by the little counter, drinking coffee and talking, as far as he could judge by gestures, about skirts.

Down the stairs there was more crowd and racket; he was less conspicuous but even more out of place. Here were fourteen and fifteen-year-olds, squawking and giggling. The juke-box wailed epileptically; a boy at the back sighted with concentration along his rifle barrel at a line of little wooden aeroplanes that zoomed erratically across a painted backcloth. Van der Valk drank a cup of coffee, watching a tall boy who stood alone, slouched against the counter staring at nothing. The other boy came back and handed over his rifle.

'Five out of eight. Not bad.'

'Do eight out of eight, in one minute, then talk. Dead easy. The ravens throw up a can, and get it in the air with a pistol.'

'They won't even let you try. Hjalmar won't allow any more anyway.' Envy mixed with admiration in the younger boy's voice.

'I can do the shooting. And I can fix it with Hjalmar,' said the tall one. He was a good-looking boy, eighteen or so, with wavy brown hair and clear pale skin, wearing a suède windcheater, and expensive fawn trousers. 'Be seeing you.' He headed past Van der Valk up the stairs. His voice was clear, superior. He would make the top rung all right, Van der Valk thought.

He walked out, and in at the door of the bar in the Oranjestraat. There was a curtained portière against draught; inside it was dim and warm. The light came from copper brackets; rugs hung on the walls – not such good ones as Feodora's. The barman, in a scarlet jacket, was polishing glasses; there were no more than a dozen people. Through an archway came a smell of good food; he could see two couples eating, and a waiter in white with a long apron. He sat on a stool.

'Quiet night, by the look of it.'

'Be busier later. Ice? Only ten now.' As he spoke another barman came through the curtains at the back, putting a comb in his pocket and straightening his bow, evidently just coming on duty.

'When d'you come off?'

'Eleven. Tonny there's on duty till four.'

'Hi-ey,' said Tonny, absently straightening a bottle. 'Boss not in yet?'

'Over the other side, maybe. You want to get a bit more tonic in, and maybe a couple of bottles of Martini while you're at it.'

'Here he is; I'll ask him for the keys.'

A short, slim man came through the curtains, treading softly as a cat. Quiet, ivory-coloured face; smooth, dark red hair, eyes between brown and green. Handsome. Dinner-jacket, with a sulphur carnation. His voice was youngish, pleasant.

'Need any stuff, boys?'

'Tonny's getting it.'

'Enter it immediately.' Keys jingled. He picked up the bar checks and leafed them through. His eyes slid round the room and met Van der Valk's.

'New blood. Happy to know you.' He held out a firm, cool hand. 'Hjalmar Jansen.'

'Van der Valk.' Hands shook. A voice spoke suddenly in his ear, rusty, like an old gramophone. 'Have a drink, hey.' On the bar stood a raven, its fierce eye studying him cunningly, its beak unpleasantly close to his finger. Hjalmar smiled.

'He does that with a new recruit. Means it, too. Kees . . .' He flicked a finger at the glass and the barman came up with the bottle. Hjalmar poured some water in a glass for the raven and added a little gin. 'Has to have one himself with you.' The bird drank noisily, licked its lips – do birds lick their lips? Or smack them? It stared at Van der Valk and remarked:

'Look out for the cats.'

'Cats?' Hjalmar was stroking the bird, which sat now on his wrist.

'Yes, he makes war on cats, but he's nervous of them, always talking about them. I'm nervous myself sometimes, that one might claw his eyes out.'

'Have a drink with me? You like anis?'

'Thank you but no. Maybe the next time. Try eating here when you come.'

'Now that I know my way here I'll plan that.'

'You do that thing. Good night to you.'

Van der Valk went home, thoughtful. Two interesting encounters.

## *Chapter Two*

'I have a very strong feeling about it. Nothing evidential, nothing to act upon, I grant. But to me it points like a gun-barrel.'

'M'yes.' Mr Boersma had a new pipe and wasn't liking it; put him in a cross-grained frame of mind.

'Cats. You and your intuition. Means what he said it did; why shouldn't it? Bird dislikes cats. All birds do.'

'Very well. But the bird said, distinctly, "Look out for *the* cats.' Specific, detailed. Two occasions now somebody speaks as though they had a houseful of goddam cats.'

'You're stretching the induction to unfair lengths.'

'Something there,' said Van der Valk obstinately. 'I got a tip that this place was a hang-out for the type we're thinking of; discontented, spoilt adolescents. And I found what could be a gang set-up. Boy talks about the ravens; that's certainly a gang. I attach no importance to that on its own. But if they call – seems likely, good mascot – a gang after this bird, and the bird – and our gangsters here – talk about cats, then that seems to me a connexion.'

'No physical connexion.'

'No. A parallelism of idea, call it. Interests me.'

'I don't see it. Ravens. Gang maybe, but boy-scout stuff. Examine their activities, which you heard described. Shooting cans, climbing buildings. Doesn't jibe with raping women and breaking flats. Real hard boys, the ones we want, don't go climbing buildings. Probably couldn't climb over a dustbin unless there was a cop behind them with a sabre. I have respect for your ideas, you know that. For your judgement, too. But these charges are going to be very grave ones. Can't make any moves, in another town's territory, unless you feel quite sure. Tricky ground. No official action possible unless backed by in-con-tro-vert-ible evidence.'

Pleased with his phrase he stuck his pipe back in his mouth. Van der Valk changed the subject.

That evening he annoyed his wife rather, by staring at space and not listening properly. To defend himself, he said that if he were free the following evening he would take her out to dinner.

'Where are we going?'

'Bloemendaal aan Zee.'

'Why there?'

'Oh,' vaguely, 'I was out hunting something up, and came across this place, and it occurred to me you'd enjoy it.' Policemen's hypocrisy. He wondered whether Feodora ever came into the Ange Gabriel. Probably not; her acquaintances in the town would not be best pleased, since they went there themselves.

*

Arlette enjoyed herself greatly. The food was good, and she had pineapple with kirsch, her passion. They ate mussels, and cordon bleu escalopes; a gigantic meal, with two bottles of Moselle wine. Van der Valk felt pleasantly unbuttoned. As seemed to be his habit, Hjalmar appeared, soon after ten, and stopped by their table.

'Ah, you came back. I'm delighted, the more that you've brought your wife. Enchanté, Madame.'

'Help us kill the bottle,' said Arlette happily. He sat down, and showed a liking for conversation.

'I noticed your place next door,' said Van der Valk suddenly. 'Do you find it worth your trouble? I should have thought it clashed a bit with your interests here, but I may be mistaken.'

'Yes and no. It can be a nuisance, but it makes more profit with less worry than this side of the house. I won't bore you with details, but it subsidises me here, where I don't make much profit really – one doesn't, you know, when one wants, and sets out, to do the job properly. But I admit to an interest next door as well. There and here, both hobbies of mine – and it is pleasant to have a business that combines two hobbies' – with a grin.

'That place downstairs is terrible, of course; frankly, my concern there is purely commercial. But upstairs I've succeeded in making a sort of club for these children, which I hope fills a gap in their lives, just as this place is intended to do for adults. After all one has to admit that this is a town where there is little real entertainment. I think I used the word hobby. It amused me to work the idea out and put it into practice.'

'And you don't find them rowdy?'

Jansen spread his hands in self-deprecation. 'I was a bit cunning, ha. They themselves discipline the rowdy element. Their prestige, you see? Self-government. To help I put a pianist in there, too. I was a bit dubious, but they ate it up. If you'll forgive my congratulating myself in this way – but since you're kind enough to show interest – I think that what really made the success was my being there a lot. I have to continue being there a lot, mark; I spend nearly as much time there as I do here. They like that: to see me there; when they realised that I liked talking to them, was not bored, nor simply out for their money, then the place clicked. They want to be liked and approved of; I do both; simple as that.'

Arlette, who had a boy of twelve and another of nine, and enjoyed talking about children, was interested in all this, and was surprised to see her husband appear a little bored. But she was a discreet woman, thought Van der Valk, watching his wife's expression with some amusement.

'Very interesting, that. Do they confide in you at all? I have children the same age – very cagey.'

'I rather think they do. Not deeply perhaps, but about their ideas. I'm quite proud of that – as is shown, hein, by my readiness to talk about it, every chance I get. – I trespass on your quiet. And indeed I trespass on your good nature too; I should be attending to my work.'

'Nice man,' said Arlette, who was very slightly drunk. 'I like it here; good place, good pianist. I must go to the lavatory.'

The waiter brought coffee, which Van der Valk sat stirring, thinking. When he tasted it he realised that he had put sugar in twice.

Yes, nice man. But he could see what Feodora had meant. The man talked to Arlette as though he too were a woman. Chameleon. Was he prejudiced, because he had liked Feodora? Well, forget the man, forget this cats lark. Just put a hypothetical case. Boersma had said that this gang had something oddly adult about it, and something uncharacteristically vicious. Now, imagine an adult, who had some motive for wishing to make war on society. And then suppose that he had a good, cynical idea, to use, for his warfare, a fifth column: the members of that very society in embryo. Now imagine this adult to be someone like Hjalmar Jansen, who seemed to be on such good terms with his adolescent customers.

In order to remain secure from suspicion and eventual discovery this hypothetical man would need to possess an unusual power over them. What could it be, and how would he apply it? Van der Valk did not think his idea would stand up to reflection. Must be nonsense. There'd be a leak at once, of course, he told himself. Since whatever the boys were, they were not discreet. And that was the great drawback to using them. Boy gangsters were efficient, yes; fanatically brave, active, skilful, quick, calm; everything, in fact, bar discreet. Secretive, yes, to adults, but among themselves, on the street, in cafés, they would boast. And when caught, at any time possible and sooner or later certain, they would not keep their mouths shut; they would sing their little heads off. And what would the hypothetical man do then? If he really were clever, he would realise that. Were there any precautions he could take? Van der Valk watched Arlette, talking to the pianist, and Hjalmar, chatting with a little group around the bar.

Could there be some legal trick – that perhaps nothing could be shown to connect him with the gang? If they tried to implicate him, perhaps their words could not be made to stick. He tried to remember his law; rules of evidence, mm. Character witnesses against anyone were suspect, he thought vaguely. Get six boys to declare that a given person incites them to criminal acts. Mm, no defence in law to say someone made me do it. Then your given person produces twenty substantial citizens to declare that such a thing is impossible. And there's no direct evidence at all. How does the court react?

I must be a bit drunk, he thought. This was all fantasy.

It was, he knew from experience, fatal to fall in love with a theory. Too easy to collect evidence that pointed the way you wanted it to point. One assembled a whole collection of suspicious incidents, made so in one's own suspicious mind. Follow people in the street, and the most blameless of them look furtive. Forget it, he told himself, lighting Arlette's cigarette. What can I get her to drink that won't make her any more drunk? Later, going home he thought, 'Don't forget it; just play it real cool.'

*

He did, so cool that no enquiry or idea helped him in the slightest. He learned that Hjalmar Jansen had been born in Sweden, but of Dutch parentage; he held a Dutch passport. He spoke to the night-club squad; never been anything fishy about Jansen's place in Amsterdam. He sent requests for any available information to all the police forces of Europe. He got replies, but wooden, meaningless. The man had lived in Sweden, Belgium and Germany; nothing was on file 'to his prejudice'. On file; Van der Valk cursed at the pompous letterheads of ministries of the interior and departments of justice – yah; he wished he could talk to these stilted writers. He knew how often in police work one can have a sharp idea that someone is shady, and that in private one might hear illuminating things, even though on the file there might be nothing 'to his prejudice'.

Meanwhile he went to a great deal of trouble finding out that the gang in the Beatrix Park had not, as far as could possibly be established, come from Haarlem, or Zaandam, or Hilversum. There were plenty of other places still, but his thoughts strayed back to Bloemendaal.

But stray his thoughts might, the answer was still zero.

Both Mr Jansen and the town of Bloemendaal were armoured in respectability. He spent several evenings after duty studying the habitués of the 'club', thinking that a quiet look at their activities might pay a dividend. It didn't; these boys and girls appeared to lead startlingly respectable lives. This puzzled him.

What did his own children do? They were younger, and they had less money. Rarely could they have orgies of lemonade in ice-salons. They spent more, much more, time at home – though less than he would have liked. Mm, his experience was still narrow, but it seemed that the Bloemendaal children spent much less time, surely, at home than those he was accustomed to in Amsterdam. But when on the streets, the children he knew – his own, say –

well, he didn't care, they seemed a fair example even if he was a policeman – did far more than anyone did in Bloemendaal. Amsterdam streets are full of life and activity; the street life is like that of Venice. Bloemendaal reminded him of an English town; bare, bleak, cold streets; not a child to be seen.

When on the streets, further, his own children did a great many things that he preferred not to know about. There might be a craze for something thoroughly respectable and conventional, like making model aeroplanes. More often, there were crazes for riding on lorries without being seen, or upsetting the greengrocer's sprouts, or the perennial pleasure of dustbin-kicking. Or they hung around the docks – what did they do there? – or they built orange-box racing cars, or they made fires and forged things. There were crazes for sailing, for judo; there were crazes for possibly more sinister things that were kept dark, when they burst into horrid laughs at meals and poked each other under the table. They had been kicked up the arse by many shopkeepers, and clipped over the ear by more than one policeman. They did, in fact, all the things that most children do.

These others in Bloemendaal seemed to do nothing. They had plenty of money, of course; they all had well-off and indulgent parents. They went almost every night to the Ange Gabriel; much to the cinema; often enough dancing in Zonnehoeck. But he could not see anything individual, anything gay, in the activities of any of them. Everything they did was sober, dull.

If they had any craze it was swimming, and two or three times a week they went to the indoor pool in Zonnehoeck, which was warmed. But even then they were dull. No shrieks or frivolity; in a dedicated manner they polished their jack-knives or their crawls. Why did they seem to have so little fun?

The ravens were easily isolated; they were the gloomiest and the most dedicated. In the mornings to their schools; deep-voiced, didactic lecturers' tones, illustrations in a scrawl of chalk; the polite laugh at a witticism; the looseleaf folder full of scribbled notes. This machinery for launching their careers they took seriously, conscientiously. They were clannish, spent little time with other groups of students. They drank coffee seriously, and spent hours in earnest talk, leaning on the saddles of their autocycles.

In the evenings more hanging about, more gossiping, listening to the record-player – cerebral cool jazz – with the same intent faces they presented to their instructors. There would be a solemn game with poker dice to see who bought the beer. Their clothes, hair and finger-nails were important; on these they spent quite as much time, money and earnest conversation as the girls. Indeed, in their habits and manners there was scarcely any difference. None seemed to bother much about what physical differences of sex remained noticeable; there was certainly never any giggling or pinching.

This glossy, slippery surface Van der Valk found boring and incomprehensible. After two weeks of most entomological observation he thought hell. Some life at home would make a change. He bought a bunch of anemones and the records of *Rosenkavalier* for a rather soured Arlette; these melted her and he got fricandeau of veal to eat, with sorrel. When she wished to punish him he got brown bean soup, repeated the next day. But Arlette's pleasure in having him at home in the evenings only lasted three days. On the fourth, a fine spring evening – they had sat on the balcony and had a beer before supper – there was another upheaval.

'No rape this time, but by God everything else: the exact same pattern – them all right. Two flats in the Schubertstraat; nothing seen or heard; they weren't interrupted or even noticed. Too easy, as long as people's doors are only fastened with these piddling spring locks you can open with a nail-file. They must have made a noise, there were people right underneath – but watching television, blind and deaf of course. Damn this telly-goggling; turns people into a lot of zombies. Sound on full blast – I ask you. They tore the place up – that typical contemptuous treatment; bottles of wine poured over bedclothes, ink thrown at curtains; you know. A dummy made of pillows, dressed in the man's best suit, stabbed several times with a bread-knife or something and then left hanging from a lamp standard. Lipstick all over the wallpaper. Not much money, but one serious loss. A nine-millimetre pistol gone, and a little six-thirty-five revolver, one of these dinky women's things. That's fun; we shall have them shooting someone,' finished Boersma sourly.

'Look,' said Van der Valk. 'If I can establish that the Bloemendaal mob were here in town last night, will you give me some rope on it?'

'So: you've kept working on that, have you? And you've got anywhere?'

'Nowhere. Just a growing conviction, that's all. I have a fair dossier on them all. If I got a break anywhere, just a crack to get a knife blade in, then I might make something out of it.'

'Go right ahead. I've had trouble with the Press, Officer of Justice, everyone. I'm at the end of my patience. Find me one tiny bit of evidence, and I'll light a fire for you under Marcousis.'

'They had a car, I suppose?'

'Usual stuff. Found abandoned at Sloterdijk. Stolen an hour earlier near Artis.'

Train, he said to himself outside; must have taken the train. First tiny piece of carelessness, perhaps. Sloterdijk would mean a Haarlem train, or had they doubled back? With a good deal of trouble he got on to all the train guards who had punched tickets on Bloemendaal trains the night before. First, the barrier at the station itself.

'Ten-thirty to eleven last night. Six or seven boys together, probably with student's subscription cards.'

The man was a fool, some self-important emperor of the ticket-office. From his voice Van der Valk could just picture him.

'Oh no, no, Chief Inspector, I wouldn't have missed them; I always notice everything. No group like that.'

He stopped himself breaking into obscenities. The guards on the trains themselves were harder to pin down, but once he had them his idea began to make some sense. Fewer people travel on season tickets in the late evening, when the commuters' rush is over. The 22.10 from Amsterdam Central stops at Sloterdijk and Haarlem, and connects there with a north-bound Alkmaar train that stops at Bloemendaal. Six boys, described recognisably, had been on this last. It was a roundabout route; anyone could have left Amsterdam ten minutes later, and reached Bloemendaal five minutes earlier, by the direct route through Zaandam. Knowing this, the official checking tickets between Haarlem and Velsen had been surprised to see their cards. He had made no comment, but had remembered. Less bad. Anyway it got him half a handful of freedom from his chief.

'Whole thing still stinks. For chrissake do nothing rash. Pull them in and they swear blind they were at the cinema in Haarlem, and I get indignant parents coming here to pull my tail-feathers.'

'Boys' own tongues will be as weak a spot as any. I won't shake any sticks at them.'

'All right, kiddo. Just don't let the apple tart fall.'

He was by no means confident. Boersma's remark was true. If he asked the boys anything they would simply look blank; he had no purchase on them. His conviction, complete now, that this was the gang for which the Officer of Justice was howling, did him no good whatever. This business was a pest, and seemed likely never to be anything else. He felt thoroughly depressed, sitting gloomily in his office doing one of the things dear to writers of detective stories – making little drawings in his notebook, which didn't help. He tore it all up and went home crossly, but an hour later was doing the same thing while his coffee got cold.

Arlette was going over a pile of mending – boys' summer clothes. She had Schubert lieder on the gramophone. It was April; leaves were unfolding on all the trees in the city; Arlette only lit the stove in the evenings; one began to see tourists in the street. He needed someone to talk to. Not her; it was his most inflexible rule never to bring troubles home with him. He watched her gratefully, an island of calm, a darning needle in her mouth, and grinned as she put a hand up her back to unclip her bra, leaning back with a sigh of relief. Behind her the melody swelled and rippled like silk flags in the wind, reflected in the water of a Tirolese lake.

His piece of paper was covered with drawings of cats – all looking more like cows – and a list of names. Six ravens. Michel, Dick, Eric, Bertus, Frank, Wim. One possible new raven – Kees van Sonneveld. A lot of wiggles round this last; it had given him a lot of thought. This was the boy in the suède windcheater; the hot shot, the progress chaser. A possible weak link. If he were not one of the gang he might be jealous – even if he were one. His loyalty might not be so firm, or – more likely – it might be the most fanatical. Either way might be illuminating.

Six girls; each raven appeared to have a steady girl friend. Elly, Lina, Marta, Lies, Paula, Carmen. Kees too had a girl, Hannie. Lines crossed and recrossed from one to the other. He had a drawing of Hjalmar, sinister tiny figure in a gangster hat and dark glasses. He was rather ashamed of his idea about Hjalmar; even for him it looked unusually preposterous by daylight. Another drawing, of Feodora; she had given him the idea, she belonged here too, somehow. He tore all this out and made a neater drawing: Hjalmar at the centre; around him, the boys in a ring. Outside that another ring, the girls. They knew, he would bet, what went on, but he would also bet that no stolen jewellery or anything else would ever turn up in their possession. Thinking about the girls he made more drawings: the angel Gabriel, blowing a trumpet, himself and Feodora linked again – now why was that so definite in his head?

He thought a while about the personnel of the building; they might know of anything odd. The cook, a rather sour Frenchman; the waiter, a pompous soul called Schut; the washer-up, the two barmen, the pianist. The counterhands in the ice-salon, the cleaning women, the kitchen-help. He considered these people, but it was not really likely that any of them knew of anything unusual. Staff were all born gossips; if they had ever noticed anything it would be all round the town. And if he asked them anything that would be all round the town too. He dismissed the idea. This business had to be worked a bit intelligently.

He crumpled his paper in irritation and told Arlette he was going out.

'I won't be all that long. Just to undo knots.' She understood. One of the nice things about Arlette was that one never had to explain anything, ever.

*

Feodora sat on the divan with her long legs curled under her, a filter-tip cigarette sticking out like a bowsprit from her jaunty mouth. To get the ash off she just blew: ha. Her flat was clean. but not neurotically clean, like so many in Holland. More Arlette's idea of clean, and that made him feel at home. The room hummed with warmth and comfort; there was a fresh faint smell of narcissus and scent, and Feodora's elastic body. He felt his mind go loose, gratefully.

'No customers tonight?' lazily.

She smiled. 'Yes, but later on; you need not hurry to go. I am glad to see you. But I have no illusions. You come because I might be useful to you, and because you can stretch out, like me.

You look happy; you feel, too, happy; isn't it so?'

He put on an honest look.

'I like you that you are not ashamed of it. Come, what can I do? You are in a mess? No, don't tell me, I see policeman in your eye thinking, inquisitive bitch. Quite right too; I hate curious women. I get told things because I am incurious.'

'You tell me something. You think Hjalmar is a dirty stinker, right?'

'My exact words.'

'Tell me why.'

'How foolish you are, why. Isn't any why, don't you realise that? He is always polite and clever, everybody likes him. You will not find one person in all Bloemendaal who says it is a stinker, except me only. I have no reason; he has never injured me. Call me spiteful.'

'But it's you I'm asking, not Bloemendaal.'

'I do not know. I think it is a bad man. I can see you think so too. What does it matter, why?'

'If I knew why it might be so, I might be surer I was right to think so.'

'Look, you have experience as policeman, how long?'

'Fifteen years.'

'You have not got so far without meeting some bad people. No reason why; just bad.'

'Very few.'

'Yes, but always some. I have myself met; I am in the right position, huh. I know without evidence, without having to see and feel. You policemen, your – what is the word? – obsessie; you must always see and touch. Too materialist. Yes, shut up; I know: you do not want it so, you will tell me. It is the judge who must have it. But the judge knows too, there are very naughty things, and there are people who do them because they like them. No good always to try to explain. I know nothing, I have heard nothing, I suspect nothing. But I tell you Hjalmar is one of those men.'

'I think I agree, but still I must be able to prove it. I can't just sit knowing things about the man; my job is to do something about it.'

'What has he done?'

'Nothing, I suppose, that the law calls a crime. Maybe he has a hand in what the boys up there, the gang – in what they do, or why they do it, or something. I've no idea why I think so; I'm like you.'

'Ask the boys. They would not tell you but you would find out.'

'I can't even put my hand on them. No proof. Nowadays we can't pull them in on suspicion alone, not when they're only boys, especially. It's frowned on. If I question them they clam up and their parents throw lawyers at me. They interest me, these boys. They seem so abnormal, and I cannot understand why.'

'I know none of them. Well brought up; they run away when they see me. They all got their own girls anyway, nasty little beasts they seduce when thirteen.'

'You know any of the staff up there?'

'I know Juillard, the cook. He has supper with me sometimes on his day off. He teach Piet to play belote; we have good fun with him there. He likes Hjalmar; says he is a good boss. You see?'

'Where do you think these boys take their girls? To make love. I suppose they do make love?'

'Of course. In the downs, in the sand.'

'They don't. They never go off with the girls like that alone.'

'You know Hjalmar has a flat on top of the Ange Gabriel.'

'There has to be somewhere, doesn't there?'

'There does.' She was grinning. 'You always work like this?'

'Like what?'

'Why do you need me? You could work without picking my brains.'

'I always work like that. I need other people. I'm not the big detective, only a poor sod of a policeman. Lousy one at that.'

'I don't mind. Change from having my clothes taken off. You want to hear music?'

'You like music more than people.'

'I can read people. I can't read a word of music. Harmony, descant, counterpoint – I don't know what any of that means. But I love music, yes.'

She put on the 'Four Seasons'. Mm, the woman was in a country that was not hers, without husband or children, in a profession regarded as antisocial. When she went to a concert it would be to satisfy a need, like women who went to konditoreien to stuff themselves with wonderful cream cakes, and to hell with their figures. She felt unfulfilled; the music filled her. Mm; perhaps that was true, perhaps all rubbish. He disliked facile psychiatry. What did it matter anyway?

The music made him think of open steppes and desert sands, a dry tingling air, the pace of horses, the flight of hawks, the little belling copper street-noises of Samarkand or Tashkent. Why? Civilised, small eighteenth-century music; baroque ballrooms of Nymphenburg, satin knee-breeches, candelabra. Ridiculous that it should bring older, Asian civilisations to his mind.

Would Hjalmar like music? Or had he contempt for civilisations, whether Asian or European? Did he see himself as a wolf, predestined to attack them? Where music brought her happiness, did crime bring his? She enjoyed her lovers; she put thought and energy into the business of releasing and rebuilding them. What did Jansen do? Had he a mistress somewhere? He had wanted her; he was not pederast. Did he have a woman? Must have, surely. That would be important, to find that out. What were the keys to the man's character? He was not a stupid man. It was important to understand.

Shit, thought Van der Valk illogically, why do I have this rage for understanding people? He went home rather sullenly; he knew that Feodora expected him to go before he had to be asked. But she liked him, he saw. She liked, too, his trusting her. A prostitute was strange company for a chief inspector of police; she could blackmail him. Did she expect him to sleep with her? Did she understand that he preferred not to? He decided that she would not try to understand – she would just accept. Whether he was a conscientious policeman, a faithful husband, or just looking for somebody's brain to pick, she would not think that her business. That was her strength. She would not meddle with his mind. Therefore he liked and respected her.

'Doesn't this job show any sign of coming to an end?' asked Arlette hopefully.

'No,' with deep gloom. 'It's one of those ones where you know almost immediately who, bloody well, but there's about as much chance of proving it as there is of demonstrating that the earth is flat.'

'Is it interesting?' Not that she was interested.

'Yes. Very, even. Odd people. If it wasn't so aggravating it would be amusing. I've been spending the evening with one of the witnesses. A whore who listens to Beethoven quartets on the gramophone.'

'Nice. You would enjoy that.'

'Yes, but it didn't give me any idea what to do.'

'I have the right idea,' said Arlette, unflustered. 'A good night's sleep. But first, hot milk, with brandy and plenty of nutmeg.'

## *Chapter Three*

Next day was sharp, bright and cold, with an energetic sun, and plenty of wind. He shaved in the kitchen with the balcony door open, the fresh air playfully sliding between the skin and his vest. He took big breaths happily, and thumped his chest like Tarzan.

'Feel good?' Arlette was rubbing a cracked egg with lemon to stop it leaking. Her hair smelt good; her face was fresh and cool. She kissed him back, gave the coffee a careful stir to settle it, and turned up the collar of her housecoat. 'That wind is sharp, though.'

'Easterly. Wind from the steppes.' It reminded him of Feodora. 'I'll have two eggs, please. Don't think much of that cheese; no flavour.'

'Everybody'd run out of farm cheese. Hey, get a move on,' she shouted at her eldest son, painstakingly brushing his teeth. 'You're directing traffic, don't forget.' It was his turn to see schoolchildren across the road, with the white belt and the 'fried egg' with which Dutch children control road crossings.

'I can't help it if Father takes such a time to shave.'

'Neither of you has any business in the kitchen anyway.'

Van der Valk regarded his child with affection and amusement. Took after him. There was a perfectly good washbasin in the bedroom, but he disliked it; he always shaved in the kitchen. Farmer I am, he thought; really I would prefer the water to come from a pump. Like the Friesians; well, if the Government insists on giving us the water, it will do for the animals, and thus far pipes and taps. But in the house, no; tea tasted better made from a barrel of rainwater. Plainly, his son would also tell his wife in another few years that tea tasted better made with rainwater. Look at that boy; helping himself to my eau de cologne, and putting it on his hair.

I am not really an unreasonable father, he thought. I love my children and devote all the time I can to them. I show maximum interest and pleasure in their thoughts, their friends, their pursuits. But I am so much away when they are at home. Often I am tired too, and nervous, and I shout at them then, or push them away, when they natter at me, or I give curt answers. I cannot call myself a good father.

Arlette was speaking, her voice indignant. 'And if anybody else gets holes in their trousers, well, they can just go to school in their bare bottom, that's all, for the rest of the week. I've just got no more trousers for you, and that's flat.' She had less patience than him, but she was a good mother. What would she feel, as a parent – no, what would I feel, as a parent, if some policeman came and told me my boy had broken into flats, or raped a woman? Would I be indignant and hostile, and not very inclined to believe or accept? Mm, I think I would.

He had lost his indecision; he knew what he had to do. These parents . . . they were more trouble than the children ever were. Admitted, he was a bad policeman, he knew; felt and did all the wrong things. He was intelligent, that was all, and tactful, and anyone who was not a total numbskull and ground at the paperwork could pass exams. He had got on by luck, and by not being too stupid, but he was not a good policeman. Good policemen did not waste their time sympathising with parents, for a start. Boersma didn't, and he was the chief. Van der Valk knew that he would be very lucky ever to get further in his profession than he was now. He was distrusted, higher up. He shrugged; not going to worry about that now; where was his notebook? How Arlette hated it when he was abstracted at breakfast.

He made a fresh list; names he knew by heart now. Bertus. Father a chief cashier in a bank, one of those upright dry men. Precise, thorough, self-righteous because they never make mistakes in their accounts. As though their stupid accounts had the faintest importance. There you are; I told you you were a bad policeman. He decided he didn't care, and made a little zero mark opposite the name. Not likely to be helpful. Lives in the Texelstraat anyway, and does not come home for lunch. Interviewing a type like that at work is a waste of time. Mm; pass to the next.

Erik. Father very rich, luxury flat, the type with automatic doors, in that skyscraper where the boulevard joins the Jacoba van Beieren Laan. Director of a textile factory, a fat, shrewd, tough man. Would be narrow-minded like so many rich people; interested in things as long as they were likely to make him still more rich. Went every year to winter sports, still played a lot of tennis to keep him active. Fantastic diamonds he had given his wife, a vulgar woman with a fearful accent, who had been the daughter of a greengrocer in the Haarlemmerdijk. The son tough too, with inherited toughness from both parents, but whereas Pa didn't care about Ma's accent, the boy did. Pa was no fool, and would, he thought, be approachable, simply because he was a very realistic man. He put a cross for Erik.

Dick. Father head draughtsman for a biggish engineering concern in Velsen. He did not know much about him. A well-ordered, meticulous man, mathematical but not lacking imagination, he guessed. Poetry in a slide-rule – ha. House in Amelandstraat. Don't really know, but a cross for Dick, he rather thought.

Frank; rich again. Flat in Jacoba van Beieren, but not on the scale of Erik's father. Doesn't bat in the same league; lives up to the limit for prestige purposes. Look how well the company – and I – are doing these days. Export manager of the big plastics factory in Bloemendaal. Very ambitious, red-hot climber backed and egged by pushful wife. Crafty; too crafty ever to compromise himself; maybe too crafty to be honest with himself. Always away in Germany or Italy, saw himself as coming man. Was, too, no doubt. A hot-shot; just my meat, thought Van der Valk regretfully. Damn being tactful. Zero, though, opposite Frank.

Wim. Father the poorest, he knew, of all this crowd. Still better off than a chief inspector of police, probably. Head of packing and despatching in the plastics factory. House in the Strawinskystraat. A conscientious, plodding man, excellent at his job but scared of being supplanted. A cross went down, but with a question-mark beside it.

Michel; big, pleasant bungalow in the Richard Strausslaan. Father an architect, a Belgian, pretty successful too. Had designed a good deal of Bloemendaal. Office here in Amsterdam. An artist, mm; might be easier than some to manage. Pleasant face; can't really tell. But put a cross. He considered his list and drank his third cup of coffee, lukewarm.

Arlette had cleared the table, and left him isolated, pointedly, on a little island of crumbs. Cigarette-ash on his plate too; big crime. Four crosses, one or more with a query, and two probable zeros. He thought that with the two who had offices here in the city he might make a useful start.

Lucky to have done this homework; without it he would have been at a loss. The information in the little book had been got without difficulty from a week's observation of the ravens and a few phone calls. He knew nothing of their characters, but their homes and backgrounds would help. He had to probe them a bit. His position would not allow him to do anything that sounded impressive, but he might find a soft spot somewhere. He might get an excuse for a big talk about arrests, but he doubted that. He had to be careful. The train episode was worth nothing without formidable corroboration, and he could not make – lacking this – any frontal assault. And no question at all of the easy way; impossible to dump them all in the nick, to sweat till they began to give at the knees.

He stood up and slapped his pockets, a hard cheerful man with a lined face; no beauty. Let's go and have a game of cards with these gentlemen. Frans Mierle and Rudolf Carnavalet; business addresses, notebook, uh. Architect was the nearest, in the Prinsengracht. He climbed into the little black Mercedes police-car and hitched the seat of his trousers with satisfaction. This, he hoped, was where humble foot-slogging paid off.

Those patient evenings, while vague feeling crystallised into a moral certainty, had been unofficial. No car. All that tiring menial work of following and observing, the tedious looking-up and checking – it was not strictly work for a chief inspector, and now he was glad of a change. He did not regret that patient work. 'To get it well done do it yourself' – a slogan he really believed in. Anyway there had been no help for it. Boersma was strict. Not petty, give him that, never went around complaining about waste of scratch pads or paper clips. But a Tartar for government personnel, and government transport.

Van der Valk knew, too, that the old man was a firm believer in his adage that good policemen were made by getting to know their districts properly, knowing everybody, slogging round. Often unofficially. Often off duty. No claims allowed for shoeleather, was one of the old man's aggravating sayings. None the less Van der

Valk agreed. He knew many lazy chief inspectors. They sat at desks, calling everybody to their offices to show their importance, doing business on the telephone like so many stockbrokers. Well, well, they got promoted quicker than he did. But he did not feel bad about it; on the whole he enjoyed his life. He liked to study people's homes as well as their offices; their wives, their bookshelves, their furniture. But he was no longer twenty years old. He preferred to do his running about by car, and now that he had the green light from Boersma, the enquiry was official. An enquiry, he thought, grinning; that useful, polite, portmanteau police word for being nosy.

At the Prinsengracht he sent in his card. People never kept him waiting. They might wish to, but they were either frightened or curious, and the rare ones who were neither had generally the intelligence to know the power of good manners. Whichever category Michel's father belonged to, he had no more than a moment to wait before the typist showed him into the architect's private office, a big airy room with light wooden furniture, red cushions, and sun shining through primrose Venetian blinds.

Carnavalet was a sturdy man, still under fifty, with a crew cut, a slate-blue business suit, and library horn-rims. Tired eyes, but a resolute, springy body.

'Have a chair, Chief Inspector. What can I do, build you a new bureau?'

'I wish you would. No doors, no telephone, and several quiet private fire-escapes.'

'Life as hard as all that?'

'Well,' grinning, 'you can lighten the load.'

'At your service.'

'How do you get on, at home, with your boy Michel?'

'Michel? What are you trying to tell me?'

'Not telling anything. Only asking.'

'Has something happened to him.'

'He's in the best of health, so far as I know.'

'Something he's done?'

'I have no grounds for being precise. I think he may have got into bad company.'

'Bad company. A police cliché. Has he done anything and if so what?'

'You're quite right, it is a cliché; I'll try to talk Dutch. Would you say you knew him well?'

'How well does a father know his son?'

'In my experience, remarkably little.'

'I suppose that may be true. I haven't the contact with him I would like, but I suppose that's a symptom of his age. They have to make their own minds up about things. He doesn't want my opinions; he wants to form his own.'

'Forgive me if I say that you sound a bit over-emphatic, as though perhaps you were fortifying yourself against criticism. Would you say, in your opinion, that you might have been a bit too easy with him, in his younger days?'

'I suppose all parents make mistakes. I do think so, sometimes, yes. Now hadn't you better tell me, Inspector?'

'We're having worries with a crowd of young men, among them Michel. My first reaction is to find out something about these boys. Any source of friction that might be upsetting their lives.'

'Aren't you being very pompous? What has the boy done, hit a teacher? I've every sympathy, remembering my own student days.'

'Breaking enclosed premises, robbery with violence, personal assault, sexual assault.'

'Good God.'

'Yes, exactly. You still think me pompous? I've come to you to learn what I can, that may help.'

'Where is the boy?'

'He's not been interfered with or even spoken to. Nothing will be done behind your back. I'd like to talk to the boy, in your presence. Our attitude nowadays is not to rush about arresting everybody, but to try to understand, first.'

'Explain yourself. Have you any proof that the boy has done these things?'

'Look. A court will take a grave view of this. It is very important to fix the degree of responsibility.'

'If any.'

'As you say, if any. Not easy to find this out without the boy's help, which he will not be disposed to give. If I can establish exactly what they have done and why – paradoxically, if you like, they, and you, will have less cause for anxiety.'

'You must take me further into your confidence, Inspector.'

'The boy must take us both further into his confidence. I want your help in that. There's no question yet of a procès-verbal.'

'I begin to understand. I fear that won't be easy. Difficult boy. Nervous, intelligent, but lazy. I do my best to get on well with him, and of course if he were in trouble . . . but it is not always easy. Sometimes – try to understand me – I lose patience.'

'I think I understand. I have children too. One sometimes says, "Blasted fool; very well, get on with it, but don't expect sympathy if you get into a fix." '

'Rather, yes.'

'What does he do at home?'

'Moons about sulkily. Hardly ever is at home; always in some damn coffee bar.'

'Just ask him to stay at home tonight, say I want a word with him. Then we shall see just what we can understand. Don't make a thing out of it; I'm not going to arrest the boy, just a few moment's talk.'

'I certainly see no objection to that.' Carnavalet seemed to be choosing among further remarks, but thought better of all of them.

His other call was in the Herengracht, right at the top towards the Brouwersgracht, where every second house belongs to the textile trade, mostly pretty shabby, to judge by exteriors. There was certainly nothing spectacular about the premises of N.V. Mierle. Dinginess personified, and only the huge aerial photographs on the reception-room walls – of an impressive modern factory in Almelo – showed the importance of the concern. Heer Frans Mierle's private office was also dingy, old-fashioned, and without the slightest effort to impress a caller. No need; Frans Mierle was an impressive man.

Middle fifties; stocky, fleshy; not soft. A face cut from a huge block of pale leather. Sharp eyes with rings under them, behind tremendous glasses – beside those Carnavalet's were cobwebs. Big rumbling voice, frequent laugh. Not a silly laugh, just completely self-assured. Hair still dark but thin. Black suit of magnificent material, superbly, almost theatrically cut. Handshake about as soft as a lobster's claw.

'You're not going to give me this no drink on duty lark. Who gets in here at all gets gin. And a cigar. Refuse, and I treat you as the fool you demonstrably are.'

Van der Valk enjoyed big business men. His technique was to adopt theirs, and be just as outrageous.

'Don't like gin,' he said pleasantly. 'Prefer brandy. Not goddam Dutch brandy either.'

'Ha. Miss Pons! Miss Pons! A big Bisquit, for my FRENCH FRIEND.' Diabolical emphasis. 'You know that suit of yours is nothing but a disgrace; you look like an off-duty bailiff, escaped from the pages of *Stubbs' Gazette*. Now, Miss Pons, when you've quite finished fussing with the little paper napkins, I may tell you that this is the police, so sit with your chair well against the safe door. Hold up incoming calls, and when Hirsch rings tell him luncheon as usual in Victoria, and I'll tell him then all that's good for him to know. Now, Mr van der Valk, shoot.'

'You're on good terms with Erik?'

'Reasonably.'

'Like him?'

'Yes. Pest of a boy, but got guts. Takes after me.'

'What do you plan for him?'

'Business here. Good head for figures, otherwise not too terribly bright. But persistent. Good close grain; hard wood.'

'That what he wants to do?'

'Wants to be a drummer in a jazz band. Soon grow out of that.'

'Does he get on well with his mother?'

'Boy's got no sense of reality yet. Looks at the outside of things. Thinks this office is a disgrace. Thinks Miss Pons too old and too plain; he would prefer a sexy crumpet secretary whose suspender he could snap instead of getting on with the work. That answer you?'

'Well enough.'

'Any more questions?'

'I'm waiting for you to ask why the enquiry.'

'Very well, why the enquiry?'

'Erik's in one of these gangs.'

'Aren't we all? Natural instinct. Wolf pack?'

'Wolf pack.'

'That's my boy. Plays the goddam trumpet, if you please.'

'Thought you said drums.'

'Hell, I don't know. Caterwauling of all kinds.'

'Ever had a burglary?'

'No. Spend plenty of money on security. If I did – wake the insurers up.'

'Suppose burglars broke into your house; tied you up.'

'Have to hold me first.'

'Five – maybe six could. Not babies. Good tough boys. Like Erik.'

'You're not telling me –?'

'I wasn't there. But I thought of having a little word with the boy tonight. At home, with you there, as bodyguard perhaps, in case he gets too tough for me to handle.'

'Have some more brandy. I've been underestimating you.'

'Been underestimating Erik, I'd say.'

'Let me handle him.'

'No.'

'I can get the truth out of him; he'll only tell you lies.'

'Less bad, but you'll put his back up. Just stay quiet; you can have Miss Pons take me down in shorthand.'

'I have a dictaphone. About time I found a use for it.'

'Seven o'clock?'

'Precisely, then; I have friends later. You'd make a good business man. Hasta luego.'

'Word of advice?'

'Maybe.'

'Don't yell at the boy. Just say he has to stay at home for once and watch the goldfish.'

'To hell with goldfish; I have birds. Very well; I'll wait to see what you have, first. Miss Pons, let my friend out.'

Pooh, thought Van der Valk; easier than I thought, but they won't all be like that. Those two are at least genuine, and intelligent, and they love their children. What went wrong? Hard to say. Erik evidently thinks Pa a loud-mouthed farmer, and Michel's been a bit spoilt, but there must be a lot more to it. Aren't I the same? Sometimes over-aggressive, sometimes over-restrictive. Aren't we all? Doesn't every father oscillate between the one and the other? Takes a lot more than that to account for what these children have done. There you are, wanting to explain everything again.

Back in his office, he considered with sour humour a situation he had heard of: that of a nervous and ambitious policeman whose son had got into a gang, and who had been blackmailed into protecting their activities. Ha ha.

These boys would doubtless think up some ingenious lies. So would the parents, of course. Gangs had an amazing capacity for fantasy, sometimes sinister in a surrealist way. Boersma had reminded him of the gang boy from Rotterdam who had gone to the German police with torn clothes and blacked eyes, and complained of having been beaten up and robbed. He had even pretended to identify two louts put up for questioning by the innocent Germans. His idea of a rich joke. As for the bogus confessions, they were an Amsterdam speciality. Yet here there was a different feeling. It just was not like an ordinary gang. Boersma had pointed out that the element of fantasy was missing.

'It's that as much as anything gives me the idea of something out of place. Then take this rape. I suppose we'll get told tripe about an Oedipus complex or something. I simply see an oddly isolated fact, an anachronism. Wanton brutality, yes, but out of keeping with smashing china and sticking dollies with a bread-knife.'

Never mind, thought Van der Valk; this evening is going to be amusing. Feeling light-hearted he went home early, with a bottle of white wine and a new climbing plant, to pacify Arlette for spending yet another evening away from home.

Why should I bring her something just because I'm going out? She knows it's my job, that I can't help it. What is the point of a present? And why, when it is so obviously a bribe, is she so pleased about it? Women are ridiculous.

Seven I've got to be in the Jacoba van Beieren; I can have a bash at friend Frank first. After that the Richard Strauss and I can take in the Strawinskystraat on the way, and last up to the 'islands' for the other two.

He knew Bloemendaal by now as well as though he lived there; after being in a snack-bar twice his visual memory was so exact, so sharp, it was as though he had been a regular customer for years. It suddenly occurred to him that this memory was a very valuable quality. He thought a bit about Kees van Sonneveld. Let him stew for a bit; he'll hear about it from the others and wonder why he was left out. Maybe make him jumpy to be left on the hook a day or two longer.

'I've got an easy evening; probably be home early. Keep some soup or something that I can warm up, and we'll have a drink when I get back. It's only a few parents; not that tiresome hanging round the streets.'

*

He was driving happily out to Bloemendaal when a big English Bentley hissed past him at vast speed, honking like an imperial wild goose; he grinned as he recognised Frans Mierle. Now what will Karel Kieft have for a car? Make a little bet it's something fancy. When he parked on the Jacoba van Beieren Laan he was delighted to see that Heer Kieft's auto had not yet been put away and was in fact a white Jaguar. The snob, he thought, almighty show-off; big deal (he had recently read *The Catcher in the Rye*).

Mr Kieft was tall and thin. Slim, that said it better; immeasurably distinguished, very neat. His wife was a small fair woman with dolly prettiness and a tiny mean mouth that made him dislike her immediately, intensely. He was in a business suit still, very exquisite pale grey. English tie, old Etonian or something, and red Morocco slippers. Madame wore a very smart wool two-piece. The flat was furnished with bareness and discomfort, which someone had mistaken for good taste. There was the type of picture one sees adjoining the windows of expensive suburban art-shops. In England these tend to be nudes by Sir William Russell Flint, and in Holland Franz Marc's 'Little Red Horses', and nasty elongated women by Bernard Buffet. Heer Kieft had gone in for English imports in a big way, and had indulged himself in a clipper ship. Every sail you could think of set, and so much sea that the wind would have blown them all away instantly.

There were Regency-striped silk cushions and velvet curtains, imitation Hepplewhite chairs and a chandelier; both candles and drinks stood in fake English Georgian silver. The place was full of Podsnappery and Wappin and Mebbery. What books there were came from the Book of the Month Club, in fake leather bindings. Van der Valk, who had been in England and seen the insides of some English houses, was not intimidated by these aspects of grandeur; he was a little inclined to snigger.

'You have not come at a very convenient time, Chief Inspector. We are on the verge of having dinner.'

'I realise that; I must make my apologies. Unfortunately I have several of these calls to make this evening.' (You're on the verge of more than dinner.)

'Will you explain yourself? Sit down, by the way.'

'Thank you; I'll try to be brief. I have some worries concerning your son Frank.'

'On what account?'

'On account of serious raids made upon persons and property in Amsterdam, by boys of his age. Do you –'

Kieft cut in. 'Acquaintances of Frank's?'

'Let me finish my sentence. Do you feel able to think why Frank should have done such things?'

'Are you making an accusation?'

'That is not part of my job. I only wish to understand facts that have not, perhaps, very simple explanations. I am trying to discover why boys of good family and education should be inclined to go off the rails so violently.'

'Mette, will you fetch Frank?'

'May I ask you a short question?'

'Which is?'

'Are you surprised?'

'That the police ask idiotic questions? No.'

'Very revealing answer.'

'Mette, fetch Frank.'

Van der Valk looked out of the window. 'I hope you never get that beautiful car dirty.' Silence, icy.

'Frank, this is an inspector of police, it appears, from Amsterdam. He has some ludicrous notion that might be better disregarded, but since you are here, if you answer a few questions briefly we can perhaps have dinner. If I stop you answering it means that I intend to protect myself against officialdom, by taking legal advice if that appears necessary.'

Frank was a calm, deliberate, good-looking boy. Van der Valk thought him both cunning and stupid, rather an unsympathetic child. He looked him over coolly, taking his time about speaking.

'There are only three questions,' he said cheerfully, enjoying himself. 'One: which of you kept the gun?'

'What gun?'

'Nine-millimetre Lüger, standard German army issue. There are plenty of them, but this one has a number.'

'Don't know what you're talking about.'

'Two: how did you come to choose the Schubertstraat? Accident or design?'

'Never been in it. Where is it?'

'Three and last: who among you had the idea of raping the woman?'

'I don't understand.'

He noticed with satisfaction that Mette's ears were as red as her horrible little mouth, and that Karel looked exactly as though someone had painted dirty words all over his good car.

'You will understand, though. You're not very bright, any of you. You see that I know all about it. Your lies are not convincing; dull, stupid, mechanical. I'm not pressing it further now; you have some time to think it over. One of these days I'll have you brought to my office. Tell lies then and you'll feel very sick.'

Kieft was furious; his nose looked like candle-grease. 'I want to know exactly and in detail the meaning of this ridiculous performance.'

'Ask your son; he knows.'

'I'm asking you.'

'And I'm not telling you. You choose to be offensive. Since this, so far, is an informal enquiry you have a right to refuse to answer anything you choose, conscious presumably of the interpretation such a refusal might bear. Instead you behave as though I had come here to pester you with fantasies for my own amusement. Which give me the right to forget that I am a chief inspector of the recherche. You are a parasite, probably the cause of a spoilt and stupid child doing things he will regret. When the judge hears you he will tear you in half. I have nothing further to do here except notify you to hold yourself in readiness for an official summons, from the Officer of Justice. Good evening.'

Big words, brother; you were just dying to say them. Admit it, you were delighted he behaved as he did. Will it do any harm? No, not really. Knowing, and not knowing, Kieft won't have the guts to face it.

He left the car where it was and walked up to the corner of the sea boulevard. Hot stuff, here. From the top, where Mierle lived, the view would reach to Ijmuiden and well out to sea. On a clear day, with a glass one would be able to read ships' names as they slid majestically between the piers. The lift was as smooth and felt as fast as a Ferrari Europa. A pretty maid took his hat and coat. 'You are expected, sir. Will you go straight in, please.'

The wrought-iron door, with stuffed birds behind glass panels – mm, décor like a fancy restaurant – slid open when he was three feet from it. In the enormous salon one complete wall was window; a single massive double sheet of glass, forged in a curve. The second wall was more glass, but with the aviary behind it instead of the North Sea; the third was glass too, but a poor effort, he decided; it only came down to bookshelf height. He found himself knee-deep in green plants and green-grass carpet. It was a tropical garden in a lighthouse. It could certainly be criticised, thought Van der Valk, impressed, slightly disgusted, and a great deal amused; but it fitted Mierle. He wore woolly slippers and had undone his tie, but had not changed his suit. He looked like a black rhinoceros, that might at any moment charge across the clearing in the jungle.

'Come in, come in, man. This is my wife.' The daughter of Amsterdam greengrocers looked fearfully out of place in the jungle, but serene and composed. A formidable bosom and appalling clothes, metallic hair and a huge kind smile, hot and bright as sunshine round her amiable brown eyes. He liked her at once.

'Mr Van der Valk, this business is worrying Frans and me dreadfully. Won't you tell us, please, what it is that Erik has done?' He guessed that she would have a talent for saying the wrong thing. Mierle looked at her indulgently; did he ever lose his patience and get mad? Were there occasionally shattering rows? This was not a good room for throwing things.

'No pictures,' Van der Valk said, in a disappointed voice.

'Ha. Next door. But they'd disappoint you. No Picassos; not worth money; sorry.'

'Mayn't I see?'

'Why, yes. If you're sufficiently interested.' A long oblong room, pleasantly untidy. An old-fashioned, massive, very ugly writing-desk piled with paper. Books and magazines falling about everywhere; spring flowers in a cheap glass bowl. A shabby armchair facing a television set had two sewing needles stuck in its arm; Mevrouw removed these, scandalised. The bookshelves were open, painted white, and full of travel souvenirs; Venetian glass, hideous majolica, an ivory crocodile. The pictures were a surprise; all were good hand-painted reproductions of well-known Vermeers: the pregnant girl in blue, reading the letter; the old woman sitting at the street door; the 'Procuress'; the 'Geographer' and the painter who admires the simpering girl holding the trumpet. Van der Valk greatly approved of this choice.

Mierle stood grinning; Mevrouw hovered, rather uneasy. They went back to the other room.

'Shall I get the boy? We don't want to waste time.' Mierle picked up a grass-green telephone, with a plastic cord like a green mamba curled round the tree-trunk coffee-table. 'Come on up, son.'

The boy had springy, wavy hair, and his mother's rather blunt features. But he had his father's small shrewd eyes. He did not seem perturbed, and sat easily with his legs crossed, dancing his foot casually. Nobody spoke; Van der Valk smoked his cigar peacefully, staring at the lazy fan of smoke. The boy was cool, but bothered by the way sweat broke along his upper lip. He had to take his hand from his pocket to brush away the tickle; to have to do this discomposed him the least bit. He ran a hand through his hair; Van der Valk said conversationally, 'Tell me about the cats.'

It went off like a bomb; the boy nearly shrieked.

'What cats?' from a swollen throat. He opened his mouth and shut it again, looked at his mother, who sat irritatingly on the extreme edge of her chair, twisting a handkerchief. Looked at his father, whose cigar was pointing like the barrel of an atomic cannon. Nobody spoke.

'Someone said, "The cats won't like it." Interesting words, spoken in rather odd circumstances, one evening in the Schubertstraat in Amsterdam.'

The boy sat stiff in the jungle, tense as the tail of a jaguar.

'Explain that to me. We'd understand each other better then, huh?'

'Would we?'

'You're brighter than Frank. He just looked stupid and pretended he didn't know. You don't want to talk; I understand. The brave ones don't talk, and you're proud of your guts, niet? Now consider. Since I know, there's no point in the don't talk line. The one with guts and intelligence is now the one with a story to tell, since that will save you all a great deal of pain and misery later. Ask your father – there's no percentage in being a hero.'

Silence.

'It bothers you that I am a policeman?'

'There's nothing to tell.'

'Not about the gun? Who found the gun? And who has it now?'

The boy was making an effort. 'I'm sorry. I don't know.'

'Don't know,' said Van der Valk pleasantly, 'went the wrong way in a one-way-street, was arrested by the police and sent to the penal battalion in Algeria. What's the point of don't know, since I do know?'

The tension eased a bit, but the boy's face remained rigid.

'You puzzled me, that's all. I still can't make out what you're driving at.'

'You can't? Ever tried to stop yourself yawning? Eventually you have to. This is like that. You'll find you will have to tell me.'

'You're threatening me.' Van der Valk smiled. 'I've done nothing; you will have to leave me alone.'

'What was it the cats wouldn't like, Erik? The woman remembered the remark, you see. You can tell us now; she isn't here. Harmless phrase; odd that you should be afraid of it.'

'I'm not afraid of some silly phrase you've invented from somewhere.'

'Is it so silly? We'll find out. When I'm gone, ask your father's advice about what you should do.'

The boy stood up, and put his hands back in his pockets.

'I'm not scared of you. I'm not telling you a damn' thing. And if I want to go out you can't stop me.' Van der Valk put his cigar in his mouth and grinned, saying nothing. The boy stared a moment and then turned abruptly and marched out.

'Would you say he was scared?'

'He's terrified,' said Ma shrilly. 'He's only a boy. You shouldn't have frightened him like that.'

'Nobody said anything frightening,' said Frans Mierle heavily.

'Young scallywag's got a guilty conscience. What's all this about cats?'

'Don't know myself. Some code-word of theirs; evident that it meant plenty to him. I think that if I knew exactly what it did mean I wouldn't be as mystified as, frankly, I am about some aspects of this affair.'

'I'll get to the bottom of this.'

'Remember that I'm the enemy now. I want the boy to feel you're on his side. But you've seen that it isn't just a nightmare of mine, huh? I got the impression that the boy was frightened of more than just having to come up against the police.'

'Yes,' said Mierle. 'I saw.'

Strawinskystraat. Small houses in a neat detached suburban row. Front gardens with gnomes, oil-tanks at the side for the furnace, flowering bushes; lilac, roses, hydrangeas. Homely, comfortable houses. Mrs Brinkman answered the bell. She was one of those honest Dutch women that go shopping with their aprons sticking out below their coat hems, spend the entire day in a frenzy of window-cleaning, and at last get tea and relapse utterly into reading knitting patterns, from *Eva* and *Margriet*, until it is time to go to bed. She let him in twittering.

Heer Jeroen Brinkman was a type of man found everywhere in big concerns. They are by no means ineffective but have the misfortune to look so – indeed they are the backbone of their firm. But because they are unobtrusive and unpushful, and flatten themselves in doorways for less intelligent men to go by, less honest and less kind men, they are trodden on by clots. But where did Wim get his height and broad shoulders from? At eighteen the boy had a cruiser-weight build that must have come from a four-square dung-fork grandfather somewhere. He was not the brightest of the boys, but quite bright enough to take the lead even when his strength and agility alone were not enough. Quick, sensitive and a bonny fighter, he was the king-pin of the gang.

The Brinkman interior was very conventional; surgically clean and showroom smart with polish and varnish. Van der Valk had to feel slightly ashamed of his cigar, a superb and gigantic Romeo and Juliet from Cuba – Frans Mierle's of course – when Mother dashed at him with a spotless ashtray.

'Is there something serious?' asked Brinkman flatly.

'Yes. It may turn out less so than now seems likely.'

'I see from your card, Mr Van der Valk, that you belong to the juvenile branch. Is it Wim?'

'Yes. But first of all, where is Wim?'

'Not here, I fear. Are you going to – do you have to take him?'

'No. Only talk. Simply that I should prefer to talk to him here, where you could follow everything.'

'Ah. He is very seldom here, unless his study absolutely demands it.'

'How does he get on with it?'

'Well, I am glad to say. His employers say that he is an asset, though his theoretical work is sometimes weak. He finds his maths a burden, I'm afraid. He hasn't stolen anything from them? Is it there that the trouble lies?'

'No, do not worry yourself with that. He is in a gang, which has disturbing activities.' Clink-clink went the teacups; Mrs Brinkman was not neglecting her duties to a visitor.

'I find the phrase "disturbing activities" rather ominous.'

'They are ominous; they've been going a good deal further than the tricks of these gangs do as a rule. On the other hand the boys may not be entirely responsible for some of the goings on. I don't only say that to reassure you. Nowadays we like to be very sure, before we talk about arrests or courts, that they are really necessary. This is, so far, what we term an informal enquiry.'

'Take another biscuit, do,' said Mother. 'We're from Zaandam; double ration.'

'Tell me frankly, Mr Brinkman; do you find Wim difficult to control?'

'I am bound to answer that he is hardly controllable at all, I'm afraid. I know something about this gang, if only that they are all boys with more money than he has, so that he feels obliged to keep his end up. He pays little heed to either his mother or myself; he finds us too quiet and tame, and I suspect that he is ashamed of our being very ordinary folk. He does show affection, and gratitude, often; don't mistake me, he's a fine boy. He knows too that we are always wholeheartedly behind him. But he can be violent; we have had painful scenes. I should take stronger steps to keep him in order, I know, but I am afraid of prejudicing his career. You may say I give it overmuch importance, but it seems the one really bright spot in a gloomy picture. Myself, I never became highly qualified, and then there weren't these apprenticeships and technical sandwich courses, and it all took more money. I am ambitious for the boy, and the engineering firm think highly of him; they will pay his expenses for further studies in Germany. I am very apprehensive in case all this should be spoilt by some foolish trick. Now you come here and make me very uneasy indeed.'

'I am sorry that I cannot reassure you much at this moment. Perhaps when we know more . . . Impress on him if you can that his career may be damaged if he is not quite open with me. Perhaps it would be best if someone were to go to the Ange Gabriel, where I expect he is to be found.'

'Playing billiards,' said Brinkman a little bitterly. 'At that he's the best in town. I will send my daughter.'

'Then I will come back in half an hour. No need to say anything, simply that I wish to see him.'

The Richard Strausslaan runs through this district; the bungalow of the Carnavelet family was a few hundred metres down from the crossing. The architect opened the door, without any enthusiasm at seeing him, wearing old trousers and a polo-necked sweater, and smoking a pipe. He led the way into a very pleasant living-room, wood-panelled, with many bookshelves, a lot of high-fidelity listening apparatus, and some fine eighteenth-century prints. Michel sat in a corner, deep in a magazine, or pretending to be; he put it down and got to his feet, whether from good manners or from defiance would be hard to say. He was a loose, lightly-built boy with an intelligent face; taut and wiry, long thick black hair carefully combed back. He looked as though for two pins he would make a dash out of the door.

Van der Valk had no fixed approach to adolescents, least of all a phony attitude of commiseration. Playing chaplain is an act boys and girls see through with great speed. He refused a cigarette; he was rather glad to have got to the end of his enormous cigar, which was beginning to bore him.

'Listen, Michel; did you ever spend any time thinking what would happen when you were caught?'

It took the boy aback; he frowned and turned it over in his mind.

'When was I caught?'

'Not realised it yet? Talk now as though I could help you, because you'll be surprised how much I can.'

'I've only your word for it. What am I supposed to have done?'

'Forgotten all about the Schubertstraat? The car to Sloterdijk? The train to Haarlem?'

'Whoever you're looking for, I'm someone else.'

'All six of you?'

'I speak for myself. Let them do the same.'

'I see; you've made up your mind to say nothing. Not clever. The cats won't like that.'

Anxiety showed for a second, like a rabbit at the mouth of a burrow. 'The cats? What have they to do with you?'

'Ah; at length someone who doesn't pretend not to know what the cats are.'

The boy flushed, and his mouth twitched. But he held firm. 'I said none of us have anything to do with you.'

'I got told different.'

'Who by?'

'One of you used the very words I did, in a house by the Beatrix Park. Recall? The woman remembered. That the cats wouldn't like it. They won't like this either, will they?'

'They won't tell you anything. No more will I. You're just singing.'

'Think so? How do you suppose it came into my mind, over there in Amsterdam, to come up here for a few words with you? Put in more work on your idea. Was it through the cats, do you think? What gave you away?' Anxiety showed there again, plain to see this time. But Carnavalet intervened.

'That'll do, Van der Valk. Too many leading questions; court would not allow that. If you have any proofs, produce them. Otherwise shut up.'

'Michel, Erik, Bertus, Wim, Frank and Dick. And Kees van Sonneveld?'

The effect was startling. The boy sprang up, and held himself in check with an effort.

'The cats will get him,' viciously, and then bit back the next words. 'I'm not saying a word. Do what you like; I'm not saying a word.' With two steps he was at the door; he turned and gave Van der Valk a look of fear and hate before slamming it.

## *Chapter Four*

'Now what does one make of that?' Carnavalet had a bemused look. 'I can't make any sense of any of this. Who or what are these cats?'

'Believe me or not I have no more idea than you. But you can see that it meant plenty to the boy. You and your ideals. Sure I was asking the boy leading questions and it would not have been allowed in a court. We're not in a court; we're trying to find out what it's all about. Wasn't doing the boy any harm, and might even have got somewhere if you hadn't opened your mouth.'

Carnavalet looked penitent. 'Are you planning to arrest him?'

'Certainly not. Serve no useful purpose. They all take the same attitude; death or glory, say nothing; but they cannot help giving things away. It is confused still, and it has to add up to something before I make any decisions.'

'I'm sorry the boy behaved like that.'

'Didn't worry me. Any boy defending himself is hostile and offensive. I'm beginning to establish a certain pattern. When I feel that one exists I will make a report to the Officer of Justice. He will decide further steps. It may take some time; I cannot tell you much more at present, but call my office any time. Good night.'

The rest of the evening was much the same. He had been amused by Wim, who had refused point-blank to come home or talk to him at all. He made no effort to coerce the boy; it would have got him no further. The other parents were no great help either, though Heer Wagenfeld turned out to be an engaging man, with a good deal of humour; odd that his son Bertus should have none at all. As for Dick's papa, the abstracted, imaginative designer of machinery, whom he had thought would prove a reasonable person, he turned out to be the toughest proposition of the evening; a righteous man. Van der Valk guessed, indeed, that this righteousness was often a source of conflict in his house. Willem

Krebbers said that no proof of his son's connexion with any misdeeds existed, that Van der Valk's suspicions were not sufficient ground even to allow him inside the house, and that common courtesy alone compelled him to listen. In short his ears and eyes were closed. He did not raise his voice, and was careful not to be rude, but he was adamantly in-the-right, and very touchy at the faintest hint that he might not know everything his son did or thought. He had more sense than to be abusive, like Kieft, or sarcastic, like Wagenveld, though he was plainly angry; he made it clear that he would contest – bitterly – any questioning of his son.

Unperturbed, Van der Valk told him to be in readiness for a possible judicial enquiry and a conceivable criminal process, in which case his objections would interest nobody. He drove home shrugging; he had enough – he had his foot in the door.

'I kept the wine till you came. It's lovely; beautiful condensation all over the bottle. You aren't too late. All a waste of time, as usual, I suppose?'

'Some gold. Not too much.'

'And when you have cleared it all up nobody will notice or thank you for all this patient waiting and noticing and tactful explanation that you always do.'

'Too true. But there, it's the only way I am able to handle this sort of thing. Come on, girl; corkscrew.'

Two things had struck him on the way home. None of these boys had sisters – or brothers – anywhere near the same age. Frank, Erik and Dick were only children. Michel had a baby step-brother; Bertus twin brothers of eight; Wim's sister was ten. Secondly, of the four ravens he had spoken to, none had offered the obvious alibi. None had said 'When?' None had said 'Then? Then I was with my girl; ask her'. All four had simply stuck stubbornly and more or less consistently to a stout denial – they had never heard of such nonsense. This he thought odd.

Common enough among adults. Yes, I did it – tacitly – and you know, and I know that you know – and I bloody defy you to prove it. But it was rare among boys. Their instinctive defence was 'No, no, mister, I wasn't even there; ask my Mum, ask my girl.'

He put it out of his mind; the wine was good. He ate supper, and talked holidays with Arlette; that lovely subject. He was in bed, stretching comfortably, before a thought struck him. 'The cats won't tell – the cats will get him' – typical that Michel, easily the most intelligent, should have given the most away. It was obvious. The cats were simply the six girls.

Legally they were untouchable. They could always – and would always – say if they were caught with any loot that it had been received in good faith as a present. 'Just thought it was an ordinary piece of kitsch – never dreamed they could be real diamonds.' Boersma maintained – and rightly, he thought – that girls were responsible for all gang troubles, but whatever knowledge they had of the boys' designs, rarely did they take part in any gang's activities. These ones, one felt sure, knew nothing. They were there for decoration, for prestige, for simple – very simple – sexual entertainment. He had heard a girl of this age say once, indignantly, 'I'm just an instrument, that's all.'

It was puzzling how they proposed to 'get' the unfortunate Kees – if indeed they did. Ostracising him would be a bit weak. Would they beat him up? More likely; he had known terrifying things done to harmless passers-by, thought up by tough factory girls, in the trains from Zaandam at knocking-off time. But that would not be much in the style of the young ladies ofBloemendaal. These girls were the new aristocracy, highly educated and trained. Where a former generation had gone to finishing schools in Paris or Brussels, these sprigs went to theatre or hotel or ballet schools. These had not needed even the year's 'household help' in France or Germany, that had become such a feature of Dutch girls' education. They had travelled all over Europe with their parents, and spoke four languages easily. They wouldn't beat anyone up. What would they do?

Next day in Boersma's office he was making his report.

'That's the score; no possible doubt, as I think you'll agree. But I can't see any grounds on which we could pull them in. Too many suppositions still; we haven't anything we could give the magistrate. Can't prove guilt, can't assume innocence.'

'Yes; false position. I think we could pull them in, mark, and let them stew. We'd soon get our material then. Those two you mention – they'd give in pretty quick. But I agree – I've thought it all along as you know – that there's some other element involved here. Leave them free for the present and we are more likely to learn something. And they can't guess how little we in fact know.

Any ideas on keeping the pot boiling?'

'Vaguely. The odd boy, this van Sonneveld child, may be a weak link, and tell us more about this cats angle. And if by any chance we are right, and this Jansen really has something to do with the gang, mightn't he be tempted to tamper with the witnesses, then we'd have some grip?'

'Mm. These girls – cats, cows, whatever you call them – useless to us, as I see it. We've nothing on them, nor are we likely to get it. I don't want any truck with these smart little bitches; quite enough trouble as it is, huh? Parents! This other boy, though, yes.'

'He'll hear from the others that I've been questioning them, and he'll wonder why he has been left alone. I think that will be making him uneasy.'

Brrrr went the telephone; Boersma stretched out a hairy powerful paw.

'Commissaris here. Yes. ... Put him on. ... Yes, with Boersma. Yes. ... You leave me to be the judge of that. ... Give me the details.' His hand scrawled steadily in precise longhand, surprisingly neat. 'With a K or with a C? Yes. ... As far as is known, clothes and passport? Money, mm? Good. ... Very well. ... It ties up with something we're working on; I'll take the necessary steps. ... Of course. ... Standing order that you notify this department in all such cases. ... I want any progress put on the telex to here at once. ... All right; 'bye.' Plonk.

'Something of a coincidence there, but not altogether unexpected from what you tell me. You've caused a panic among these boys all right. That was our friends, the Bloemendaal bureau. Your birdy. Young man called Kees van Sonneveld. They report his disappearance, early this morning.'

'Well, for once a stroke of luck. And given that, we might be able to open the can. We can hold him for that; obstruction of an enquiry, huh?'

'It'll be easy enough. Took a passport, so headed over a frontier. We'll get him in Belgium or Germany.' Boersma pressed his intercom button. 'Sanders? Come on in here.'

Duty brigadier, with a shorthand pad.

'Disappearance; we want him quick; usual notice to passport people, customs, foreign police and interior. Photo and full particulars on the way from Bloemendaal. Probably over the frontier by now, but check Roosendaal and Zevenaar first, because odds are he took a train. He'd have to steal a car; might reckon it would lead to him quicker. I want him held for this department, understand, and not Bloemendaal; we want him. Directly he's signalled I want to be notified, and one of your boys, Van der Valk, can go and pick him up. Should be easy.'

'What do you think of my getting out to Bloemendaal?' said Van der Valk. 'I'm thinking I'd better get Marcousis into focus, and he can help. Unless you'd rather talk to him first?'

'Not at all. Leave that to you.'

'There's a couple of other angles. This boy's girl, for instance. If he's in it, so will she be.'

Boersma gave a look of patient disgust.

'Yes, I know; leave them out of it. But now that the boy's vanished, I have a logical approach to her. I'm thinking of the tie with Jansen. This club in the ice-salon – Jansen's flat is immediately above. And I think that they play games up there. Sofa games.'

'Use your own judgement.'

*

Commissaire Marcousis, head of the Bloemendaal police bureau, was a handsome, commanding personage, with a fine profile and a resonant voice. He was immensely good at the social side of his work; on the best possible terms with anyone who could conceivably matter, and his sports club was the best run in the province of North Holland. He was always accompanied by two beautiful setter dogs on a lead; both he and the dogs were always perfectly brushed. Van der Valk disillusioned him in a few words.

'Oh Jesus Christ. Now look, Van der Valk, this absolutely must be handled tactfully. You seem to have gone absolutely blind, on no logical premises at all. Huh? Isn't that so, huh?'

'Quite right.'

'Mm. Well, I feel bound to point out that if you've made any hit at all, which still seems insufficiently demonstrated to me, it was pure chance. No evidence to support you, and you go blundering about, and that may have serious consequences.'

'You will agree, Commissaris, that if I had found nothing I would have been able to let the whole thing drop and no one would have been the wiser. Now that the evidence tends to support a stray idea, the first person I notify is you. I've been careful, agree.'

'Yes, yes, I appreciate that, you've been as tactful as possible, I suppose.' The tone implied rather that he would have been a lot more tactful. 'Well, you've found trouble, and it concerns your department and offences in your area – we have no juvenile department here of course, it all falls on the recherche. We've had no trouble here, otherwise we'd have found this out, of course. Now you've begun you'd best handle this, I suppose, but I must insist on your doing so very discreetly indeed. And I'll deal with the Press.'

'Mr Boersma hoped that you would. Thank you, Commissaris; rely on me.'

'Oh Jesus Christ, some of the most important men in this town! Slip up and I'll have your scalp; is that clear? It's unheard of. Don't expect that I can lend you a lot of spare personnel, either; two of the recherche staff are on leave. And what proof have you got anyhow?'

'None at all,' cheerfully.

'Oh God, you people in Amsterdam seem very irresponsible. Now I must emphasise that you are to keep me minutely informed. This is a very grave allegation.'

Van der Valk said nothing about Hjalmar Jansen. Crowd-pleaser, he thought as he left a greatly disturbed policeman planning how to practise tact on the Press.

*

Arie van Sonneveld, father of the unfortunate Kees, was an account executive in an advertising agency. Commendably, he had gone as usual to work. His wife was a copywriter in the same concern. She was a very smart, cool woman in a black two-piece, and fire-engine lipstick. Equally commendably, she had not gone to work.

'Come in, Chief Inspector, do, and make yourself comfortable. I'm afraid everything is a pigsty still here; we haven't exactly been able to get on with the routine this morning. Sit down, do; can I get you a drink? Whisky or anything? Or is it too early still – would you like coffee?'

'Coffee would be nice.'

'Elise, dear, can you be sweet and make us some coffee?'

It was a five-room flat on the boulevard; very modern, like the window of an expensive shop. The chairs were covered in some sort of shaggy stuff; imitation bearskin or something. Daring colour-schemes, obscure abstract pictures, ugly furniture on knitting-needle legs, labour-saving gadgets everywhere. The walls were too thin; fizzzzz went the supersonic coffee-mill in the kitchen; wheeeeee went the electric kettle. The fire was electric – everything was electric, including Mrs van Sonneveld.

She talked too much, and smoked exaggeratedly, flicking ash about with over-bright fingernails. Her skirt was too thin and too tight; one could trace the outline of her girdle stretched over her neat little buttocks. Her eyelashes were too black and her breasts were too pointed; Van der Valk taped her promptly as a tiresome bitch; a restless, unsatisfied woman who really needed to be raped by three drunken sailors. These surroundings must have been enough to drive the boy Kees silly.

'We got up a bit late – have you heard all this? I did tell it to the inspector at the bureau.'

'I'd be glad to hear everything again from you, if you don't mind telling it again.'

'Not a bit. Well we were up a bit late, and we'd slept heavily; we'd been to a party last night, and taken a fair amount of gin on board, not so much that I couldn't drive, of course. Arie – my husband – never will drive at all after a party,' she added rather hastily, as though she had made a slip.

'Well, at breakfast Kees didn't appear, and he had classes of course, and it was really getting late, so I went to call him, and found some of his clothes were missing and he wasn't there at all. The bed had been slept in, otherwise I might have thought he'd spent the night with some friend. Then we found a good deal of money was gone, and our passports are kept in the same place, and I saw his was missing, and then it dawned on me he was really gone, and hadn't just got up unusually early for some reason. He's been so queer lately, you see; rude and abrupt, or just silent, and we had been rather concerned even before this. Black for you?'

'Good, that's very clear. Now I must do a little explaining, on my own account. You'll have noticed from my card that I'm from zeden-en-kinder-politie in Amsterdam. That's quite normal; my department has a central organisation connected with it for missing persons, and they notify us when it is a question of a boy or girl, automatically. It just so happened that we had known something of Kees before this morning. You ask us, and yourself, why Kees has run away like this; I'm afraid we have a shrewd idea why. We found that he had become involved with a crowd of other boys – all from this town – who have formed a gang, and to be brief, they've been doing some very disturbing things. I must add that in fairness we have no reason to suppose that Kees has actually been doing anything classifiable as criminal – or you'd have been notified, naturally – but he is connected. You follow me so far?' Big wide doe-eyes nodded, yes.

'We have quite an account with these boys, but the enquiry, of which I am in charge, hasn't got as yet beyond initial questioning. No one has been arrested, or anything. And so far I had left Kees out, for the reasons I gave. Now, either he's got alarmed at knowing a bit too much of what the others were up to, and frightened of being questioned in his turn, or he may have rather more than just guilty knowledge. I don't know yet.'

'Oh dear. Oh dear; is there going to be a scandal?'

'I cannot deny that it is serious. There are sensational features' – one could never quite rid oneself of these clichés, this police jargon – 'and there will, I'm afraid, be publicity, and bluntly, this bunk the silly boy's done won't help.' Not much it won't help, he added silently; not telling you that.

'Forgive me just one sec. – Elise. There's a shopping list on the kitchen table; would you be a lamb and do it for me? It doesn't look as though I shall have time. – I'm so sorry to interrupt you; do go on. Will you be able to find Kees? I'm afraid this is a ghastly blow for me, rather.'

'Oh yes, and easily. In another country in particular he'll stand out like a lighthouse. A day or two, at latest, I expect.' The front door of the flat closed with a resonant snap. 'I should like to ask you, Mrs van Sonneveld, a little about this odd behaviour of Kees you noticed and mentioned just now. It can wait if you are in a great hurry. Would you prefer to talk to your husband, and perhaps either of you would come to see me at my office?'

'No no, I'd rather get it over. And I must stay in anyway; Elise has no key. It doesn't do to give them keys; they slip out when one's not there. Will you arrest Kees?'

'I think it likely that we may hold on to him a day or two. Whether we keep him depends on what he has to say for himself. Have you any idea, now that you look back, what can have made him silent and abrupt to an unusual degree?'

'No, I'm afraid I can't. I can see now that he had something on his mind, but I thought it would settle itself if left alone. My husband and I are kept so busy, and have ourselves so many problems occupying our attention, that really we did not give an awful lot of thought. . . .'

She got up to bring him an ashtray, and sat down again alongside him, on the studio couch. She put her chin in her hand and crossed her legs elegantly.

'It's very good of you to be so considerate, Inspector.'

Van der Valk said nothing. She's got something to confess, he thought.

'I do wish I could help in some way to keep poor Kees out. I've been thinking that if anyone can you will see that things – aren't dramatised too much, if you see what I mean. You can understand that we want to avoid that kind of publicity. I know what papers are, I deal with them at work a lot, and they can be fearful. If you could help me in that – well, I would be very willing to cooperate with you, in any way I could.'

She leaned over to put her cigarette out, letting him smell her hair. What's coming, he thought.

'The result of these investigations, when someone as obviously very intelligent as you are is in charge, hangs so much on how they are conducted – isn't it so?' She was sitting on his left; she made a slow half-turn and subsided gracefully on top of him. Merde, he thought; I was slow; shouldn't have let her sit next to me, idiot that I am.

'I'm so dreadfully nervous at all this; feel how my pulse jumps.' She had picked up his momentarily-undecided right hand and pressed it against her breast. He grinned at her flickering eyes.

'I'm afraid your ideas might lead to difficulties.'

'Do be nice to me; I am so upset, I need consoling.' Irritation, boredom, lechery and amusement were nicely balanced inside him. She was showing a nicely calculated strip of rather scrawny thigh above the tops of her stockings.

'Oh, damn this skirt; it's so tight.' Her knickers were shocking-pink, a shade he found rather distasteful. All we need now is a photographer.

'Darling. I want you so badly.' He cleared his throat in a pompous way, which made him think of Marcousis – now how would he have handled this? – and cursed the deep cushions and the sloping back of the studio couch. He got both hands under her and with a heave of his stomach muscles got on his feet, carrying her, with a strong desire to laugh. Better not; only make her furious.

He put her carefully in a chair.

'Look; let me get you a drink.' She showed neither anger nor embarrassment.

'Perhaps you would. I think I could do with one. Whisky and dry ginger, if you don't mind, rather weak.' He had the same himself, with much the same sentiment. It was rather nice.

'I think that on the whole you'd be wiser not to influence me.'

'I suppose you're right, yes. You can't blame me for trying. I'm sure you too know how to be discreet.'

He gave a little bow and sketched a polite smile. 'I'll see that you're kept in touch, Mrs van Sonneveld. You have my card. Ask your husband to come in and have a talk with me.'

Outside, he got into the driving seat of the little police Mercedes with a crash, puffed loudly, pushed his hat back and reached for a cigarette.

Hannie Troost. Good honest-sounding farmer's name. He reflected that she was a very pretty girl indeed. Would she now go winding her legs round him and whispering invitations to pull her knickers down? – tight white cotton, he had no doubt. Ha, he rather thought not, and guffawed aloud; a woman passing with a shopping bag looked scandalised; well she might.

Terschellingstraat; right up at the north end of the town, where the sea-boulevard curved inward to the pleasant district called the 'Islands' after the street-names. A house like the one where Bertus, the bank manager's son, lived; comfortable houses for comfortably-off people; this one very neat-looking, and clean with fresh paint against the brutal, destructive sea air.

He was not sure what Pa did; there was a younger sister at school still; mm, Hannie must be a little younger than some of the other girls; could not be much over seventeen.

'Mevrouw Troost? Van der Valk, recherche Amsterdam; here is my card.'

Not flustered, this woman; quiet eyes read the card carefully.

'I'm cooking, but come inside.' Fat, unpretentious, been pretty, wore her clothes well. Rather like the woman in the Beatrix Park. She fiddled a minute with the saucepans on the stove and sat down calmly.

'Your daughter Hannie has a friend, a young man called Kees van Sonneveld.'

'Yes, I know. Pleasant boy; nice manners. He's been here once or twice.'

'Do you know his family at all?'

'No, not at all. I believe they live on the boulevard, and have a lot more money than me,' with a pleasant grin.

'The children get on well together?'

'I think so; they've been out together often.'

'And what do you think of it? Not opposed?'

She smiled. 'I don't take these things too seriously, you know. Why should I be opposed? One's always anxious about one's chickens, but he seems a nice quiet boy. Unless your being here means – ?'

'Yes, I was just coming to that. I was going to ask whether you've noticed any particular change in Hannie's ways; any alteration in her normal behaviour. In the last few weeks, say? Only because the boy seems to have been behaving oddly.'

'I won't say in the last month or so, no. These last couple of days she's been perhaps a bit moody and disagreeable. I guessed she'd had a quarrel with the boy, maybe, or found some new charmer – or he had. I paid no attention; these things come and go, don't they? Adolescent tantrums, but you know that what they regard as nosiness in parents is not well received.'

'You get on well with her as a rule, then?'

'Oh yes indeed; she can be difficult – what child isn't at that age? – but she's a sunny girl; sings all day as a rule.'

'Is she intelligent?'

'Not outstandingly so, no, but certainly not stupid. Shows a considerable talent in her art classes, which she's very keen to follow up.'

'Tell me; did she behave at all oddly this morning?'

Something like a tiny cloud of suspicion or fear puckered the skin between her eyes.

'Queer that you should ask; she's out of sorts this morning, hasn't gone to her classes. Complains of headache and 'flu pains. You're not breaking anything to me gently, are you, Inspector? She's not in your bad books in some extraordinary way?'

'I've no reason to think so. She's no period troubles or anything of that sort?'

'No, no; I'd know at once.'

'Well I haven't any secrets to keep from you, Mevrouw Troost; the aim of all this was only to throw a little possible light on the boy Kees. He's missing from home, and in a tangle generally, and I was curious to know whether Hannie knew anything about it, or whether his troubles had infected her perhaps. Since she's here I'd be glad of a word with her.'

'I'm afraid she's in bed. I suppose you could talk to her if you really wanted – I'd prefer to be present myself.'

'Let me be frank with you. As a policeman I tend to be something of a specialist. I have to let children feel their confidence is quite safe, and since it concerns another I think she might tell me what she knows. But will you understand that she might feel reservations, concerning the boy, with you there? As to being in her room I agree that is not suitable. It would be best if you ask her to put on a dressing-gown and come down for a quarter of an hour, after which she can go peacefully back to bed and I won't bother any of you any further.'

'Very well,' a little dubiously. 'I do understand that. I'll call her since you wish it.'

The girl was down after a wait of a cigarette; a really startlingly pretty girl in the daylight, with long silver-blonde hair that she had tied back with a ribbon. She had found time to paint her mouth carefully, he saw with amusement. With even more amusement he saw her make good and sure that her mother was not listening at the door. She had not put on a housecoat, but trousers and a sweater. She had a rough manner, a blend of shyness and sulkiness.

'I thought there were some cigarettes around here somewhere.'

'Take one of these.'

'All right; thanks. You're some sort of policeman, Mother said.'

'Some sort.'

'What's Kees done? Mother said it was something about him.'

'A bunk.'

'How, a bunk?'

'Took his passport, and a few clothes, and all the money he could find, and just walked off somewhere.'

'Oh dear; I was rather afraid of something like that. Where is he, or don't you know?'

'Soon will. Germany or Belgium. Were you worried about him?'

'Well, he said he would, but I didn't really think he would.'

'What was it all about?'

'I don't really know. He had a fight with one of the other boys, and he was fed-up, the way one gets sometimes, and he was talking a bit about cutting loose.'

'At the Engeltje? Last night?'

'Yes, but I came late; I had a bit of work to do, and I don't know quite what happened earlier, but there'd been some sort of row.'

Michel, thought Van der Valk.

'But you don't know what?'

'He wouldn't tell me.'

'I see. How are things between you?'

'All right. He was just fed-up. We all get that way.'

'Weren't the other girls there? Didn't they tell you?

'Some might have been there. But I don't go round with them all that much. We're not quite the same crowd.'

'So you didn't particularly want to ask them?'

'No.'

'You've had no rows, then, with Kees, these last few days?'

'No; why?'

'Your mother thought you might have.'

'Mother? – what does she know about it? She always thinks she knows everything.'

'Kees' mother thought he'd been a bit broody for a day or two now.'

The girl shrugged; she was not interested in what Kees' mother had or hadn't thought.

'So no fight?'

'No, I tell you.'

'You go together? Steady, I mean.' Nod, casual.

'Go to bed together?' That woke her up; she blushed furiously.

'Hey.'

He grinned. 'All right, your mother's not listening. I know how things are. You do don't you?'

'Well . . .'

'Not pregnant, are you?'

'You do ask some questions, don't you?'

'Ach, that's the way I live. Good old Professor Pipi.'

She laughed. 'No, I'm not. Good heavens, if Mother heard this she'd have a fit.'

'Why d'you think I wanted to see you alone? You're sure?'

'Too true I'm sure.'

'Mean you got the thing now?' Nod, indifferent.

'We'll find Kees soon enough. But that's less important than straightening him out, right? If he just ran away because he had a fight with his family . . . You know them?'

'I've met them.'

'Like them?'

'Yeees. His father's all right, or would be if he ever stopped talking, but I didn't take to his mother much; in fact to be honest I thought her a perfect bitch. Kees can't stand her even if she is his mother.'

'So you reckon it must be on account of her?'

'Don't know what else it could have been.'

'Well, if that's all it is, I can't do much.' She was coming along nicely now. 'I thought he might just have slipped off because the police were picking up the ravens.' He said it casually and watched her go white.

'Oh no . . . but . . .'

'Affects Kees, doesn't it?'

'But . . . how do you know about the ravens?'

'Professor Pipi knows all; in other words, it's my business.'

'I can't tell you anything about them.'

'Or the cats?'

Silence. Angry frightened eyes glared at him.

'You're one of the cats; you know all about this business.' She bit her lip. 'All right, Hannie; go on back to bed; I won't push you now.'

He went back through the kitchen, where Mother was clattering pots about, rather ostentatiously not listening at the door.

'Thank you very much, Mevrouw Troost, that was a lot of help. There's an involved story, which we'll get to the bottom of when we've seen the boy. I think she probably has a lot of influence over him; I might ask her to come along to my office, maybe, when I have the boy there. I'll phone you if I think it becomes necessary. Thank you again.'

He drove thoughtfully back to Amsterdam. Did the ravens – or the cats – know yet that Kees was missing? In his office he gave some instructions. One was that Hannie Troost's movements should be watched with some care. She would hardly be going out today, but after seeing him, maybe . . . The other was that the phone should be tapped.

When he got back from lunch the message lay on his desk that Kees van Sonneveld had been picked up registering at a small hotel in Keulen.

Van der Valk talked briefly into his phone. Bring the boy back under escort, rub in the fugitive from justice stuff a bit, lock him up. He sat thinking. Three hours now hanging about in a depressing German police bureau, waiting for the unwelcome sight of some clot of a Dutch policeman. Then the dreary journey through the Ruhrgebied, the tedious lingering at Emmerich, the wearisome landscape of central Holland, and then instead of a warm, lit, homely Amsterdam the chill of the police bureau; the ignominy of being stared at as unimportant, entered on a form, searched, locked up, not knowing what the morning would show. Kees was a sensititive boy; his knees would buckle.

Van der Valk looked out of his window. The variable, treacherous spring weather had hauled around again into the west; the clear cool sunshine had vanished. The wind had almost dropped – the scud of cloud had slowed into a sort of grey vapour that hung over everything. A tedious drizzling grey rain stopped and started, and could make up its mind neither to blow over, nor to rain and be done with it. He disliked it most because it was undecided, like him.

## *Chapter Five*

This wretched child now – bah, he had not had a good lunch – he could of course bring the brat into a thoroughly confessing frame of mind within a few hours. If he knew anything – and presumably he did – it would be evidence enough to roll the gang up. And then would that be that? Suppose nothing that he then heard from any of them served to implicate Jansen in the slightest? Would that still be that, and he be forced to forget his instinct, that shadow of doubt that had deepened to a certainty as the affair ripened? He could not drop any hints; if he encouraged the boys to implicate Jansen no doubt they would; they would seize any shadow of excuse in mitigation. Anybody could see that with no evidence, concrete evidence, of an adult being in any way involved, the prosecution would be very sharp. They were all around eighteen, liable to be treated almost as adults – and the rape, the tying-up – there were ferocious scores against them.

This part, too, was just what he did not understand. The rest – the breaking in, the stealing, the destructiveness especially – that was standard gang behaviour, nasty no doubt, but not really serious, save in the emotional minds of prosecutors, laying about them in court with hot flushed phrases. For those things there were explanations – not that they did anybody any good.

One could not even blame the parents overmuch. One could not say that their laziness and their selfishness alone were at fault, any more than one could go canting around whining that it was all the fault of the bomb. Men, and children too, did fearful things. That could not be sentimentalised. He considered those people whom he could never understand, who blamed the bomb for everything and themselves for the bomb. They seemed to be mostly English; why was that? They had made a scapegoat of the thing, it seemed to him; get rid of the bomb and all our sins will be wiped clean. Would they now? He would rather be red than dead too, he thought, but for rather different reasons.

Society was at fault, always had been. For its sins we would send these children to houses of reform, and even if we sent their parents too it would not improve society. To go on about the bomb was hypocritical tripe. Hiroshima was a plague epidemic. We cured the plague and invented the bomb to take its place. Camus' plague was fascism . . . names, names. We didn't get rid of them. Plague in the Borinage was the mines – poor old Zola, who had seen, or thought to see, the germ of a new world grow out of the plague-pit of the mines ninety years before. History was full of plagues; this was just the latest.

History was full, too, of examples of young men who formed gangs and terrorised the innocent. Often they had been of rich families; more often than not, he dared say. The Mohawks of the eighteenth century had been worse than anything he knew of today; these events remained common coin. As for this gang he had here, it was simply more bourgeois, less imaginative than the boys in Paris who chased each other through the Bois in cars, at night. Really his job was a ridiculous one.

Society, he thought, was a fermenting mass, like a huge farmer's-pot of pig-swill, boiling on fires of hatred and envy, of bad education and war and outrage, of poverty and starvation, homelessness, joblessness. The scum rose to the top, where he was supposed to skim it off with a ridiculous tiny spoon. He could never reach the ferments and instabilities inside, let alone the fires below. He too was part of that sinister boiling in the pot. Tied, too, to these boys, with a strong band. What would he have felt, and done, had it been Arlette who had been raped? And what had he been like at eighteen years of age?

There you were; it had been nineteen-forty, a plague year, that. Everyone had said that his generation had been unlucky, to have to go to war instead of finishing its education in peace. If he hadn't gone to war no doubt he would have been in a gang. Unlucky! Had he been older he would have eaten the bitterness of unemployment, of the Chiappe riots. He had thought himself very lucky; he still did.

He had been given a gun, and an official licence from the state to kill Germans; a fine hunter's licence. He remembered his immense pleasure in that gun. Young men of eighteen were natural warriors. Hunters; raptors. To alter those instincts, channel them into a petty little world of commercial throat-cutting and financial rape – an unworthy ambition.

He shrugged. His amateur comments interested nobody and were very dangerous to himself. If he talked like that, anywhere, he would be branded atheist, anarchist – every generation has its little ism. I am everything, I contain multitudes. Sure I'm anarchist, sure I'm fascist, sure I'm communist, I admit it gladly. But as a professional policeman that wouldn't do; he'd be out of a job in a week, and that was just; he wasn't paid to trot about being sorry for either communists in the Borinage or fascists in Algiers, however much he sympathised with either.

He was paid by the state to call these pathetic boys to account; be it so; he had his duty to the state. Privately he could think the state a fool, and did; why, so it was. But Befehl ist Befehl. To do one's duty is important. People despised the Germans for obeying the state. That was surely illogical. They might be blamed for creating that state, but not for obeying it.

Look at the Swiss Guards – Christ, they were not even French, and they came from Liberty-land, bonfires on the first of August. Foreigners and mercenaries, and they died fighting like tigers to defend an empty royal palace, worthlessly, senselessly. Yes, but how admirably. They had their place in history for doing their duty. Only a sentimentalist would have respected them had they torn off their uniforms and joined the ragged idealists driven by hunger, most just of causes.

One admires the men who manned the barricades under Louis Philippe, and one also admires the soldiers who fired upon them.

You sit here being high-minded, Van der Valk, but there's work to be done. But I am trying to understand, he thought. My job is to defend society, to resist and contain those attacking it. Were the ravens attacking it? Weren't they making a gesture, only, against a society that sent them to classes to learn how to make money – classes which they all followed scrupulously? What about Jansen, the respectable restaurateur? Was he a defender of society? He considered Mr Jansen.

Van der Valk had started his recherche career on the night-club squad – the comically named 'brigade mondaine'. The society troop; not so comically misnamed, he had always thought; quite the contrary; named both justly and shrewdly. In that work he had come to know a bit about the night-club business.

Men who keep bars, restaurants, cabarets, are predators too, more than most men. He had always thought Victor Hugo acute, to have made Thenardier an innkeeper; in this business it is instinctive to despise society. The waiter sees captains of industry drunk and maudlin; he observes with cynicism the table manners of millionaires. He knows which women are prostitutes. He sees the petulance of the most respected members of society – bored and whining children, banging on their high-chairs and screaming to be amused. If such a man were an artist he might be a considerable artist. Like any Amsterdammer, Van der Valk knew Frits Schiller. And he had often thought – if I had a bar I would hang it full of pictures by Ludwig Bemelmans. Dodo from Hamburg dancing in the Crazy Horse saloon – go on, look at yourselves.

But if a barkeeper was a weak character, and intelligent enough to be bored by the tedious business of making money from society's frivolous hours – why then, he might become a dangerous man. He might become an outlaw, a pimp, a pornographer, indulging his hatred and contempt for this miserable society and taking it by the throat.

In his young days he had often thought about this. It had been this thought that had jumped back into his head when he first heard about Jansen from Feodora, and this thought that had stuck in his head after seeing and hearing the man.

He went to the lavatory and washed, and combed his hair, and was distracted from fine thoughts by a button gone off his shirt. Raincoat weather too, and his summer raincoat was at home. He put on his long black leather coat crossly, and got heavily into the little Mercedes, rocking it on its springs; a hundred and sixty pounds of honest policeman. Idiot that I am, he told himself, turning the nose of the car towards Bloemendaal.

At three in the afternoon the Ange Gabriel stood aired and cleaned. Doors and windows had been open all morning, but were shut now; here, by the sea-boulevard, the greyness was coldest and wettest. One could still smell the fresh air inside. The log fire was giving out a pleasant warmth; the barman, in shirt-sleeves, was cleaning the shelves behind the bar. Hjalmar Jansen, with typed lists pinned to a board, was checking his bar stocks; Van der Valk wondered how long he had been out of bed – he could scarcely have got into it before five-thirty. Nobody else was in the bar. Doubtless some came at lunchtime for an aperitif and a business talk over the poker dice.

There was a thick sea-fog hanging over the boulevard; the North Sea slapped idly at half flood; a few mothers were pushing prams lazily along the pavements of the Oranjestraat, stopping to peer into show windows, or gossip. Jansen wore soft, dark blue trousers, and a white polo-necked sweater, like a gymnastics instructor, young and healthy and innocent. His dark auburn hair hung over his forehead; his clear pale skin looked fresh and rested.

'Now that's a pleasant surprise. Don't bother coming down, Harry. I'll do it. What are you going to drink?'

'Picon, thanks; bit of lemon and a slosh of grenadine. Got a moment to talk?'

'As though I needed any excuse to stop this idiot job. Let's go and sit over there.'

They faced each other across the oblong table; usual Dutch café table, covered with the usual Oriental-design cloth with fringed ends. The barman brought the Picon at last, and coffee for Jansen. A lighter snapped, and the first, aromatic smoke of American-blend cigarettes drifted in blue ribbons across the clear air. Van der Valk brought out one of his business cards and tossed it across the table.

Jansen studied it carefully, while he studied Jansen carefully, learning nothing. The man turned it over to look at the back – why does everyone always do that? – and handed it back slowly, looking at him with indifferent eyes, lowering them at last with a look almost of shyness. Policemen have a trick, of staring with a glaucous gaze; Van der Valk did it now. There are few people who do not shift uncomfortably; Jansen was one, though.

'So, so. Official visit, since you show me that? You're not the less welcome.' The voice, too, was unchanged in timbre, and nothing changes a voice like fear, however well controlled.

'Ah, official, no. But having been here before anonymously, call it, I thought it unwise not to identify myself today. I have to talk a bit of business.'

'I have a faint idea that I know what your business is.'

'Likely enough.' No menace or irony in his tone. Was there any emphasis? If there were it was disregarded.

'I noticed that some of the boys were in a stew – been questioned about something or other by the police – yourself perhaps?'

'Myself. Did they tell you what it was about?'

'No. Can't say I have any knowledge of that. There was some whispering in corners going on, but rather a conspiracy of silence. What I just said I pieced together from words let fall here or there, but I didn't pursue it.'

'You are in their confidence, however.'

Jansen smiled. 'That little word police, you know – puts a stopper on confidence.'

'Think I don't know? But not, I hope, on yours.'

'By no means, but I cannot help you much. I had only an impression that something was amiss, but I thought it unimportant, and I paid little heed. It seems I was wrong.'

'Were you surprised?'

'That's rather a difficult question. I would in a way be surprised; they have harmless methods enough of letting off steam, but really, not knowing what they are supposed to have been doing, I cannot say. On the other hand I don't let myself – so to speak – ever be greatly surprised by them; one never really knows what goes on in their minds. Boys do fall foul of the police after all. I'd say that I would be surprised to hear it was something serious, but is it?'

'You know, I have my own conclusions about that.'

Jansen was not disconcerted. 'Ah, I beg your pardon.' He sipped his coffee, found it cool enough, and drank it off.

'I should nevertheless expect you to pass the benefit of your own conclusions on to me,' said Van der Valk pleasantly. 'You may form your own impression of how serious the matter is.'

'Yes, of course. I must say that I would feel a bit averse to forfeiting whatever confidence the boys might have in me. I take it you want me to pump them. If I became known,' pleasantly, 'as a mouchard, shall I call it, that wouldn't do my business any good.'

All this fencing, thought the policeman. Does he know? Has he realised why I've come?

'You knew, of course, there was a gang.'

'A gang, mm; a gang. Doesn't that imply something criminal? I knew of course that they have a sort of élite, with some pre-eminence among themselves. These boys and girls who use my upper room as their club, as we call it, have a uh, disdain – that's the word – for the herd downstairs, I haven't discouraged that; rather amused me.'

'And the ravens?'

'My word, Chief Inspector, you seem to know as much as I do. They form the committee, one might say; they make the rules. Self-government – it's quite a society in miniature; amuses me to study it. Antics if you like, but the ravens, as they call themselves, are the coming rulers of Bloemendaal, really. All sons and daughters of the most influential figures in this town.'

'Where's your bird today?'

'He's in the flat; he gets in the way when I'm stock-taking. Yes, the bird. They took it as a symbol, call it that, for this, uh, top layer of aristocracy.'

'As a compliment to you?'

'I do believe it was, yes; made me laugh.'

'You weren't aware that this top layer had a tendency to go out and break into people's flats.'

The irony was unmistakable this time but Jansen stayed unruffled. 'I had no notion, stupid as you may think me, but I'm not a trained observer, like yourself. I did pick up a hint that the police have this theory, since apparently the questioning was along those lines. Have you arrested any of them?'

'No need. I can put my hand out at any time I judge fit.'

'Seriously, though, are you entirely satisfied that they have done whatever is imputed to them? They're thoroughly nice boys, you know.'

'I agree. It's a question of fixing the degree of responsibility.'

There was a second's silence, while Jansen appeared to consider the meaning of this remark.

'Ah. That is a question for a professional. I could not pronounce upon such things.'

'Are you upset about this?'

'I am, rather; from what you tell me it sounds as though it might be serious.'

'No more personal reason?'

'My dear Chief Inspector, I hope you are not going to be angry at my encouraging these boys upon my premises. It is, after all, my profession.'

'I should like you to satisfy my curiosity upon one subject.'

'Gladly. What is that?'

'The cats.'

'The cats.' His voice was neutral. 'What about them?'

'Know what they are?'

Pause at the loaded question. Was there a slight apprehensive flicker in the greenish-brown eyes, or was he imagining that?

'There are a good number of girls in the club; the cats, I think, are a sort of élite among them, like the ravens in fact. They have these names for things; you know how seriously they take all their little schemes.'

'Just so. The cats now – do they sleep with the ravens?'

Jansen laughed. 'How on earth do you expect me to know that?'

'You aren't as observant as I had thought you.'

'I don't know what goes on outside my walls, Inspector. They have their little emotional affairs, no doubt, which come and go, and in any event do not interest me. Doubtless something of what you suggest does go on; they aren't made of plaster, these children.'

'I haven't much doubt that they do sleep together, though.'

'Ah, to be frank I have not much doubt of it myself.'

Van der Valk licked at the melting ice in the dregs of his Picon. Was it a good idea to pay out any more line? This smooth bastard knew how to stay away from hooks. Not yet, he thought; let him wonder how much I know. He put his glass down on the mat.

'I ought to be buzzing off, but you know something? I'll have another of these. Go on, join me.'

*

It was after four when he went. He wondered whether he had got anywhere or not. He thought so; hadn't learned much but had sowed seeds, valuable seeds, dragons' teeth. Doubt, yes, and fear and suspicion. He could have gone further; mentioned Kees van

Sonneveld – did Jansen know yet about that? – and the interesting behaviour of Hannie Troost. Ja, he could have developed his idea that they all used Hjalmar's flat for making love. Prove that and he had caught the fellow in a fine piece of hypocrisy for a start. But it was not criminal to let an eighteen-year-old couple play games on your sofa, though it was a natural thing to lie about. It didn't need explaining, and the fellow was quite cute enough not to try. No, he could not get much further yet. That boy Kees had better know something. And would Hannie have phoned any of the cats, to tell them there was a tiger about? He stopped at a phone-box.

'I'm in Bloemendaal. Anything on that Troost girl?'

'No. Bart phoned in. Not been out of the house and no calls.'

'Tell him to sit tight.'

On an impulse he left the car in the Anna Paulowna, and walked up to Feodora's door, thinking that she would probably be out. She was in, though; she had just finished washing her hair, and was in underclothes with a towel round her neck.

'My policeman.'

'Don't remind me; I'm fed up with it.'

'So; crime palls?'

'Tastes of ashes. Arresting people; what good does it ever do?'

'My poor friend; come in and collapse. And the affaire teddi-boy? It is finished?'

'Goddam, it's hardly started. It's slower than an old cow going through a gate. I don't know why I should be so nervous, but I don't like it at all.'

'Ah. No sense in telling you to forget it, but remember too that in the world outside are important things. Not to us, huh, because we know not enough about them. Others do not know about your worries. We measure importance by how great extend our own interest; no more. To prove what I say tell me your worries; you will find me not interested and the matter will lose importance. Here is a change from your stinking atmosphere of criminals and policemen. You don't know the story of Alphonse Daudet, about le Sous-Préfet? He went to practise his speech in the countryside, and was so happy with the landscape that he writed poetry instead.'

'Everybody tells you their worries. You hear all the secrets, my dear.'

'I think I hear more secrets than anyone in this town. It is a fact well known about whores.'

'I don't ask you to tell me any of them, though some would undoubtedly interest me.'

'That is so,' with amusement. 'I am undercover agent. I am knowing who does all the dirty tricks in this town. The business deals – I plot them. I will tell you something, which breaks no confidences. I have one very good friend. He has a son; you are interested in this son. Rich man with big car. Poor fellow, he would like to bring the big car coming to see me but even he does not quite dare.'

'I can put a name to your friend.'

'Yes, I dare say. Well, my friend Frans tells me too what worries him – and what pleases him. When he is bloody clever he comes here and laughs very hard. But now he is worried. He try to find out the answers too, which you are wanting. He can't; the boy tell him nothing. Frans thinks the boy is not refusing to tell, but frightened to tell. He is worried about that.'

Van der Valk smoked in silence.

'We will have a drink. You like marc de Bourgogne?'

'I love it; years since I had it.'

'I found shop – cheap because no sale. Dead stock must out, so good bargain.'

'I've been talking to Hjalmar.'

'So. The holy hypocrite.'

'You know that sometimes you are not too stupid. It was you made me aware of that fellow, and he stinks. I've not proof enough to tread on a cockroach, but somehow he is the spring behind these boys, I'm convinced, and until I know more I'm unwilling to drop any guillotines on them. Confidence, to hold against the ones you give me.'

'Horrible man, but interesting.'

'Do you get ideas in the night?'

'No, I am innocent woman, the night is for making love. Ideas come in the morning, when I go to swim in Zonnehoeck, all fresh and alive.'

'Ha. I'm a poor man; I get ideas at night. Only time I have. At first they were all that he was mixed up in this business. But he's not frightened; not enough anyway; maybe this business is less simple than I think. I may get something out of the boy.'

'Frans? His boy?'

'No. One ran away. We picked him up in Germany; I'll see him in the morning. Excuse is good to hold him a day or so. And there'll be a little paragraph in the Press, to show I mean business. The parents will see that. I dislike the Press, but it has its uses. That's where you can help, maybe.'

Feodora watched him quietly.

'You want me I think to do some espionage on your business. No. I do not want anything to do with Press or police, and I will not be mouchard. I like you; I help when I can, but this not.'

'I'm not asking you to be mouchard, and I'm not threatening you. Just show a little more curiosity than you do usually. You don't have to break confidences; just understand that I don't want to hammer these boys, but I must have the truth. I will keep your name from the Press and the local police and anyone you care to name; my sources of information are my affair. Just tell me what you see and hear; I need help here.'

'I am sorry to be stupid. I have had much trouble. Many men have come at times to me, saying tell, tell, or you are hurt. I do not want to be found dead; I am no Rosemarie. But yes, I know more. I also know Arie van Sonneveld.'

He laughed. 'I had a tender moment with his wife this morning.'

'Yes, I have heard all about her.'

'You are the sponge, aren't you, that wipes them clean.'

'Yes, they come to me like to confession in the church. All their dirty little vices they confess to me. I will tell you anything I hear. But I will not be the finger, that not ever, you understand. I will not come, even to you, and say – that man has done so and then so. I would not live long after, and I could not live with myself.'

It occurred to him that Marcousis was not the man to stay putting in more time at his desk than his importance demanded, and he drove over to the bureau to hear about the Press release. The big chief was, in fact, looking with impatience at his watch.

'If you have any arrests to make, why don't you make them? I think, now that it's going to leak anyway, that it would be better to sweep these boys in. I can clear that with the examining magistrate. Be over then, with less gossip.'

'You wanted me to do it, Commissaris, got to let me do it my way. Gossip is what I want. Loose mouths and frightened mouths.' Van der Valk did not tell him either where he had been or what he thought.

'A good arrest keeps the public quiet; you don't think of that but I do. Well, yes, I won't interfere with you. Come on then. Good God, and I told my wife I'd be home early.'

*

The morning paper carried the fruit of Mr Commissaris Marcousis' conscientious desire to keep the public both quiet and properly informed. It was not too bad, on the whole, thought Van der Valk, eating breakfast next morning; no sillier than usual.

'A certain K.v.S., student at the Technische Hoge School, living at Bloemendaal a.z., 18 years, left his home in the early hours of yesterday, after laying hands on all the money he could find. We learn that the previous night several of his associates had been questioned by a chief inspector of the Amsterdam zeden-en-kinder department, acting in conjunction with the local police. The student v.S. has now been apprehended by the West German police in Keulen, and is being held in Amsterdam for interrogation. We understand that numerous attacks upon persons and property are in question, from which various households in Amsterdam have suffered during these foregoing months. It now seems likely that several young men in the town of Bloemendaal may be involved in these outrages. Chief Inspector van der Valk of the Amsterdam juvenile bureau, who is conducting the preliminary investigation, has refused to say more at present, stating that the affair is not yet a judicial enquiry, but it is believed that he is confident of rolling up this band of marauders.

'Commissaire Marcousis, head of the Bloemendaalse bureau, yesterday told our reporter: "It is not thought in the public interest to disclose details of this sort before the Officer of Justice sees fit. The Nederlandse youth is not inclined to escapades properly called criminal. It is necessary to distinguish between hooligan and criminal elements in this instance. The authorities have the matter firmly in hand, and a report to the Officer of Justice will shortly be made." '

He guffawed over these hardy clichés. Arlette snorted.

'This Marcousis seems a jelly-fish. Is it true?'

'I've nothing at all concrete; this is just to show we mean business, and start tongues wiggling. I could lock up the boys now, but we believe that isn't the root of the matter. Today I see this child they mention.'

'I'm more interested in your children. Do you realise that they again both need new shoes? Now listen, this is important. Yesterday I was in the Nieuwendijk, and in the Bata ...'

*

In the office he got Arie van Sonneveld on the phone. 'Will you be kind enough to come over? Twelve o'clock? All right. Yes. ... Yes. I'm going to have a talk with your boy now. Then we learn what we learn ... I can't tell; I'll let you know when I've decided.'

Frans Mierle. 'Can I drop over and see you after lunch for a few moments? Just an idea I'd like your opinion on, that's all. Two-thirty? Very well.'

His staff. 'Keep that girl sharply under your eye. After this morning's paper she'll be up and doing. Still no phone calls?'

The report to Boersma; his conversations of the day before; the way Jansen knew how to side-step a question that might become tricky.

'A holy hypocrite all right. No fool, though.'

'Wait and see; let it ripen. I'll handle the examining magistrate if he queries your method; I've spoken to Marcousis and told him to mind his own business; nothing to do with the parquet over there at all. You're talking to the boy?'

'Waiting outside my office now.'

'Don't hold on to him unless you feel you've good grounds.'

Van der Valk walked back without looking at the rather miserable figure sitting on a bench outside his office. He sat down at his desk; he arranged himself to look severe. Threatening papers strewn about, a hunt for a ballpoint, an abrupt order – 'Bring him in.' Some acting, now. When the boy came limply in, he was writing busily.

'Hamlet, Macbeth, Othello and King Lear are farcical comedies by William Shakespeare, all giving excellent examples of what to avoid in police procedure. Faulty reasoning, and hasty jumping to inaccurate conclusions, lead most of the characters into bed with the wrong women.' Boy was pretty well dissolved by now.

'Sit down,' curt-voiced. He threw the ballpoint down severely, and turned his paper upside-down in a security-minded way.

'What have you got to say for yourself, young man?' He began with a classical tirade. Trouble . . . anxiety . . . waste of time . . . public money . . . unjustifiable . . . information withheld . . . pilfering . . . irresponsible children . . . perfect pest. He carried off all this easily; the boy had had nothing but sandwiches for thirty-six hours, was tired, dirty, and thoroughly demoralised. Van der Valk reached his peroration, and slid easily into the soothing syrup of the 'chansonette'.

'Now this escapade of yours can hardly be overlooked, can it? You took your mother's money, and you've caused a great deal of nuisance. However, serious as all this is, I might be able to find a way to gloss it over if – only if – you give no further trouble. Run away because you're in a tangle with work, or a row with the girl friend – that's one thing, and can possibly be excused. But run away to avoid questions, as you did – questions you know very well the police want answered – that's very grave. Deliberately obstructing or misleading a judicial enquiry is an article of the criminal law. Denials, evasiveness, lies, excuses – any of that now will make your position a very uncomfortable one indeed. The time is over for fooling about; I hope you realise that.

'Now I intend to settle with all this straight away. You know that I have more than enough reason to hold you under arrest, until this business is sorted out – which may well take weeks. Whether or not I let you go depends entirely on your being scrupulously truthful in answering questions. And I have material enough to check the truth as you go. Understood?'

'Yes' – sounding properly quenched.

'Now how long have you been in with the ravens?'

'Only a week.'

'And did you know, before, that they went about breaking into houses?'

'No, honest; how could I?'

'When did you find out?'

'When I – joined up.'

'That day? Straight away? You got told secrets?'

'Yes, but not much. Just that they made raids.'

'So you got accepted. How? On Hjalmar's say-so?'

'Well yes, in the end.'

'You mean that they accepted you but Hjalmar had to agree?'

'Well no; they didn't want to have me; that was what made me mad. But I asked Hjalmar and he agreed, and then they more or less agreed too.

'What does it have to do with him then, whether you were in on this or not?'

'He's strict about the club, and who is sort of boss. He says as he is the owner, he has to agree to any rules.'

'So, you got accepted. What then?'

'Well, they said I couldn't go out with them till I'd been – sort of tested.'

'Ordeals and things?'

'I suppose you'd call it that, yes.'

'What did you have to do?'

'Pinch things from three different shops.'

'And did you?'

'Yes.'

'What did you do with them?'

'Threw them away. I – I didn't want to keep them.'

'What were they?'

'A cigarette-lighter, and a transistor radio, and a – a pair of – of girl's pants.'

'I see. What did Hjalmar have to say about that?'

'Oh, he didn't know; how could he have? He wouldn't have allowed that.'

'He's friendly with all the ravens. He's there continually. You mean he doesn't know?'

'He gives them privileges; you can get drinks on credit and that. But they keep things very quiet. He couldn't know about the raids.'

'You mean he's too stupid to notice, or what?'

'I don't know.'

'Mm. Your girl, Hannie Troost; she joined in too?'

'The ravens all have girl friends. The cats, they're called.'

'What did she have to steal?'

'Nothing, I don't think.'

'I won't bother to stop and ask if you're lying. If I find you are, it'll be just too bad.'

'I'm not lying, honest. I don't know; she didn't tell me.'

'What did you think?'

'I did suppose she might have to do something, but she wouldn't tell me.'

The boy was in a pitiable state, certainly. The sweat was rolling off him. Fear was acting as a barrier; a greater fear, it seemed, than that of being locked up. It was interesting.

'The ravens go out on raids, then, that's established. We'll have something to say to them about that. And what do the cats do? They have some way too of making life exciting, no doubt?'

'I don't know; I haven't been on any raid. Honest.'

'Not in the Schubertstraat?'

'Never, I swear it. The others went, I know, but I didn't. They said' – unwillingly – 'I'd give them away because I wasn't enough trained. I can do anything they can, but they said I was scary' – indignantly.

'What happened when they got back?'

'I don't know. They wouldn't let me in. Or Hannie.'

'Let you in where?'

'The flat. You see, the ice-salon closes at twelve, but Hjalmar lets the ravens in the flat to play records, and they can stay late sometimes. He's over in the big club, but they can get out that way without anyone seeing them.'

'What were they doing in the flat?'

'I don't know; they brought drinks, and things to eat. Hjalmar doesn't mind, they say.'

'Cats there too?'

'Yes.'

Mm. Whoopee, party. Boy hadn't seen anything evidential. Not much good; get demolished in a court. But enough to arrest the ravens, anyway.

'You've been in the flat?'

Hesitation.

'You've made love with Hannie there, haven't you?'

'Yes, once. Hjalmar wasn't in that night, but the ravens had the key. They said we could play records.'

That was clear anyway.

'Now. Michel Carnavalet had the idea that maybe you'd given them away to me.' The boy was biting his nail, haggard.

'He said something to me. We had a fight.'

'I know. What did he say?'

'I don't know; something that made me mad.'

'Now watch it, boy,' irritated.

'He said – that the cats would get me.' The boy was melting; looked half-paralysed. It seemed exaggerated; Van der Valk suspected that it was put on.

'Well? What could they do to you?' contemptuously.

'He said they'd kill me.' The boy burst into hysterics.

Going too far: that's pure melodrama.

'Stop acting,' sharply. 'That does you no good.' Ach, leave it for now. He called the policeman outside. 'Take him away to cool off; I can't do anything more with him in that state.'

He was annoyed. He had got something out of the boy, and could doubtless get more, but it was not worth much. The over-emotional witness is the most unreliable. Came too easy; he would have preferred more sulks and lies, and less weeping. The boy was a nervous child, yes, and thrown off balance, admitted, but oh, oh, how these types could act. Being locked up and interrogated by the police was meat and drink to them; a drama. Do better to let the boy go; his word was not worth much. When they got theatrical they said anything that came into their heads.

He sighed; witnesses were always a nuisance. Cowlike denials and obstinate stupidity, or phony confessions from the hysterical ones who wanted to appear important. There had been a look of genuine terror, but a policeman of his experience had been taken in a time or two, and knew how persuasive and convincing hysterical people can be. Medically, isn't it a mild paranoia or something? He couldn't remember but didn't care anyway.

The gang had presumably made threats. Michel had wound them up to terrify, no doubt. He remembered the American boys who had bound and blindfolded the adjudged traitor, and put his head on a railway line. When a train passed on the other line the boy had been gibbering. Something of that nature, perhaps, to silence the boy. But the story was rubbishy. Policemen shouting at boys in an office – it wasn't good enough. To get a check he needed to think up something more clever.

He turned over his idea about Frans Mierle; one never knew; it might work. Daft enough. His experience was that the daft ideas, ridiculous and unthinkable by the book of rules, often did work. He had known ludicrous tricks succeed in throwing a witness off balance.

He rather doubted whether he would get much out of Miss Hannie. He had nothing to threaten her with, or bribe; the two classic methods of interrogation – he detested both. He liked witnesses that gave things away to other people; then there could be no hanky-panky later about police coercion.

As for Hjalmar Jansen, he knew all right. But the parties in the flat after the building was closed, the rest of it – was there a criminal charge there? One would never be able to prove complicity. He would go on, quietly, thought Van der Valk. Won't arrest anyone yet. Let them ripen a bit. If they do beat up the van Sonneveld kid, that might loosen somebody's tongue too. The pressure on them could be made just as great – greater – as though they all sat in a cell being grilled by relays of policemen. An idea he, personally, had no use for.

# *Chapter Six*

It really looked, today, as though the weather might turn into a spring heat-wave; the best kind of all. Not yet hot enough to be disagreeable; not the heat that comes to Holland from the steppes, upon the east wind, and brings the jelly-fish by thousands on to the North Sea beaches. Too early for that kind. No, the anti-cyclone from the south, that almost brought with it the scent of thyme and mimosa from Corsica. It was April still, though; the air had a fresh sharp tang. Sunday tomorrow. If it stays like this there will be women in cotton frocks like enchanting butterflies, fluttering along the boulevard. Van der Valk stared out of the window, longing for a beer. The prosaic phone rang in his ear. Bloody Bloemendaal.

'Chief? The Troost girl had a call, some girl called Carmen. Asked if she were going to her afternoon classes. Said yes; they've arranged to meet for lunch in that snack-bar on the Singel.'

'Less bad. Get on to Bart, tell him to go after her, hear a bit of what's said if he can get close enough. Keep them tagged.'

Now what about this boy Kees? He wondered what Arlette had for lunch; at weekends they generally had dinner in the middle of the day. Mm, he was inclined to let the boy go, yes. What is to be gained by holding him? And free he is one more seed of discord among them. They would be wondering whether he had given them away, and how much. If he released the boy, and made no move to pick the rest up either, it might be concluded that he had abandoned them; even that they had got away with it. Boys were optimistic and impatient; they might construe his inactivity as impotence, which would be very handy. On the other hand wasn't it a great risk? Wouldn't he risk censure in not arresting them all immediately, since the boy admitted the existence of the raids? He would have to get Boersma's opinion. Perhaps if Marcousis kept them all under observation, just for the weekend. So far as he knew the ravens had all kept to their ordinary routine, showing no sign of uneasiness or disturbance; he had two of his own inspectors keeping an eye on them, besides Bart tagging the cats.

He could screw the boy some more, but what would he get? Boy would say a lot, no doubt, whatever he thought Van der Valk would like to hear, and would that be any good? And keeping the boy – it could be made, afterwards, to sound like duress, and the courts didn't like that; they wouldn't like the statement either; too easy to recant. And Jansen. This party business was no good. He wanted evidence of the man's actual connivance in a crime; he felt that existed, somewhere, and when he got it he would take the fellow to the cleaners with much pleasure. His intercom burred.

'Yes?'

'Mijnheer van Sonneveld to see you.'

'Ask him in.'

Arie van Sonneveld was a thin, almost meagre man, whose bony, excitable face was accentuated by the thin hair slicked down flat. He wore a nylon shirt, a terylene suit; he had an overall synthetic look. Even his teeth looked too good; must be plastic. He was very smart; his eyes were sharp and clever, his smile a bit over-ready. He was reputed to be extremely good at his job, which consisted of spending his days persuading rich manufacturers to increase their advertising appropriations. He spoke like a machine-gun; was more than a little nervous.

'Sorry; I'm a bit before my time, if anything, but I had to squeeze in between two appointments. Please don't think me callous, Inspector, or unfeeling for the boy. I'm very worried about him. The truth is that we're up to the eyes at this moment in work; we've a man on holiday and I have no one to whom I can delegate this job. That is just the trouble in my business – it's extremely personal – depends entirely on contacts and conversations.'

'Take it easy. Sit down; unwind the dog.'

'This is a very upsetting affair, Inspector; I simply can't think what can have come over the boy. He has a good life, does well at school, and now he does a fool thing like this. From what I hear from my wife, you think he's got into some lunatic gang or other. I must thank you for calling like that to explain things to her. I'm only too sorry I wasn't there myself, but you see how I'm placed, always in the squeeze. I suppose the boy ran out of fear that he would have to speak up, huh? Has he told you everything? Will he have to go before the court? What will happen to him?' He crowded his phrases together like a television jockey, squeezing as much commercial as possible into thirty expensive seconds.

'Don't jump so fast. We want to find out a bit more before we decide anything. The boy's very strung up at present. I've had a talk with him, but I'm not very satisfied. He seems to be frightened, and that's why he ran away, but he has nothing particular to fear from us. If he really is frightened, and it isn't an elaborate act, I wish to establish what it is he's frightened of and why. The best way is to show him that in fact he has nothing to fear, certainly not concealment, and with that in mind I am at present half inclined to let him go.'

'I have no idea why he should be frightened of anything. But I knew nothing at all about all this; it's taken me utterly by surprise. Of course I'd never have let the boy get in with some gang – it's all so unbelievable. Do you really believe that the boy is mixed up in something criminal? I mean these boys are sometimes wild, I know, but this story of assault; he can't have had anything to do with that, surely?'

'He assures me vehemently that he's never done anything criminal, and I think that is true. He certainly has some guilty knowledge – I cannot say what view the magistrate would take of that. What he's mostly scared of, by his own account – and this is where I'm more sceptical of what he says – is that he imagines himself to have been accused by his former friends of giving them away to me – which is quite untrue – and that they will take horrible reprisals; refuse to speak to him or something. Very childish but it seems to bother him. I arrived at certain conclusions from another angle altogether; he has done no more than confirm, under questioning, various ideas of mine. But I get a strong impression that he imagines things too readily, and I treat his remarks with some reserve.'

'Inspector, you don't need to keep him in jail, do you? I mean, it surely isn't very logical to hold him when others are free who, as I judge from your words, are more deeply involved.'

'I am aware of that,' said Van der Valk a little tartly. 'The boy has been kept in here just twelve hours, after involving us in considerable trouble and work. The machinery for tracing a disappeared person is elaborate and expensive. If I had questioned him, as I intended, in his home, it would have saved me trouble also.'

'Yes, yes, I do realise that; of course.'

'Now, Mr van Sonneveld, if I release the boy it is into your custody and responsibility; you're his guardian. I do not want to keep the boy shut up; I dislike that except when it serves a clearly useful purpose. I may want to question him again, in which case he had better appear promptly. The Officer of Justice will decide whether he will be proceeded against, when he considers the affair. That may take time.

'These boys have a great deal to answer for; Kees, very possibly, considerably less. You can impress upon him that he may think himself extremely lucky that he has only very recently become deeply involved. When he's been at home a day or so, cooled down and thought things over, I want him to realise that he has nothing to worry about except making a clean breast to me. At the moment his story does not altogether make sense; I appreciate that he's steamed up, and that it isn't cold-blooded lying, but I'm not convinced I've heard all that he has to tell.

'Furthermore, he has to sort out this nonsense of being threatened. If anybody hits him, he's capable of hitting back, I should hope. I recommend you to show him sympathy without becoming emotional. Try to get on terms, get his confidence a bit, so that he feels he can rely on you. These other boys won't gang up on him; that would be an admission of guilt. They aren't being arrested, for judicial reasons, at the moment, but they would be, of course, at once if they misbehaved. Now do you still want me to release him, having heard my conclusions, and knowing that I'll hold you responsible for his doings henceforward?'

'Well, yes, Inspector; I should be glad if you could do so.'

Wants to see in the paper that the boy was let go, thought Van der Valk.

'Very well. I'll probably be ready to let him go this afternoon, but the Commissaire may have something to say about that; he may even decide otherwise. If he's not home by six you can give me a ring. And I rely on you to keep him out of any further trouble.'

•

It was a good lunch; carbonade flamande, the beer stew with onions he was very fond of. The metal of the car was surprisingly warm, from standing in the sunlight.

On the way back he thought with some amusement that this affair would give the Officer of Justice headaches. And what a fool I am, in parenthesis, to share the worries that belong to the magistrate. All I'm called on to do is to arrest the boys, promptly.

That's the way we were trained. How a criminal is handled, judged and regarded is the province of the magistrature, upon which the police officer may in no way intrude.

But in the juvenile branch he had learned that this elaborate machinery of magistrates and judges, although greatly simplified for children, is still often too slow and unwieldy. The experienced police officer could and should settle minor misdeeds himself, and even in serious cases he should use his sense and training to simplify and disentangle and when possible adjudge, instead of turning a confused and conflicting situation over to the magistrate, and going happily off to wash his hands.

Ja ja, thought Van der Valk on the Herengracht, to 'reform' twelve adolescents or so, all well educated and of wealthy and successful parents – it would need thought. Could you send these boys to a state training school, or let these girls mix with juvenile prostitutes? But there, these charming children had done pretty things; he thought of the woman tied and raped; of the slashed and daubed furniture. His job was to protect those people. The job of protecting the children came later.

He made one of his little drawings for Frans Mierle. Like a target; wobbly concentric circles.

'What the hell is that?' Smell of Cuban cigars over his shoulder, of 'Moustache', of a healthy man.

'That, on the outside, is our six tough boys. Wondering rather uneasily at present when my hand is coming down on their shoulders. Doesn't come because I'm wondering still about this circle inside. That's the six girls, mainspring if you ask me of everything the boys do. Inside that again, a rather sinister shadow. The owner of the Ange Gabriel, a certain Jansen, a character in whom I am interested. I am being indiscreet – to you – for a purpose. I am very frequently indiscreet; it is the perpetual complaint of my superiors. It is fair to tell you that these six boys have so far remained at liberty largely because I hope that some word or sign will show me that this personage is, as I think, involved.'

'And if you could establish such a connexion the boys, I take it, would not have to carry the whole burden of answerability.'

'That's so. To get them to realise that is not so easy. They'll think it's a bribe to get them to talk.'

'Why tell me?'

'Tell me first: how's Erik?'

'Like someone going about expecting to be hanged.'

'If things go on like this, the Officer of Justice will demand, on the evidence I now have – and he'll have my report on Monday – the immediate arrest and interrogation of all the boys. He will probably think it not worth proceeding against the girls at all, on the ground that it would be impossible to lay an adequate charge and get a conviction. Our sinister figure won't be touched. If the boys sought then to implicate him he would simply deny it, claiming that they are inventing anything to beat the rap. Even if they all independently accused him it would still look like a concerted job; wouldn't carry much weight; too easy to refute. I make myself clear?'

'Brutally.'

'You'd be surprised at the extent of my brutality. I have thought up a cock-eyed scheme, which you may like. Instead of leaving Erik, this weekend, to run about with a lot of kids, I'd like you to take him out, buy him a good dinner, give him a bottle of wine, let him feel his oats a bit.'

'And then?'

'I had thought then it might be a good idea to introduce him to Feodora.'

'Ho! And how do you come to . . .?'

'I have the most unlikely friends, like you. I know something of your character, otherwise don't imagine for a second I'd come out with an idea like this; as much as my job is worth. Just that I think – I've tested it – that a man, or a boy, will tell things to a woman without distortions or evasions. I did it once in a murder case; nearly got myself hanged for it; fellow shot himself, or rather I shot him; it came to the same thing, a bollocking for me. But it worked; the fellow talked. I may add that it's no speciality of mine. Old classic Gestapo technique. But not respectable.

Lucky I'm not respectable and neither are you. I add too that Feodora refuses to be a police nark, but if you agreed she'd help us to get the truth out of Erik. You'll agree that it's time we got it.'

Mierle laughed harshly. 'You're an imaginative bastard. So I'm the only man who's not hypocrite enough to pretend to be shocked. The idea is not bad. Fé's a good girl. Do Erik a lot of good too.'

'Better influence than these teenage amateur whores he mixes with. They're the root of this mischief.'

'I'll see what I can arrange.'

*

Boersma had had calls from Kieft and Krebbers, the two outraged parents. Both had been full of self-righteous indignation; he had sent both away with a flea in the ear.

'You'll have no more lip from that pair,' he concluded grinning.

'I've decided more or less to let the van Sonneveld child go too. What do you think? I'm hesitating, frankly, and wondering whether you wouldn't insist on my pulling the whole lot in. Spoil my weekend. I'd base my report to the Officer of Justice on what you thought. I'd prefer to leave them loose. You know what it means, hammering them till they bust, and neither of us likes that. I have rigged a couple of gags to get them to give the whole show away anyhow, but maybe they ought to be behind the shutter, the way Marcousis wants.'

Boersma put his hands in his pockets, not an easy job sitting down; he was putting on weight alarmingly.

'I read the boy's statement. I incline to agree with you; when it's just acting – and how these little stinkers can act – 's not worth much. Would provide enough of a spring-board to pull them all in if we need, but yes; I see it the way you do. Let the child go, I think, and leave the others loose too as long as that serves a purpose. I can handle the magistrate on that basis, as long as I convince him and myself that it is serving a purpose. This Jansen – don't let that become an obsession. There'll come a time for him. As for the girls – probably hopeless. They stoke the boys up, of course, good old sex; but your worry about morals – bad as old Slotemaker de Bruin. Legally, sleeping with the boy friend isn't even a bloody misdemeanour. No, take your weekend with a quiet conscience.'

*

He took an enormous pleasure in his free Sunday; everything went right. The weather was perfect; he took Arlette and the boys sailing on the Loosdrecht lakes. But he only just made it. On Monday morning, while he was still at home, looking with disgust at a nose peeling from sunburn, he got a hurried gabbling phone call from the bureau in Bloemendaal. Kees van Sonneveld had been found at daybreak by a shrimp fisherman, after a hunt of some hours. Found drowned on the beach, some distance – a kilometre maybe – north of the 'Islands'. Found drowned! Found drowned?

'What are the indications?'

'Like nothing more than an accident.'

A rechercheur called Visser had been first on the scene, and was still making a careful examination of the ground. Van der Valk knew him slightly as a good chap, serious and careful, even if no great ball of fire.

'The boy had one of these frogman outfits, what are they called? – aqualungs, that's it. Was trying it out I suppose in the sea, lost balance in some way, got a cramp maybe, lost the mouthpiece and started inhaling water. That's the best I can do anyway. No marks anywhere on the body. Didn't drift much; tide flooding, dead calm sea, no offshore wind; sea just floated him up to high-water mark.'

Van der Valk scowled like a thundercloud.

'More to the story than that. Where'd he get it, this aqualung?'

'The father gave it him on Saturday; special present; the boy had apparently been wanting one for a year. He was playing with it in the pool at Zonnehoeck yesterday; we've been keeping an eye on him and these others, but that's your affair, isn't it? Still, what happened here is obvious enough, I reckon. Wasn't accustomed fully yet to the apparatus, got entangled with it in some way. It's a fair weight. Plenty of compressed air left in the cylinders still. They're buoyant naturally, I suppose, but can't be more than barely, can they, since one's supposed to swim under water?'

'Funny coincidence department,' said Van der Valk sourly. He was ready to vomit; could only feel disgust and frustration. They had thumbed their nose all right. Was it to stop his mouth, or as a fearful warning – or both, or neither, or what? But nobody seemed impressed by anything the police could do. Poor little wretch.

He slammed into the car and drove much too fast down the boulevard back to the bureau.

'Medical report yet?'

Marcousis, thoroughly harassed, was just back from a disagreeable interview with the parents.

'Fine thing. Now I'm in trouble with everyone. Burgomaster on the phone, a dozen parents, the Press – lucky I can choke them off. Strong assumption of suicide.' (Suicides are not reported in Dutch newspapers.)

'Suicide,' said Van der Valk, 'my aching fanny.'

'Oh, I quite agree; just a handy excuse to stall them a bit. Accident as plain as daylight, but very unfortunate.'

'Unfortunate, accidental, population-worrying, burgomaster-flustering homicide,' furiously.

'No no, surely that's out of the question?'

'I think it very much in the question; intend to find out, what's more. What was the boy doing swimming then and there, anyway? What's the number of the hospital; I want that medical report.'

'You don't need it. Doctor's coming here as soon as he's finished his examination. Look, Van der Valk, you can't seriously have grounds for supposing this. I agree that it happens very inopportunely, but coincidences do come about like that.'

'Coincidence, shit.'

'No sign whatever of any attack. Visser examined the body and the whole scene; he's both competent and experienced.'

'Refuse to accept this as a homicide – and I don't like the idea, any more than you do – and our whole effort to cut down this gang collapses. We are held to ransom then by a mob that starts with violent robbery, goes on to rape and takes in a cute little murder on the way without turning a hair.'

'Impossible; all the boys were being closely watched.'

'Why wasn't this one watched?'

'Come now; you yourself released him. Besides, he was watched.'

Marcousis had lost his self-importance; he was not only harassed but genuinely troubled; he had, as well, the policeman's instinct for something unreasonable.

'The boy went home; we left it at that. Can't just sit outside their doors all night. None of them had done anything worrying. This one hadn't been near the Angel; he sat in the café in the Ruyterplein, with his girl; there's been no contact with any of the others and that, after all, was where we suspected trouble. Once they were all safely home we left it at that.'

'What about the girls?'

'The whole lot, girls and all, were all quietly at home by about eleven-thirty. The parents say that the boy came in, stayed about a quarter of an hour, and then took his aqualung thing and went out saying he wanted to show it to someone. They thought it queer, but the boy was proud as Punch of the thing and it seemed natural to want to show it off by any chance he got. We didn't check on all the girls, but none of them were hanging about in the town after eleven.'

The doctor was shown in; a bleak man, with a glacial eye.

'Well, gentlemen, I have made a fairly detailed examination for you.' He knew Marcousis, but was not at home with Van der Valk; he kept glancing uneasily at this furiously smoking figure, who looked liable to arrest him at any moment, for – for abortion – or something equally outrageous.

'This is a chief inspector of the Amsterdam recherche.'

'Mm, yes, delighted. Well, you will get my full report in writing, of course, and the results of certain tests are still to come, but briefly, death was by drowning, seemingly somewhere about or a little after midnight – I certainly cannot commit myself to any time limit. There are no injuries or bruises; it appears likely that the boy went swimming and got a cramp, and died as a consequence of asphyxiation. Nothing to have caused any failure of the heart, which was quite normal. No sign of any embolism or any such condition. He had eaten a substantial meal, but several hours previously; digestion well advanced. I am making a blood-test for alcohol, but I do not expect a high figure; the boy had maybe drunk three or four beers in the course of the evening.

'Perfectly healthy boy, no history of tuberculosis, no respiratory infections, no damage to heart or nervous system. I am the doctor to his family, and knew him, of course; the boy was splendidly healthy; organically sound and good muscle tone. If there exists any contributory cause, it might possibly be the aqualung.'

'That's what I've been thinking,' said Marcousis. 'Although it seems to be in order, it might have confused or hampered him. We'll get the apparatus examined by an expert; air-regulator might not be in order, or a valve choked, or something. Tell me, Doctor, were there any unusual features at all?'

'No, I would not say so. There was a certain amount of fine sand in the lung, which might be thought unusual, possibly, if the sea was calm.'

'Would that be accounted for by his diving and perhaps getting into some difficulty near the bottom? Would a struggle stir up the sand, and enter the lung in that way?'

'I should say that it sounded feasible; it is not, strictly, my province.'

'Sand in the lung, in calm water deep enough to drown in,' said Van der Valk gently. 'It did strike you, Doctor, as unusual?'

'Unusual, yes, I have already called it so. But not, Inspector, unheard of. It is not uncommon in cases of drowning on this coast. Even in deep water there is a quantity of sand in suspension.'

'When the water is rough.'

'That is the feature I remarked upon as unusual. I do not venture to call it unheard of.'

'This sand,' said Van der Valk. 'How did it penetrate the mask of the aqualung?'

'Perhaps in a struggle he tore the mask loose in a panic, imagining that it impeded his breathing.'

'I understood that the mask was found in place.'

'That is so,' said Marcousis, 'but the action of the water and the way the rubber is moulded to fit the contour of the face could have worked it back. It would slip easily into place.'

'Hm.'

'Action of sea-water has been known to do stranger things than that.'

'I never believe half what I'm told. I don't believe these things could ever pull one under water, even if that's where you wanted to go. They're designed to be buoyant, I believe. One carries weights, and Visser told me the body carried no weights. I mean to find out.'

The doctor picked up his driving gloves.

'Such questions are not within my competence. I can only assure you that the boy drowned. My report will be at your disposal in an hour or two, gentlemen. Good morning.'

Van der Valk watched him go, sourly.

'He seen the parents?'

'Yes. Treatment for shock; little spot of barbiturate. You want to see them?'

'Don't suppose seeing me would do them any good. Or me, come to that. Better to stay away. Where did the father buy the aqualung, d'you know? Locally, or in Amsterdam? Not many shops sell a thing like that.'

'I asked. Here; sports shop in the Strandweg. Same side as the Hema; 'De Roos' it's called. It was a present, to show that they didn't hold the running away or the money against him.'

'Only way these people appear to know of showing sympathy – spend more money.'

Marcousis passed that. 'Apparently the boy had been longing for the thing for months. He was a fine swimmer, and very keen on this assisted diving lark. He was very happy and excited with the thing.'

He had forgotten to look dignified; he had sharpened a matchstick with a razor-blade lying in an ashtray, and was picking his teeth. Van der Valk watched him with some amusement, easing his tension. When he's not playing figure-head, the fellow looks more like a policeman.

'It stinks, Commissaris. I'd better warn you; it stinks.'

The man was not a fool, either. He went and stood by the window with his hands in his pockets, chewing on his matchstick, with intelligent eyes fixed on the other. He was in a quandary, Van der Valk could see. He knew the man had been transferred from somewhere sleepy down in Brabant, where crime means chicken-stealing; he was newly promoted too; his first command of a metropolitan district. Van der Valk had met the type before. Big contrast to himself. They were pushed up the ladder fast for being predictable, reliable, and conforming exactly to the official image of a good policeman – one who caused his superiors no disquiet.

Smart, certainly, even brilliant; smooth speakers, good exam-passers; excellent administrators.

This one certainly had ability. But he lacked Van der Valk's experience. Never been on a homicide in a senior capacity. And secretly perhaps he envied the aplomb, the readiness to disregard rules, the unorthodoxy and flair of the Amsterdammer. He had, moreover, the faint deference towards the capital of which the provincial can never quite break himself. Here, too, he was nervous of a fussy Officer of Justice, with an ogrish reputation; he had been most impressed by Van der Valk when that gentleman had said calmly – 'Bugger the interfering old whoreson; just tell him I don't know myself yet.'

'Will you tell me what you do know?' Marcousis suggested.

Van der Valk was flicked by the tiny shade of deference.

'As you know, I let the boy go,' he said slowly. 'Boersma agreed that there was nothing to gain by holding him. He was melodramatic; big weeps and prayers.' Marcousis nodded sympathetically. 'He had a tale that the gang would kill him if he talked. I judged that to be an act, put on to attract a little sympathy; self-pitying type. It looks as though I was dead wrong. The boy knew something, since he showed absolute terror. I think they did get him. How I can't see, yet. The boy goes home; twenty-four hours later he's dead. I can no longer disregard what he said himself – 'They'll kill me' were his exact words. Suicide is out of the question; no one puts on an aqualung and goes out to drown himself; it'll do for a day to stall the Press, maybe. And what is the motive for a homicide? I hardly know. To begin with, to stop everyone's mouth. That seems exaggerated, but this isn't an ordinary gang. High score against them, firstly. Eight cases of breaking into dwelling-houses. Thieving; maybe five thousand pop worth, maybe more. Assault on person. Rape. Next, there is an obscure and unusual factor, which is the reason I didn't rope them in at the start. I've been trying to get a line on this; without much success so far. This Jansen; you may know him. Owner of the Ange Gabriel. Something fishy about him. But we can't hesitate now, of course; the magistrate wouldn't stand for that. These boys have to come in.'

'Jansen? I know him slightly. I don't understand you. He's mixed up with a gang of boys? I know they go there, but is there any further connexion? You mean he's a pederast or something?'

'Nothing like that, I think; I got the van Sonneveld boy to admit what I suspected, that Jansen has been allowing petting parties in his flat with the girls. The connexion is something intangible. The behaviour of the boys had been inconsistent with their usual ideas; I don't believe they thought it all out themselves. And look now at this death. Too bloody neat. Adult hand somewhere, and I'm very curious about this Jansen. But I've no proof of anything, of course.'

There was interest now in Marcousis' face; maybe it was just this stupid office that had turned him into a stuffed shirt. He was studying his surroundings, his neat desk, Van der Valk's face, the plants on his window-sill. The blades of the sansevieria could do with a damp sponge. A policeman came in, with two cups of coffee.

'The burgomaster, and pretty well everyone else in this town, except, maybe the Officer of Justice, wants this to be an accident. They're steamed up already about this gang of yours. It isn't them that's been attacked, you see; their attitude is let Amsterdam look after itself. Bad for business to have scandals here. Maybe you think I'd prefer just to sit here and play politics; I wouldn't altogether blame you for thinking that; I'm pretty sure it's what your boss Boersma thinks. I can't stop him; he's older than me, a lot senior to me, due to retire soon anyhow. But I'd like to tell you something.

'This town's not a bit like Amsterdam. Isn't like anywhere else, for that matter; too new. Everything brand-new and sort of self-conscious. Nothing like this has happened before, and everyone wants to keep the varnish from being scratched. Like driving a new car; showroom polish still on it, say. You're all nervous; everybody's dirty greasy fingers make you mad. As much as breathe on it there's an outcry. That's you, at present.

'Don't think I'm trying to be funny, Van der Valk, but they all take the line here that you're just stirring up shit. I haven't forgotten how to do my work, but you know what any senior police official has to take into account always – cooperation. Here there isn't any, except in putting a quick firm stopper on anything that sounds like it might grow up and become a scandal. Now if I come out in the open on this, calling it a homicide investigation, you'll hear the screams from here to Venlo. Not to speak of the grindstone, sharpening the knife for my throat. You don't appreciate it in the city – believe me that isn't meant for criticism – just that my experience has been in small towns. I was inspector in Tiel; chief inspector in Breda; I knew before coming here that being chef de bureau in a smallish town is no sinecure, but since I've been here I've really learned a few things. A whispering campaign can ruin one. I've known it happen; a chef de bureau in a town of say, fifteen thousand folk. Chap had to ask – to ask – to be suspended, and beg for a special investigation to be held by the state police. Did his career no good, as you can imagine. He was reinstated, but he'll be in towns like that all his life now.

'I'd prefer to put this to you another way. Personally, I'm entirely on your side. I'll use all the means at my disposal to help you, back you up, get this business clear. But officially – for the books – I'd like to see it docketed as an accidental death, but needing investigations as part of your enquiry – since the boy was your witness – into gangsterdom in Amsterdam. Good rhyme, that.'

Van der Valk grinned. He had seen which way the cunning bastard was heading. Trouble-shooter, all right.

'Witness dies suddenly; it needs explanation; you widen the scope of your enquiry. I'll have a quiet word with the magistrate. I'd like you to take charge of the whole thing, with all the help you need; use my offices, personnel, anything you want, and afterwards I'll make a very strong commendatory report; help your own promotion record, if you'll forgive my being personal.'

Tact. But Van der Valk was not entirely displeased.

'All right then. Agreed. Then let's start. To forestall the Officer of Justice, all the ravens had better be picked up straight away. And no contact with one another; they'd better be pinched individually. They're all at their classes now. Tonight, quietly, when they come off the train. Avoiding publicity as much as possible. You agree?'

'Certainly.'

'I would like to ask you to write official forms of summons for all the cats to come to the bureau and be ready to answer a few questions. Once again, without being able to contact each other and cook up tales in concert. I plan to interview the whole lot here tonight. You could tell the magistrate if you liked that I'll make a report tomorrow on this for him – anyway, as soon after then as I can get it written. I'll be going to Amsterdam, but first I intend to have a word with this sports-shop. Will you authorise all that, Commissaris?'

'I'll do what you ask, certainly; formal summons has to be in my name; that's judicial. I don't quite follow your idea about these girls. Never get anything legal hung on them, surely?'

'I agree. But I'm going to have a damn' good try.'

## *Chapter Seven*

The sun shone brilliantly on clean bare brick streets; the thin sift of sand drifted into every cranny, squeaked under his feet. Surrounded by its ramparts of sand, blinking in the pale warm sunlight, the town was peaceful and innocent. Shopkeepers stood in their doorways with complacent smiles; careful housewives were bothered about the dancing dust-motes in their kitchens. Less careful housewives had got up early, slapped at their window-sills with damp dusters, and were now headed for the beach, in playsuits and sunglasses and Garbo hats, languidly pushing energetic toddlers – also in Garbo hats – in go-carts. Down on the beach it was low tide again.

Over beyond the boulevard limit four rechercheurs were making a methodical sweep of the half-kilometre-wide strip between where Kees van Sonneveld's clothes had been left in an tiny untidy pile, and the spot where his body had slid gently ashore, the face pillowed on a little hummock of soft yielding sand. Van der Valk thought about this pathetic body; the water running in little rills off the bare shoulders and digging tiny pits under the hips and knees and toes, as the tide slowly abandoned it.

Those two points had been marked on a large-scale map, and Benny Visser had been sent with this to Ijmuiden to talk to the tide experts of the Ministry of Sea- and Water-ways. How far, did they think, had this body ever been out to sea? How deep had the water been in which the boy had been drowned? If one drowned in calm water, would one collect this much sand in one's lungs? – they'd be sarcastic about that last one.

'De Roos' was an expensive shop, with fascinating gadgets strewn about in studied carelessness. In winter it would be skis and boots, anoraks and fancy sweaters, the chi-chi of après-ski. Dark snow-goggles, suncream and tickets for the cheap K.L.M.

flights to Garmisch or Chamonix. Now, in summer, it was alpenstocks and rucksacks, cunning little French butane stoves and the chi-chi of le camping, huge rubber water-wings, pétanque sets and elaborate German beach toys; snorkels and flippers and carbon-dioxide harpoons, leopard-spotted Bermuda shorts and espadrilles. Books on mountaineering, spear-fishing, dinghy-sailing (perched on an exaggerated-looking aluminium outboard motor) – yes, and aqualung diving. Huge photographs everywhere of naked nubile dollies, capering about at silly old Saint Tropez.

'Manager?'

'Owner at your service.'

'Van der Valk, Chief Inspector.'

'Police?' An involved intonation, in which vulgar curiosity, servility and a slight censorious sniffiness were blended as elegantly as a Lancôme scent.

'Zender-kinderpolitie, Amsterdam. Subject of visit – aqualung.'

'Yes?' a bit cagey.

'You sold one on Friday. The boy who got it has been drowned.'

'Oh. But that's terrible; dreadful disaster. I know what you mean, of course; I sold it myself. But how could such a thing come about?'

'Ja; what we're all asking. You can help, you see, considerably. You must explain the whole technique of the thing to me. You demonstrated it?'

'Certainly. Not only here, dry, but in the pool at Zonnehoeck. The boy came to me, here, on Saturday morning, and I went with him, to teach him. He didn't get drowned using it, surely?'

'He did, but whether there's any connection is an open question; that is what I'm here for – to close it.'

'I cannot believe that the apparatus could provide any cause.'

'Are you an expert in the use of this thing?'

'Naturally, Inspector, I am diploma'd in the use of all the equipment I sell here – and that covers some wide fields as you will readily believe – but I have a special certificate in underwater swimming and aided diving. Without undue conceit, yes, I am an expert.'

'You're exactly the man I want to meet.'

'I don't say this to forestall criticism, believe me, but I simply do not believe that anyone would ever drown through wearing an aqualung.'

'Tell me why you feel so convinced.'

'Simply, they are so safe. Children can – frequently do – use them; you'll see that on any beach. The mechanism is very simple. I've never known an accident with them, and I was one of the original members of the subaqua club, and I've dealt in them since they came on the market. I've sold many, and demonstrated – I wouldn't care to think how often.'

'You're convincing, Mr – ?'

'Van den Bos at your service.'

'And I like a man who knows his job. But I can't just take your word, however enthusiastic I am. I'm an officer of the court conducting a judicial enquiry – you understand. I'd like you to do something further for me.'

'Be glad to.'

'Can you leave your shop for an hour?'

'An hour, yes. My wife can cope. Monday mornings are not heavy.'

'Would that be time enough to repeat your demonstration?'

'Yes, yes. By all means.'

'I am not a very good customer,' with slightly ferocious jocularity.

'Perhaps you have never thought of buying one yourself?'

'Too dear.'

'I assure you, Inspector,' earnestly, 'they really aren't dear, not dear at all.'

Dutch shopkeepers, he thought good-humouredly. Turn a bit of business over, whatever happens, even a murder.

'Well, you can convince me with that. Shall I run you up?'

'I will just get the demonstration model. Ada ... ' whisper, whisper.

'Believe me, only too glad to help, Inspector, I don't want people frightened of buying aqualungs, of course – ha ha – but I am most anxious that you should have no shadow of doubt. Poor boy; what a disaster ... Are you only concerned with how it came to happen?' Tactfully nosy; what's a chief inspector from Amsterdam doing here? That piece in the paper, hm?

'That's all. Just want to know; calm water, huh? safe beach, excellent swimmer. Bathing accidents do the town no good, hey?'

'No, no; indeed no.' Stopper on him; silence the last minute or so to the rather bleak concrete blockhouse of Zonnehoeck.

This building, which nobody can deny is very unimaginative indeed, has even enemies who say it is a disgrace to Holland and looks like nothing more than a Hitler-bunker. The owner is a famous skirt-chaser; there are many local jokes about the Wolf's Lair. Flowers do not do well in the beach air, but he has done his best to soften the rigid outlines with awnings, and parasols above the terrace tables. It looks a little, now, like a sergeant-major in a bonnet.

The pool was beyond the restaurant, handily next to the bar; a long green shimmer of water looking pleasantly cool under the glass roof, which had heated the atmosphere to stuffiness. There was nobody there; what swimmers there were at ten-thirty on a Monday morning were gathered today in the sunshine round the open-air pool on the far side. This was not warmed, but was more attractive today, catching the reflections of the bright fringed parasols. The terrace here was half-full, and white-jacketed waiters were scurrying round; the summer staff had just been hired, and had that look of not yet belonging. Van der Valk decided on the indoor pool; no point in drawing attention to himself. He paid a shilling to hire shorts, and dived in untidily. Ha, the heating had been turned off – the owner was not a man to miss a chance for little economies – and the water was sharp and fresh as a lime, for all the stuffiness of the air about.

The cold water cleared his brain pleasantly; he prepared to give his close attention. He sat on the tiled surround and dangled his legs with almost a holiday feeling; he wished he could buy one of these things (last year, it had been the little French stove for le camping that he had lusted for, and surrendered to). Childishly, he entered happily into the delusion that this was for a customer's benefit, and not a police enquiry at all. Unlike most policemen, he had two sides to his head. He had swallowed a little water; he yelled at the barman for a beer, while his enjoyment grew slowly to fascination as he watched Van den Bos, tanned still from his damned winter sports, perform the classic aqualung tricks.

With a few pounds of lead fitted neatly into a belt he sat comfortably on the bottom, took the mask off with deliberation and waved it around, put it leisurely back on, and blew the trapped water out with a trained snort. Next he calmly slid out of the whole harness, and stood immobile a few deliberate moments before buckling it on again, swallowing, as far as Van der Valk could see, whatever water there was in the pipes. He had to put it on himself then, and try it all in practice. He found himself doing everything the other had done with complete ease and assurance.

The lung was heavy out of water, but so finely was it balanced with the heavier element that once in the water he scarcely noticed it. It was perhaps even slightly buoyant – Van den Bos told him it was, and would become neutral after a little air had been used – he found this most ingenious. Only with the weights could he plane down leisurely to the deep end, where he breathed without noticing, save for the fine waving train of bubbles to the surface.

After half an hour he was quite happy that there was no danger whatever of being confused or flustered by the apparatus; there was no interference with either swimming or breathing. He did not see how one could drown. Under water he could shout; he could laugh. He could not talk, because the mouthpiece slipped, but he could have done anything else, from making love to playing chess. He could lie flat, hover, slide backwards, turn lazy somersaults; goddam, with this thing one conquered the element. Captain Nemo van der Valk.

'I hope you're satisfied, Inspector.'

Satisfied: he was enchanted; he wished as passionately to possess one of the things as that poor sad little bastard Kees had done.

'I hope you will not be inclined to put any – how shall I say – onus? – at my door.'

Idiot, full of clichés.

'Not the least, Mr Uh, make yourself quite easy. And my deepest thanks.'

'Not at all, Inspector; quite at your service, any time.'

He went and had a shower and dressed, and came back to sit on the terrace for another beer, breathing fresh air gratefully. Ha; he was supposed to be in an uproar with a homicide case, and there is the bastard sitting on a terrace, drinking beer. He thought about it among the shouting, laughing swimmers, one-tenth of his mind registering his surroundings in flickers, like a worn-out film.

The comic crescent of a girl's bottom under the hem of her too-tight swim-suit; a man's hairy legs all plastered flat and dripping in a primeval way. Smells of 'Hero' and 'Chocomel' and Heineken, all mixed up with sea and sun-warmed concrete and far-off frying onions. Flap-flap of bare wet feet on tiles, the clink of glasses and the whisper of a small change and the heavy breathing of the water. A lovely day in early summer in Holland.

Last night in the gentle silky sea, there, twenty metres away across the boulevard, the same sea that fluttered softly in the pool at his feet – yes, that identical water there – a boy had drowned. Correction: been drowned. He sat working it out while his beer went flat. The mask limited one's vision slightly; that was really the only physical drawback. Suppose you got a cramp; it would be easy to rest quietly, and stretch and wiggle the affected limb till the muscles unknotted. And this boy had been an expert swimmer – could swim without arms or legs if need be. And to dive at all, weights were needed, to overcome the pressure. What had the clown said?

At ten metres' depth the atmospheric pressure doubled, huh. The way you breathed made a difference to your carefully adjusted buoyancy; yes. Fill your lungs with air and you tended to rise; it was easy to follow. Whatever happened, you did not plummet down like a stone, nor did you shoot up again. Everything was naturally along gentle slants. And safe as sitting at home in the living-room.

Below ten metres sudden changes of level – pressure thus, huh? – might give you a momentary earache, like coming down to earth in the dear old Dakota planes used to. You might get stars before the eyes for a second. Nothing worrying. Anyway, even at high tide on this beach you would need to be out over the first bank to get over ten metres of water. And if the boy had been out that far surely the body would have drifted further. The tide people would know about that. But even if he had been deeper that was no reason to expect trouble. Van den Bos had said calmly, 'If you can go ten metres there's nothing whatever to stop you going to sixty except that you'd have to come up more gradually!' And however deep one was one had no fear of being under water. And the boy's mask was in place, but there was sand in the lung. A second Wilma Montesi, sweet merciful blood and bones.

On his way back to Amsterdam he called at the sports shop and got a handful of literature about aqualungs, and a technical handout in rather difficult French from the makers. He arranged for the lung Kees had worn to be examined, and an expert opinion given whether any part of the equipment could have been tampered with or rendered even temporarily faulty, perhaps by a blow.

Back in his office, he went to see Boersma.

'What d'you know about Wilma Montesi?'

'Nothing much. Didn't the Italian police make a balls of it?'

'I mean the technical details.'

'Forget. Some nonsense about whether the sea current couldn't have taken her bra off.'

'We'd better look out that the current here doesn't take our bra off. This one's phony all right. Homicide for sure, tied up with the ravens. No indication how; Jesus, what a pain in the neck.'

'Let's hear.'

'Suspicion would fall on the boys straight away, huh? Also he'd be wary of them; he wouldn't risk being caught in a deserted place and done up by them, presumably. I think, maybe, on reflection, the girls have had a hand in this. We have no good legal hold on them – we don't even know much about them. I think this business was planned, and maybe they banked on that.'

'I might agree. Too much coincidence by half. But what have you got that's concrete to support homicide? Not just goddam surmise; you know that's not enough. This one'll make headlines.'

'Haven't been too far into it yet. But here's what I've got so far. The boy went to the beach in his aqualung. He went of his own accord; that seems certain. But why so far? It's two kilometres from his home. And why choose total blackness, when half the pleasure is seeing things. Where the boy was is a kilometre past the boulevard limit and black as a coal-hole. Now why, if he just went to swim? Then again there's no path along the dunes there either. Lot of old bunkers from Hitler's time, and the dunes are shut off by barbed wire. Only access is along the beach itself. Seems pretty laborious.

'Second point: the parent's story is that the boy came home at about half-past eleven, and then getting on for midnight he went out again to "show the aqualung to someone". Doesn't make sense at all, does it? What someone? He had plenty of opportunity during the day. Why come in, and then trot out at midnight? The parents haven't the guts of rabbits or they'd have stopped that. Conclusion: it was an excuse. Further conclusion: the boy had a date. Well, to take the lung in the sea is plausible, just. You or I wouldn't do it, but a boy might. But not alone, wouldn't you agree, in the dark, and pretty cold at night still. To go swimming at night you need romance, huh?

'Now, I added those two facts together and I got a picture. It's established that he was going home with his girl, after hanging about with her the whole evening and going to the pictures and after that a café. Not swimming, notice. Let's say, just say for now as a hypothesis, that on the way home they run into some of the other girls – the cats. Oh let's go swimming, someone suggests, for a gag. You come too, Kees, and bring your machine; we can try it too. He can't resist that. Goes home, gives his parents this story after hanging about a few minutes, and joins the girls on the beach, where they won't be seen or noticed.

'Now I've stood on that boulevard at night and looked out to sea. It's swamped in light, of course, and everything beyond, out to sea, looks black as a mute's overcoat, but after a while one can see, and one can certainly hear. So someone suggested – let's go up beyond the islands, boys, where we shan't be disturbed.

'That's all fairly simple if one thinks about it. Marcousis could have done that, say. Made out a case that he wasn't alone, and went up there on an errand. In that case, even if it *was* an accident, there was at least one witness, and where the hell is he? It won't surprise you to hear that Marcousis didn't want to think about it at all. The local politics are stacked against him, it's his first big case, and he's leery of this affair already. He doesn't want to get on anybody's sunny side. He wants to keep treating it as an accident, even after I told him the facts of life. Keep it as enquiry into my witness. Gives him time to get everything prepared, so that it will be tidy before anyone rumbles, and lights a fire under him.'

'Uhuh,' said Boersma, 'and if there are any cans to carry, you can carry them.'

'That's about it.'

'Your argument rests on a bad premise, though, which makes what I agree is a likely hypothesis cock-eyed. Listen: the boy had been told "The cats will get you". Meaning, we're agreed, the girls. Now according to you he goes swimming with them.'

'I've been biting my nails over that all morning. Only thing I can see is this. If it was planned, and I think it must have been, then they thought up some inducement that he wouldn't be likely to refuse. A bait. I mean they would have realised too that he would be scared of them.'

'Go on with that.'

'We suppose all the time that they said "Let's go swimming" because that way I've worked it out, maybe. They present this as a sort of sudden fantasy, spontaneous. In other words, beach party. That they'd all go swimming naked, and the boy would get sucked in by the notion of hanky-panky. "Here, I'll dry you" – that sort of scheme. Might have hooked me, I reckon, at that age. I was trying to think how I might have been caught at that age in that situation.'

'Wonderful childhood, yours,' said Boersma, lighting his pipe.

'Well, wouldn't you?'

'If I'd been out at all after ten at night I'd have felt the stick.'

'Well, so would I, of course. But to imagine these types, who aren't controlled the same way, isn't it fair to suppose?'

'It'll do as long as there's no better story. I grant that it fits this business as far as we know the facts to check the hypothesis with. But I don't much like it.'

'Neither do I, but Marcousis has pushed it on to me, and I must make what I can of it. I propose to test it.'

'Whole thing falls now in two halves. No evidence to link this to the ravens.'

'I bet they don't even know. That's the point. Neat.'

'Slow down, now.' Boersma blew smoke across the room. 'You say the girls did it, and you've shown how a set-up could have been constructed. But why? Leave aside the how for the moment; if you're right you'll find that out. The why is more important. Why should these girls commit a crime – and that crime a homicide – when they couldn't be touched, whatever the boy had told or would tell? Why are they going to combine on a risky tricky murder of someone who couldn't harm them? They're quite crafty enough to realise that, and also that suppression of a witness, now, only draws attention to them. Now why?'

'Jesus, I don't know. Maybe the boy knew much more than I thought. Blame me for letting him go. I did think, though, he'd never be much use. I thought he'd be much more useful out there – I hoped something would happen to him, poor little sod. Didn't think it would come to that.'

'Don't work yourself up; you did nothing wrong and I'm not blaming you. I saw no point in holding on to the boy either. What could he have talked about, that would have sparked off killing? I'm coming, now, to agree with you. I think, by God, the boy was murdered. But I suggest, first, that you're wrong about the plan. That it wasn't premeditated. Sometimes easier to kill people than it looks, huh? How many accidental murders do we get, compared to the thought-out, cold-blooded crimes? Maybe they only meant to beat him up.'

'Not that. Wasn't a mark on the body.'

'Frighten him in some way. Not more than semi-accidental, certainly. They did something to him that could have killed him, and in this case did. Held him under water or something. Hardly, with no marks. The boy would have struggled. But that's all how, how. I prefer to concentrate on why. There was violence. It's unexplained.'

'We've had it before. The rape was unexplained violence, and it is incontestable anyway.'

'Don't be stupid, man; the girls didn't rape anybody.'

'I don't have any goddam handy explanation,' said Van der Valk, crossly. Boersma smoked in silence.

'Get illogical acts of violence like this,' he said at last, 'and there is one explanation. Portmanteau – a bloody catch-all. But possible, and you might bear it in mind. You know what *cannabis indica* is?'

'Yay. Marijuana.'

'That's right, in Spanish. Always some floating about, especially in seaports. You might not think of it, because you might not have had any direct experience with it. Never been on a harbour squad?'

'No.'

'Well, I have, in the days before this department was a separate one. We used to see a lot of it – people were poorer, had a harder life and took their pleasures where they found them. But even now students get hold of it occasionally. I've known trouble with it before now, before you came to this department. It's a weed, even grows here if you take enough pains. That's important because it makes it hard to control. No regular sources of supply; nobody makes corners in the stuff. Result is there's always some hanging about, especially in the jazz cellars where some bum trumpet-player wants to kick up high. But we don't take it all that seriously, because officially it isn't even a drug of addiction. It doesn't hook you – that's strictly for the picture papers.

'Has a well-known effect, of course, as good stuff for a sex jag. And occasionally – and that's where the danger lies – with some types it leads to sudden, otherwise unexplained acts of violence. I've been thinking about it since you started this. I don't know what this Jansen has been up to, but I get the idea – these parties you've been hearing about – been filling them maybe with tea.'

*

He was in his office an hour later, scribbling in the intervals of staring at the wall, when the intercom told him that Frans Mierle was asking to see him. The big man sat down without a word and crossed his legs, heavy and sullen. Van der Valk said nothing; scribbled away at his draft report to the magistrate.

'Fine thing for me to be doing . . . walk into a police bureau. . . . I hear a piece of news that is very disquieting. Not an accident, hey?'

'No. We have reached that conclusion.'

'You'll arrest the boy, now?'

'Yes.'

'I see. You know he was with Feodora the whole night.'

'Can't be helped. Of course he had nothing to do with this death, and that will be shown too, but the Officer of Justice can't be denied now. Overrides my authority. But I would agree with him – the Press will get this story within another twenty-four hours, although we're trying to stall them. The boys are better off, now, inside.'

'I see.'

'Tell me about last night.'

'I saw her myself this morning. It didn't work. Confidences stopped short just where they might have become interesting.'

'I'm breaking no confidences when I tell you that this case of death on the beach will be obscure. Between an accident and a premeditated, cold-heartedly planned killing there is a lot of border territory. But it's homicide from the police angle. That leaves no room for any fantasies of mine. If I took any chances now it would be my neck. These boys will be told that unless they all come clean as a packet of Omo, homicide may be added to the charges against them. Some people are going to realise that fast – if not quite as fast as you. Directly it becomes known that the time at which this boy died, last night, is important, every parent is going to cover up for them. Including you. I don't blame you. But I can no longer allow my ideas of last week to influence what I say or do now.'

'Now listen you, to me. I know that everybody is waiting for you to arrest these boys, homicide or not. Has been waiting for weeks. Let me tell you something, so that you know where I stand. Half the legal talent in the country is waiting for the chance to make a monkey out of you, and the Officer of Justice, and the Procureur Général, all put together if need be. That bastard Kieft – a man I don't like – a chap I don't know called Krebbers, this architect Carnavalet, and a bank manager I know slightly, Wagenveld. You've met them.'

'Not scared of them, either.'

'Possibly. But they've formed a syndicate, and I gather that according to the legal eagles you'll never get away with prosecuting.'

'Tell it to the magistrate. I'm not prosecuting them; I'm just trying to make a living.'

'Just listen, you damned fool; I'm an expert on making a living. Just shut your mouth for once and listen.'

'Very well, talk; make it good.'

'You've no proper evidence. They've guessed that. So you've got to rely on a confession, and that's not enough to make your case out, in their opinion. They've briefed the kids to stay clammed anyway, whatever you say or do. They'll raise an outcry; allegations of torture; talk about Algeria; big stink. Plenty of money against you.

'Now why am I not in on this, huh? They all ran to me; I was supposed to take the lead in this crusade. I didn't say yes, and I didn't say no; they're counting on me. They're going to be disappointed. I've more money, more good name, more reputation than all that crowd of churchwardens put together. And I've more guts. They think – you think too maybe – that if my son commits a crime, I'll use all my pull to get him off light, and spend the rest of my years enjoying the idea. I haven't told these vultures, but my mind works differently. So does yours; say that for you. I'll tell you. Christ, with my connexions, I could have had the boy in South America by now, no strain.

'Erik does some dirty tricks. Right, he's got to pay for that, as the law allows, and I won't kick. But he's done no murders and you know it. Could prove it too, but that would give Fé away. And I won't have my son booked in a stinking jail on suspicion of murder. So, I have my own method of squeeze.

'Feodora doesn't like this country; with what's happened she likes it even less; don't blame her, either. She wants to go to Spain. I have good friends in Spain. Got good friends everywhere, and this is how I make them, by being honest. If I want to break a law I'll break it and the hell with it, and damn the consequences. I've got no use for this legal jiggery-pokery those stinking sneaks are so proud of. Now I've told Feodora that I'll set her up in Valencia, with all the police permits she can think of, if – and because she's fond of me, too – she gets the evidence for us that you – that both of us think is there. She trusts me. I trust you, because you trusted me. Good laugh.

'She didn't want to. She won't put the finger even on this Jansen. She was sorry she ever gave you the idea in the first place. Also she's scared, and hearing about this death will make her more so. I've put a tape-recorder in her room. She'll be gone. What you do with it is your affair. I'll see you get it, but as far as you know Valencia is a place where melons come from.'

'Why are you telling me all this?'

'To let you know that when you come to arrest Erik he'll be missing. He thinks that I'm pushing him off to Spain with her. He's struck, you might call it, with Fé.'

'If I found him out of the country I'd arrest you in his place, whatever you'd said or done.'

'I know that. D'you take me for a fool? The boy will be there, you clot, and he'll answer, for whatever he's done, no more. But if we're right in our ideas – and we generally are – so will this Jansen.' Mierle spoke without irony. 'I've taken the trouble to learn a little about you, buster. As a policeman, you're a fake. As a man, you're a friend of mine.'

Van der Valk dropped his pen and started to rub his nose.

'The local police have been instructed to rope in all the ravens, this evening, on the way home. I'll be there tonight, myself, when I'll conduct a little research into what the girls were doing last night. If one of the boys were missing, a look-out would be kept. If he hadn't been seen by morning – then a general call would go out. That what you want to know?'

'That's all.'

Van der Valk made three or four phone calls and went home. Jesus, he thought, I never learn to stop sticking my neck out. 'I'm going to bed for an hour,' he told Arlette. 'But with any luck, I might have this broken, this time tomorrow.'

## *Chapter Eight*

At six he was in Bloemendaal, fresh from sleep, food, and a shower.

'You may as well use this office,' said Marcousis. 'Everything's been done as you wanted. I'm going home, but I'll be back later, of course. The two girls you wanted to begin with are being brought in, and the others have been rounded up; all the parents have been warned. Expect me about eight-thirty, to see the colour of the blood.'

'Did you know that under water it looks green?' asked Van der Valk, grinning. 'You know, I'd like one of those things myself if I could afford it. So long.' He pushed the buzzer on the desk. A policeman came in, a young one, impressed by all the commotion.

'Got the Troost girl and the other outside, Chief.'

'Keep them waiting. Apart, and not allowed to speak. Nice hard wooden bench, good for the conscience.' He settled down to read the medical report. Clipped together neatly – Marcousis was no slouch at clerical work – were the reports on the aqualung – in perfect order and showing no sign of any mishandling – on the findings at the beach – damn' little – and a couple of terse paragraphs from the harbour master's office at Ijmuiden, about weather and tides. From this last it appeared that it would be very unlikely that the boy's body had ever been more than twenty-five metres off shore, or it would certainly have drifted further.

Lastly there were the statements of the van Sonneveld parents; that strangely unsympathetic couple. Shortly after he had finished reading and making notes, the inspector who had been charged with rounding up the ravens came in.

'All in the bag?'

'All save one. Erik Mierle. Went off in the afternoon somewhere; hasn't been seen since.'

'Very well,' unperturbed as the superintendent from Scotland

Yard. 'We'll pick him up later on, at his home perhaps. Any trouble?'

'All tame except the big one, Wim Brinkman. I know him; he's a tough boy. Gave some lip and got a smack.'

'Girls see this? I wanted a bit of drama. Injured innocents, brutally handled by callous policemen.'

'Saw them brought in and searched. Didn't say a word, but big eyes.'

'Good. Give me five minutes, and then shoot in the Troost kid.'

He took a sheet of paper, headed it 'Troost' and shrugged his shoulders. Going to start bullying the little girls now. Big beast. Till one found that they were as hard as nails. Seven little murderesses – oh no, he had no longer any doubt, not after reading those reports – all prim and demurely charming, on his unwilling hands. Peach of an enquiry; sex all over the shop. Already he had had a whore and a career woman of easy virtue, and now he was going to tangle with the immature emotions and tediously intimate physiques of a lot of eighteen-year-old sweeties. Spoilt, depraved little bitches about one-tenth as feminine as Feodora. He sighed, with deep and distasteful anticipation. And now the cold-water voice. L'eau froide. Slow freight.

'Sit down, Miss Troost. You know why you've been sent for?'

'No.'

'Let's not be stupid, shall we?'

'I know Kees is – is dead.'

'And how he came to die?'

'He went swimming with that thing of his, didn't he?'

'Did he? Uh, did he now. I'm not very satisfied that he did. Very well. You have been summoned here on an official notice signed by the Commissaris of the Bloemendaal police, to answer questions I put, which will form part of a judicial enquiry into the manner of this death, conducted by myself, in view of a possible connexion with a criminal investigation into juvenile gangster activities in Amsterdam. Is that clear? . . . Be sensible. No tears and no theatrical performances; this is murder.'

The flat cold remark knocked the colour out of her face, he was tempted to think, with a thump upon the floor.

'And I will tolerate no lying. All of you have deliberately been given no further chance to cook up a concerted tale, to bolster the original effort agreed, I have no doubt at all, between you. There are seven of you in all; I propose to question each of you separately; if I am then still not satisfied with what I hear I will begin again. I have plenty of time; it won't worry me to be here all night. Even if I get only two different versions of some detail it would mean that someone was lying, wouldn't it? And lying will not be a light matter. The next set of questions may be asked by the Officer of Justice. And if he is not satisfied either the next after that by the President of the Assize Court. Now you were with Kees all evening; tell me what you did.'

'We just walked around a bit, and then we went to the cinema, and then to a café, and we just talked and had a couple of beers and a sandwich, and then, well, we went home.'

'Together?'

'I went as far as his house with him.'

'And then?'

'I met one of the other girls that lives near me, and we got talking.'

'Carmen. Yes, I know. And how long did it take you to reach home?'

'I don't know exactly; we met Elly, and we went into her house to see a new suit that she'd bought, and well, we were trying it on, and . . . time passed, you know.' Nervous giggle.

'A couple of days ago you told me you didn't know any of these girls well. Yet the next day you were having lunch with Carmen in a snack-bar – yes, you were seen – and yesterday you were trying on Elly's clothes. A sudden change. Explain it.'

'Things change.'

'I see. Tell me what Kees was doing on the beach after midnight.'

'How can I? I wasn't there.'

'Weren't you indeed? Very amusing story, Miss Troost. Kees goes home with you, but leaves his house again almost immediately, carrying his aqualung. To show it, we are told, to "someone". We now know that he was headed for the beach to swim. Meanwhile you are on your way home, but are delayed by meeting your new friends – these suddenly intimate friends. You try on their clothes, though two days ago you had little in common with them because they were rather older than yourself.'

'Like I said. And I don't know the time because I wasn't wearing my watch.'

'Nobody asked about your watch. Helpful of you to remember.'

'The bracelet hurts my wrist. Ask my mother.'

'Who, do you think, did Kees meet on the beach?'

'How should I know?'

'Perhaps it was another girl.'

'I don't know that he met anyone.'

'But he told his parents he was meeting "someone". If it was another girl, would you be – sorry, would you have been – jealous?'

Shrug.

'Do you think you're behaving normally, Miss Troost?'

'I would think so.'

'It surprises you then to hear that I don't believe a word you say?'

'You've no right to call me a liar.' Indignantly.

'Why should I need a right when I've such good reasons? Your every word is a phony posture.'

'Say what you like if it amuses you,' angrily.

'You were fond of Kees, weren't you?'

'I suppose so.'

'You suppose so. You suppose also that if you hadn't been fond of him – I don't use the word love – you'd still have gone to bed with him.'

'I did love him, of course.'

Van der Valk purred. 'For someone who loved him, Miss Troost, you're very unconcerned about his death.'

'How dare you say I don't care? I was very upset. I still am. If I seem queer it's because I'm in shock. Who wouldn't be upset?'

'Just so. Who wouldn't? You're shocked all right, but only by my seeing through this rigmarole quicker than you expected. Why pretend unconcern? Why be unnatural? He went out with someone unknown, and you – who loved him, you assure me – weren't jealous. An hour later he was dead, and you're about as bothered as if you'd lost a hairpin. When did you hear he was dead?'

'This afternoon. One of the girls saw the police on the beach. It got around.'

'She brought the story to class. And you believed it?'

'Well, yes.'

'Very remarkable reaction. Do you know that I have brought news of death to many people, and never – not once – have I known it believed as you pretend to have believed it, complacently. Not true, they say; can't be possible; you must have the name wrong. They're always convinced that there's been a mistake. Yet some girl comes to you with gossip about police on the beach; the boy is dead, they say; the boy to whom you said good night on the doorstep last night, and you believe it all implicitly.'

'It's not true, it's not true; ask any of the girls.'

'I have no doubt you had a piece of emotional acting laid by for the occasion, Miss Troost. Which you did not quite dare repeat for my benefit. You judged it better and more convincing to be calm and brave. Because you knew already. You knew last night. And, I think, with eyewitness certainty. Consequently although frightened by my presence, you are not surprised. How many of you were on the beach?'

Silence. He pressed his buzzer.

'Bring in the girl Elly Visser, and keep her outside. I'll see her when I'm ready.'

'Right, Chief.'

'The truth will not go bad with an hour's keeping,' in a meditative voice. 'Carmen is waiting too, in patience, and, I have no doubt, in considerable fear. I advise you, Miss Troost, to be the first with the truth. Such details will interest the Officer of Justice.'

'I am telling the truth.'

'Miss Troost, why aren't you curious to know my reasons for thinking this a murder?'

'I didn't like to ask. It's not my business.'

'Ah. Your boy, your steady, is murdered, and you tell me that it is not your business. You can wait outside, till you decide to tell me the truth. I'm not finished with you; I've scarcely begun, but you can sit now in the waiting-room, on the wooden bench, until you make up your mind not to waste my time. As a liar, you are pitiful.'

He buzzed again.

'Hang on to this one until I want her again.'

The man took the girl out, and then returned.

'Her father's outside stamping about.'

'All right. Move the girls into the charge-room, and if any

parents turn up they can sit in the waiting-room, so there's no friction. You can bring the girl Carmen. I'll see these parents when I have the time. At present I'm too busy, tell them. And bring me some tea. Keep the atmosphere chilly out there. Forbidding silence, a bit churchy. No smoking or talking at all. Got all that?'

'Understood.' The man was grinning. Acting; thought Van der Valk; why can't one have police work without pretending to be Gestapo Muller? All wrong, not the way to handle these kids. But this was a judicial enquiry. Homicide. Circumstances ... Officer of Justice ... manual of instruction for the conduct of investigating officers ... article thing in the code of criminal law. ... Crap.

'Sit down, Carmen. So; you were on the beach last night.'

'Who told you that?'

'Nobody told me; I know it. Concentrate on telling the truth; I'm aware it's an effort.'

'Did Hannie say that?'

'What interest have you in what Hannie said?'

'Because it's a lie, that's why.'

'Has Hannie departed from the agreed story, then?'

'What agreed story?'

'But if Hannie was on the beach, why shouldn't you have been? You were with her, weren't you?'

'Yes; not on the beach, though. I don't know when she could have been on the beach. She went home after leaving me, I thought.'

'Lying, my child. Obvious to everyone, I'm afraid.'

'I've no reason to lie.'

'Certainly not. Nothing illegal about being on the beach, is there?'

'I don't know why you keep harping away about the beach.'

'Perhaps Hannie is lying. She was frightened. You're not frightened, are you?'

'No, why should I be? Not exactly pleased, at all this Gestapo stuff.'

'Would you be frightened if I told you that Kees van Sonneveld had been murdered?' ...

It all took time, lots of time. He had to go and squash the papa Troost, who was ramping about, talking to anyone who would listen about lawyers, and citizens' rights, and the Constitution, and who was unwilling to believe enormities and calumnies about his daughter. By this time he had a whole flock of doves fidgeting about on their slim little behinds in the gloomy surroundings of the inspector's room, and they had to be kept waiting, to ripen. It was when Hannie Troost's turn came round again that he began to make headway. She had had to bear the silent inquisition of the other girls for over two hours, and resistance wore thin. She had neither the experience nor the control of the others, and her imagination was against her.

'We thought we'd better say nothing about it.'

'Why not? You all went swimming, and Kees was still in the water when you all came out because it was colder than you had expected. That's it, is it?'

'Yes.'

'So you got dressed, and there was still no sign of him, so you all thought he was still under water, but you weren't worried. So you went home. Right?'

'Yes.'

'To finish recapitulating: when today you learned that he had drowned you were frightened to go to the police. Why?'

'We knew that he'd been – in trouble with the police, and we began to think – that he might have killed himself. We were frightened. And then I was frightened when – when you started talking about murder.'

'Not frightened enough, Miss Troost. We shall see.'

First stage accomplished. They had been on the scene, and had denied it.

The girls were tired and miserable now, frightened and confused, unable to give support or encouragement to one another. Their lies, from being far too plausible, now began to sound unlikely even to their own ears, and they began to disintegrate. They had been given tea, and sandwiches, and escorted to the lavatory in turn by a wooden-faced inspector. Three or four parents were fuming in the waiting-room, but Marcousis abolished them; he had been sitting by Van der Valk listening, and realising that the questions now, were beginning to get the answers they had expected. He was back now; Van der Valk pointed to a line in the doctor's report. He had not wished to play his high card till the right moment.

Lina was in the chair opposite; a gay and intelligent-looking girl, with pretty curling brown hair and a tilted nose. With calm and a show of sympathy he had got her in quite a good frame of mind.

'Well, then, we've that definite at last. You all went swimming.'

'There's no harm in that, is there? I just didn't admit it because I don't see why I should be questioned about my private life as though I were a criminal or something.'

'And you decided all this on impulse – have I got it right? Just let me be sure. Kees was showing you and Elly the aqualung?'

'Yes.'

'And he said he was going swimming with it, because he hadn't yet tried it out in the open sea?'

'That's right. We just suddenly thought it would be a funny idea to go as well. First time this year in the sea.'

'What puzzles me is why you should have gone a kilometre beyond the town, along the sand.'

'Well, to be quiet a bit. People here are so old-fashioned; they can't understand that one might feel like swimming at night. All nosy-parkers too. Like you. I hate that.'

'Nice for me that I'm paid to be a nosy-parker.'

'You said it, mister.'

'I have a notion that you also went so far because you had no swim suits, mm?'

'I suppose, yes.'

'You were all naked.'

'Is there a law against it? You seem easily shocked.'

'No, I'm not very easily shocked. Neither are you, would you say?'

'Certainly not.'

'Good, that's very good,' said Van der Valk with false and hearty bonhomie. 'Now: when you got a bit out of the town, far enough for nobody to see or hear and come being nosy – pity about me – you all undressed. With Kees?'

'Dirty-minded as well, I see. We made him go further along.'

'Fine. Continuing my dirty-minded train of thought, I should like to know whether he came anywhere near any of you in the water.'

'Of course not. He went further out, with his machine. We didn't go in deep, and we didn't stay in long, and we all stayed together. It was cold.'

'So in effect you were none of you near him the whole time you all spent on the beach?'

'Correct, sir.'

'Good. Definitely, then, quite impossible for him to have made love to one or more of you?'

'Do you mind?'

'Come, Lina, don't be shocked. I see that you haven't the experience of beach parties you like to pretend.'

'I'm not shocked. I object to your being obscene. It may amuse you. It disgusts me.'

'Aha. I note both your objection and your delicacy. Excellent. But I'm pleased that you're not easily shocked, because we have one or two delicate points here. Have you studied any biology?'

The girl, haughty sniff still on her face, was taken out of her stride a little.

'At school; why?'

'Good. No need, then, for me to have to explain to you the biological facts of human reproduction?' Despite himself, despite the horrid seriousness of the situation, despite Van der Valk's bland diplomatic face, Marcousis had to struggle to hide a grin. The haughty sniff became outraged.

'Now we're really getting on. I'm going to read to you a little from the doctor's report, that tells us the results of the examination made of Kees' body. Quite usual, that, in cases of unexplained death. To find out whether some obscure physical condition might not have caused a sudden collapse. This seems straightforward; there was quite simply nothing. Mm; these pathologists – they're very thorough. One minor detail here – bothers me slightly; perhaps you can help. From what you tell me I won't have to explain the slight technicality, though I will if you want me to. The sentence reads, "Spermatogenesis was occurring." Do you understand that?'

The girl stared, with consternation in her face, struggling for some defence. She looked as though her queen had been taken first move.

'Yes.' Slowly. Fairly caught.

'Now, leaving, or rather applying these biological generalities to this particular occasion' – this sort of jocular brutality was typical of Van der Valk at work – 'what ideas does that give you?'

There was a long painful silence.

'I suppose,' dragging her voice out of her throat, 'that it means he had some sort of sexual climax.'

'Precisely. Which to my obscene mind,' cheerfully, 'means he'd made love. Now I want to know who with.'

'Couldn't he,' furious look and blush, 'have had that without anybody else?'

'Quite correct, he could. Only in this case he didn't. He wasn't alone when he went into the sea, and when he came out of the sea he no longer had such things on his mind.'

The girl's face screwed as though he had hit her with a whip.

'And now which of you was it?'

'Well – I don't know – ask Hannie – she was his girl, after all. It wasn't me, I can tell you, and that's all I will tell you. Bastard!'

'That'll be all for now, thank you, Miss Wijsman.'

Troost again. The fresh girl was at the end of her tether; looking very haggard now.

'So you did make love last night?'

'That's my private life,' snivelling.

'When someone dies by violence he no longer has a private life. His actions, and those of people concerned with him, become legitimate subjects of enquiry. Answer me.'

'I can't tell you.'

'Under a handy lamp-post?'

'I can't tell you.'

His voice went soft; he leaned forward.

'Did you perhaps make love in the water? And did the others perhaps grab him? So?' His flat hand hit the table with a sudden terrifying crack. The girl burst into hysterical sobs and started to shriek.

He gave her a glass of water, and went out to the glowering parents in the waiting-room: he cut short the indignant protests at the audible sobbing.

'This is a very serious matter indeed. A case exists, here, to charge your daughters, individually and collectively, with wilful homicide. Do you realise what that means?'

Horrified silence.

'There are not adequate facilities to keep women here. They will be given food and drink and allowed to rest, while arrangements are made to bring them, tonight, to the House of Keeping for women in Amsterdam or Haarlem. They will be looked after. Your daughter, Mr Troost, is, I can assure you, suffering from no more than hysteria, induced by confessing to a criminal act. She has not been ill treated; the Commissaris here was present throughout. Tomorrow the Officer of Justice will decide what is to be done. He will certainly want to question your daughters; application must now be made to him if you wish to be present or for lawyers to be present. No statement to the Press will be made unless authorised by him. I must now advise you all to go home immediately; your further presence here impedes justice.'

When he walked back into the office Marcousis was standing by the window, apparently absorbed in the empty street.

'I'll have to make arrangements for all this,' he said. 'These girls can't stay here. Don't disturb yourself, Van der Valk – I'll use the phone outside.' He glanced meaningly at the girl. She was quiet now, a soaked handkerchief balled in her hand, staring at the wall, her smeary face dull and shapeless. Marcousis closed the door softly; there was silence. Sometimes, Van der Valk told the door, you are not too stupid.

He went over to the wash-basin and soaked the end of a towel in cold water. She was passive, let him throw the crumpled handkerchief in the waste-paper basket, and buried her face obediently in the cold towel. He lit a cigarette and watched her quietly. He was pleased when she got up, wrung the towel out, and spread it carefully to dry. He gave the smoking cigarette to her as she passed; she sat down again, drew on it, and breathed out in a long tired sigh, her head back against the rim of the chair, her eyes shut. In repose her face had become pretty again; the towel had wiped away the hysterical glare.

Van der Valk said nothing; the silence seemed to him to heal the words that had stained the atmosphere, and still hung in the room, putrefying. Fresh tears stood at the corners of Hannie's closed eyes. Her lashes were long and vulnerable; against his training, Van der Valk felt pity.

'You said I didn't love him,' she said suddenly. 'That was

unfair. That was what I couldn't stand.'

'Hannie,' he said, and was astonished to hear love in his voice. It had been meant as a word of tact. A stabilising sound. He felt no particular sympathy for her. Pity, yes, but pity is unprofessional. Damn it, his voice should have been neutral. It had no business to sound the way it did.

He had just broken her; he felt as though he had raped her. The struggle had been like an act of love; his bowels felt pinched and empty. He could not help it – at this moment, he loved her. Did she feel it too? She opened her eyes and looked at him; the two released tears trickled away and she wiped her cheek like a child, using the back of her hand.

'You shouldn't have said I didn't love him.' Her voice was gentle, as though reproving a child. Yes, she had heard the fact, implicit in his tone. For a moment now, he entered her private world. Certainly her face was still stupid; it had to be. She was a stupid girl. But it had dignity, now. Van der Valk was furious with himself. He wanted to take her in his arms and comfort her.

'I need another handkerchief,' she said. 'I want to blow my nose. And I want to go to the lavatory.'

He passed her his handkerchief, which she regarded with approval.

'He had to be killed,' she said gently. 'But I was quite determined that if he had to die, it would be with me loving him and no one else.'

Words strangled in his throat. He saw himself in the deep water, with Arlette's body in his arms, and Arlette's breath roaring in his ears. And the loving, implacable hands of every other woman he had ever loved – Hannie, too? – were on his shoulders, dragging him under. He could not struggle. Arlette's strong, long thighs were gripping him like a vice. Hannie's voice, telling him why she had killed her lover, was small and distant, but clear and reasonable. He did not know how long it took to tell him; he knew that because he loved her, and was in her world, he understood. Then the door opened and Marcousis came in, and everything was gone. He thought he still understood, but he was not sure; he felt horribly tired. He no longer loved Hannie. He was a policeman, doing his job. In an instant of detachment he realised that because he loved Arlette, and Feodora, and Hannie, he was sometimes a good policeman.

'All right, Hannie,' he said. 'I understand.'

Marcousis took no notice, the tactful bugger.

When she had been brought out he could talk; his voice was recognisable; quiet, unemotional, professional. Marcousis was smoking and chewing on a Bic, turning over the pages of notes.

'That's established. You were right: they killed him.'

'Yes. Believe me, I want no credit for making her speak. Poor little calf. I'd appreciate your help in wording the procés-verbal.'

'We'll have to get confirmation, though, from one or more of the others. They will shake loose, now.'

They drank a cup of coffee together.

'Horrid story,' said Van der Valk. 'In some way they enticed him – with themselves – and ducked him; held him under till he was lethally full of salt water. I don't believe he had the lung on at all. Brought it with him of course; it made an admirable blind. They fixed it afterwards and towed him a little out to sea; simple. It was the game of thread-the-needle that made it all possible with no struggling or yelling.'

'Just the one thing gave them away.'

'I might not have given that any great weight. Been with the girl all evening. The sand in the lung stuck in my throat a bit, and then the fact that it just isn't easy to get into trouble with an aqualung. And then someone he was going to meet. I'd asked the father to keep an eye on the boy; maybe they never thought he would be fussy enough to ask where the boy was going. Look at these girls. All out till after midnight, and not one parent knew or, apparently, bothered where they were. These people deserve trouble.'

'What I still don't understand is why.'

'And neither do I. Not – altogether – fully. But that's not our worry, huh? It'll come out.'

'We might try and drill into them a bit more.'

But nothing more was to be got out of the girls. Sullen silence. They knew nothing, had seen nothing, done nothing. Troost was hysterical; she had made it up just to stop the questioning. They didn't know what she was talking about; no more did she, probably.

Quite likely they had realised the weakness of the case; it was not compelling as long as it appeared meaningless. No, they knew nothing about what the boys did. Ordeals, initiations? – never heard of Hjalmar Jansen? – he was a good pal. Yes, they had used Hjalmar's flat to make love – he got that much out of them – and so what? He knew nothing about it; if he had known he would have forbidden them going in. Raids? Parties? Kees had imagined it, or made it up. He must have been unbalanced, committing suicide that way.

He kept on stubbornly, though it was not much use. All right, they had lied about being on the beach. Naturally; they didn't want the whole of Bloemendaal to start talking ... To have run away and concealed it wasn't a crime. And they defied him to prove anything. He decided to stop; he didn't want to be accused later of having been brutal. He could just hear a defending lawyer.

'Innocent, nervous girls ... highly strung ... tricked and bullied ... kept up till midnight ... bright lights ... shouting ... disreputable methods of interrogation ... putting words in their mouths ... agree with anything to be left alone ... humiliation and discomfort ... escorted to lavatory by grinning man ...' No, let the examining magistrate carry the ball now. He had enough to hold them. More than enough. Too much.

He drank a cup of stewed lukewarm tea, and said, 'I'm thinking of going up to the Ange Gabriel. Can't be accused of torturing Jansen by talking to him at midnight.'

'Bit imprudent, perhaps? We haven't proof enough, regarding him, to cover a sixpence,' said Marcousis, warily.

'Perhaps. And again it might be politic. Let him see the eye that never sleeps. I only want to shake his nerves. Let's go and tempt him a little. Maybe he'll be indiscreet.'

'Still, remember that we have nothing proved yet, won't you, and that man is good friends with just about everybody of consequence here, and that includes the burgomaster.'

'Yeh. He can add me, too.'

*

The Ange Gabriel was still and shuttered. Only reddish light seeping through curtains, and the faint tinkle of a piano, gave signs of life. A policeman was standing, bored, on the pavement opposite. Marcousis beckoned.

'Everything as usual?'

'Quiet as a mouse.'

'Many in the bar?'

'Dozen maybe.' Boots sloped off; gritty noise on the sandy bricks. Marcousis rang the bell; within a minute Jansen's face appeared at the judas.

'Why, Commissaris.' The bolt snapped and light spilt on the pavement. 'It took me a second to recognise you; forgive me.' His bow to Van der Valk was ironic. 'I think a friend has been expecting you. He's certainly been very patient; read the whole of last week's *Elsevier* right through three times already. Even the advertisements; perhaps he's looking for a better job.'

'Poor sod,' said Van der Valk amiably. 'He'll have to forgive me. I got held up talking to some girls. You know, the cats. They'd been hunting, and damn if they hadn't caught a mouse. On the beach too; funny place for a mouse.'

'You don't tell me.' Unconcerned as an old woman asking what cake there is for tea. We'll see: thought Van der Valk, ordering Mrs van Sonneveld's favourite drink of Scotch and ginger-ale with ice. The drinks were on him, Jansen said smoothly.

'Not every day we entertain the higher ranks of the police.'

Comfortably, Van der Valk reflected that he was this man's equal in intelligence and nerve, and his superior in courage. That's what it will boil down to. Very bold, crafty, tricky, but has he got courage? If this was to be a fight, go to it, boys. Jansen sat down with them; with young Bart there drinking beer – he had joined them thankfully, still clutching his *Elsevier* – they looked like the four tea-drinking old hags, wearing hats like nothing on earth, of Van der Valk's active imagination.

'I suppose I can't flatter myself into thinking this a friendly call – the whole building resounds to the tramp of boots. I must admit my curiosity, but perhaps you are here to explain?'

'I'm afraid I've taken away all your best customers. They're all in jail. Females included.'

'Really? Have they been doing naughty things in Amsterdam too, then?' There was gaiety in his voice; it seemed to say: 'Stupid clot; you'll never understand.'

'They had a beach party last night, and drowned a boy. Young Kees van Sonneveld, the new recruit.'

'I did hear there'd been some mishap. And the girls were there? Good heavens.' Young Bart Suykerland was out of his depth; he took a drink of beer and wiped his lips nervously. Marcousis, idly poking at the ice-cubes in his glass, seemed to be keeping score, as the two circled cautiously, feinting.

'They had quite a party. Rather similar to the ones they've had in your flat; no clothes on, and kissing games. Though I don't suppose you've ever found a dead body in your flat.' A left hook, chalked up non-committally.

'Come now, Inspector, even just between us here, in a friendly way, I can't let you talk like that; the joke is coarse. You're talking of what you don't know. They've all been in my flat, there's no secret about that – but parties, kissing games – that's merely insulting. I have a fine collection of records – you must see it some time.' Cross-counter with the right, not a bad one. 'I'm really sorry, though, to hear that you appear to be bearing down on them. Delightful girls.' Sparring, almost playfully.

'You've never married, have you?'

'Why no, Inspector, but why the personality?'

'I wondered whether you ever caught yourself fancying one of these delightful girls.' Vulgar body punch, rather below the belt, but Jansen did not lose his nonchalance.

'Bit outside my age-group,' smiling.

'I'll take you up on this offer to show me the records.' He had to crowd the fellow some more. He wished anyway to see the flat; never miss seeing where people live. He was pleased that Jansen seemed a thought hesitant.

'Tell me, is this an investigation? Am I supposed to be under suspicion of something?' His tone had the same ironic calm, but was there an edge of surprise. As though he could not quite believe that this cretin of a policeman would seriously intrude upon him? 'Not going to have to become irritated, am I?'

Marcousis answered.

'It's an investigation, certainly, and into very serious happenings. We expect, of course, the fullest cooperation of anyone who – however remotely – might have knowledge that bears on the subjects of our interest.' He sounded as though reciting a lesson; his voice was cool and sweet as ice-cream. 'As to being suspected, Mr Jansen, ask that when you are accused of something. What we think, or even suspect, does not concern the public.'

Jansen seemed about to answer, but thought better of it, looking at the Commissaris as though the referee had suddenly punched him from behind.

'I'm at your service, gentlemen, naturally, in any way I can be.'

He led the way through the curtains behind the bar into a service area; a door led to a lobby.

'Leads to the ice-salon,' indifferently. 'Is that of any interest to you? No? This way; allow me to lead.' A stairway; plain wood and painted walls. 'Any material for the club upstairs is generally brought this way.' On the first landing a door, bolted; he tapped with a fingernail. 'This is the club, where these children you are so interested in are accustomed to meet.'

'I've seen it,' said Van der Valk. 'I've been observing their activities for some weeks.'

'So?' unconcernedly. 'Shall I lead the way further?'

The staircase made another turn, through a hundred and eighty degrees The walls were painted white here, hung with flower prints; there was a carpet on white-painted stairs. At the top a plain door.

'Welcome to my home, gentlemen.'

The flat was not large. Indeed it could not be large, since it covered one floor only of the narrowish, tower-like building that faced the sea. A good-sized sitting-room, one bedroom, a generous bathroom and a little kitchen. It was not at all remarkable; it was comfortable, and that was really all that could be said about it.

The furniture was expensive, in no particular taste either good or very bad, and looked as though it had been chosen at random in a large dreary shop. Unpatterned linen curtains in a three-colour weave, a carpet that was just a carpet, a big business desk of bleached wood, very neat. A long studio couch; small arm-chairs, a brass-bound teak coffee-table, rather ugly. A few shelves of books in one of those split-level wall fittings; this held as well a drinks cupboard and extra speakers for the big radiogram that stood against the adjoining wall. Beside it stood a large cabinet; several rows of neatly docketed record sleeves. Central heating, like the rest of the building.

It was not even very clean. Tidy, yes, in the sense that nothing much stood around, and nobody much really lived there. No flowers, and few personal things. A good deal of military bric-à-brac; a little brass cannon on an oak carriage stood on the coffee-table; on wall brackets a model of a sailing ship, a mahogany box, open, containing in beds of green felt a pair of good eighteenth-century duelling pistols. On another bracket a silver-mounted musket, or arquebus of some sort. The only picture was an engraving, Breughel's 'Divertissement sur la glace, à Anvers'. The windows looked out to sea; on a little occasional table stood a large brass ship's telescope. It was a pleasant enough room; nobody would have thought it striking.

Van der Valk glanced through the records. A fine collection; going back to the roots of jazz and full of its canonised saints. Many heavy scratched old seventy-eights, lovingly wrapped in padded tissue, alongside more popular personages transferred on to modern long-players. He recognised many dimly-remembered characters from his own youth; Bix and Miff and Bunny, Jelly Roll and Fats, the King and the Duke and the Count. Records of the 'twenties and 'thirties, made by players who had then been better, perhaps, than now. Now they were bishops, beaming episcopally down at their public from thrones.

Jazz on these shelves was a microcosm of a religion, with theologians and dogmas, orthodoxies and heresies, schisms and reformations, wild hairy prophets and bland cardinals in rimless glasses, and everywhere fanatics. He laughed heartily; he had sat in holy rapture too in his day. Only a year or so back he had been delighted to see the Pope pass through an Amsterdam street, in all his glory of diamonds and silk handkerchiefs, on his way to the Concertgebouw to proclaim there the coming of the Lord. He grinned at Jansen.

'Wonderful collection. I understand the attraction.'

He went on to look at the bookshelves; he had a vague feeling that Jansen was not quite so happy to see him examine the book-shelves. Books are, he knew, the best of all guides to a man's character, though here there were not enough, really, to help him much. A colourless lot too, by the look. Oddly chameleon-like, this man; promises to be an interesting and vivid person; why are his rooms, his books so drab? Van der Valk felt he did not yet fully understand.

Technical books on the bar and restaurant business, several; some chi-chi about food and wine; many guides, tourist handouts and chatty travelogues. A handbook of the licensing and sale-of-food laws, and *How Not to Pay Too Much Income-tax*. A shelf or two of English paperbacks, thrillers. And an odd assortment of rather antiquated juvenile works. Dumas, Jules Verne, *Heroes of Aviation* next to a volume of Maupassant. *Famous Ghost Stories*, *A Hundred Tales of Horror*, Poe, Blackwood, James. Three or four volumes of Stevenson, and Pierre Louys' *Aphrodite*. Weird bedfellows. The thrillers were rather the swordstick-on-the-tower type. Hm.

The door to the bedroom stood open. Here again little furniture, and no very strong individual tastes, unless those of a man who believes in physical exercise. A divan bed, a dressing-table with a triple glass. A rope ladder bolted to the ceiling and swinging free; a very magnificent one with nylon ropes and bamboo rungs. A punchball; a pair of Indian clubs. Only one picture; a glossy, highly worked gouache of three naked women in a palace, in seventeenth-century Spanish America, judging by the architecture. One was trying on a hat in front of a very ornate looking-glass – the painter had excelled himself with this reflection. The other two looking on in attitudes of fervent admiration, with a little Negro page playing the guitar in one corner. A grin grew on Van der Valk's face as he inspected all this art with close attention.

Again, the bathroom was ordinary; the usual white-painted cupboard, which he opened with unashamed nosiness, contained nothing less banal than after-shave, aspirin and indigestion pills. No dexedrines or barbiturates or anything in the least exciting. There was, in fact, nothing, anywhere in the flat, that was not evidence of a blameless, healthy, rather unintelligent life. It seemed a bit unexpected. Almost too good to be true. But everything looked permanent and well settled-in; nothing looked staged or rearranged. An anticlimax. Nothing for the policemen here but a dignified retreat, mm? What on earth could Van der Valk be finding to grin at?

He made remarks of conventional politeness, and several broad and rather bad jokes. Jansen saw them off the premises with an inscrutably polite face, and was full of little courtesies to Marcousis.

## *Chapter Nine*

'Well,' said Marcousis outside, 'didn't get very far with him. I'm not sure that that wasn't a mistake.'

'We got further anyway than he thought. Flat had a more honest face than he has.'

'You're still convinced that he is involved?'

'Not only convinced. Now I see.'

'Mm.' Marcousis had evidently seen nothing very informative.

'Let's all go home and get some sleep,' said Van der Valk. 'I still have a job, but it's only routine.'

'I only wish I felt as confident as you seem to,' a thought acidly, getting into his neat Taunus at the bureau parking lot. 'Strange business. Obviously serious, and I take it so, but nonsensical too, don't you find?'

'History's like that too. Ever read Plievier on the last days of Adolf Hitler? You don't know whether to laugh or vomit.'

Marcousis did not look quite sure that history was approved reading for good policemen. 'No getting round those girls, certainly. Officer of Justice will have his hands full. I'll say good night to you, Van der Valk; my wife will be fussing. We'll work out the details of the paperwork tomorrow, and I suppose you'll be wanting the boys moved over to Amsterdam.'

'Sure. Good night to you, Commissaris. Come on, Bart.' They got into the Mercedes and he started the motor.

'D'you mind my asking, Chief, but what could you see about that chap? All night he never turned a hair – and that flat, well, it was just ordinary, wasn't it?'

'Didn't see anything. Nothing evidential, that we could write on paper and give to the magistrate. Just another card turned over. Ever deal a pack of cards, one by one, waiting for the ace of spades? And it was the last card of all? Old Black Jack. Something like that happening here. Out you get. We turn over a couple more cards, here.'

When you ring at the house of a woman like Feodora, and there is not an immediate answer, you do not wait; you go away. Useless, and tactless, to ring twice; you should have made an appointment. Van der Valk seemed not to know this; he rang again, the bossy double peal that means police all over the world – open up or we'll kick it in. They don't, but one does not disregard it. Feodora's sensitive early-warning system brought her promptly to the speak-box.

'Who is it, please?'

'Van der Valk.'

'My dear, I am sorry, but I have a guest.' Bart Suykerland had round eyes.

'I'm afraid I have to insist, Fé. You see, I know about the guest.'

'Ah . . . I understand. . . . I hope you will be intelligent.' The latch clicked; the time-switch killed the passage light as they reached the upper door.

No one in the living-room, and in the bedroom only two people; both had been in bed and been wakened. Erik Mierle was still in bed, upright, with frightened eyes. Feodora, in a nightdress, was sitting by him. Van der Valk came in and simply sat down.

'You wait in the living-room, Bart; better still, put the kettle on and we'll have some coffee, if Madame will allow you.'

He leaned back and shut his eyes a moment, feeling fatigue at last. He took two or three slow breaths, hunted a cigarette out, lit it slowly. Feodora reached a packet off the table and lit one for herself, and another for the boy; the table lamp shed a soft orange light on the two figures. When Van der Valk did speak it was to the boy, in a quiet voice, the tone sharpened only by his holding the cigarette between his teeth.

'It goes this way, Erik. You've found out that you're a man. I see that, so I treat you as a man now, and not as a boy. Your father is proud of you; I see that Feodora is too. They are two people whose opinions I respect. Nobody has peached on you; I knew where you would be because it's my job to know such things. I thought it out. So, with my job to do, I'm here too. I don't make bargains, as Fé will tell you, but I promise you two things.

'First, you are not being asked or going to be asked to account for anything you haven't done. I know perfectly well that you had nothing to do with Kees van Sonneveld's death. However, that death means that all the other boys, and all the girls, sit tonight in the police bureau. They might have to face a charge of murder; a judicial enquiry, certainly. It depends on you a bit; those girls could really be in trouble. As for Jansen, the sand is running out for him. I'll have my hands on him tomorrow.

'What you are asked to do, now, is to behave like a man. I'm not arresting you or anything; as you see, I'm just sitting here. I've come to drink coffee with two friends. When we've had coffee I want you to get up and walk out of the door with Mr Suykerland. He'll lock you up for the night. Tomorrow all this will be settled. That is absolutely all.

'The second thing you have my word for is that when all this affair is over – a process, by the way, which you can speed up a great deal – Feodora will not have disappeared. You will find her.'

The boy did not move; he stared at the policeman with steady eyes. They sat for two or three minutes in a peaceful silence, the cigarettes glowing and fading.

'I'm going to make the coffee,' Feodora said. 'Get dressed, darling, won't you.' Van der Valk got up politely, and strolled into the living-room, where a puzzled Bart was scratching his head over Feodora's records. It was interesting to compare them with Hjalmar Jansen's. She had an eighteenth-century taste; with Brahms she came to a stop. No Sibelius or Tchaikovsky, no Mahler or Strauss, no Wagner and certainly no Stravinsky. But she had all the Mozart operas, most of the Beethoven quartets, lots of Haydn. She evidently loved lieder, and like 'Doc Ricketts' she loved Gregorian chant.

When she came in she had put on a housecoat and tied the sash, not to offend policemen's modesty. Van der Valk grinned at her and quoted the little poem by Lorca.

'Cuando llegue la luna llena – Iré a Santiago de Cuba.'

She raised something of her old smile.

'You're a smart stinker – you've been making a conspiracy with Frans.'

'Frans worries about the boy. So do you. So do I. Oddly enough, we all love you.'

Bart in the corner was tactfully wondering what 'The Well-tempered Clavier' could possibly mean.

The spoons clinked in the coffee-cups; Erik came out of the bedroom dressed. He took the cup she handed him with a smile like his father's.

'I'm ready.'

'You cheer up, my lad,' said Bart. 'This isn't the last supper, hoor; Pontius Pilate's retired.' This moss-grown policemen's joke broadened the boy's smile, but he looked anxiously at Feodora; she made a little moue of reassurance.

'Hungry?' she asked everyone. She buttered rye bread, and cut slices of cold rollade with gherkins inside. The boy could not eat, but the two policemen did, with loud appreciation. To have eaten at the same table, thought Van der Valk, means that one has thereafter a bond; a sort of confidence. Bread and salt.

'Well,' he said, stretching with satisfaction. 'Let's cut the cake.'

The boy kissed Feodora frantically; she hugged him, and put on a brave rueful smile for the benefit of all. She made a little cross on his forehead with her thumb.

'In Russia, my mother used to do that. To protect you, till you come back to me.' Bart and the boy went off together, strolling amiably like the best of friends.

Feodora lifted the lid of the pot to see how much coffee was left, and poured him another cup. He put his hands on her waist, and gave her a little affectionate shake.

'We're like an old married couple.' She sat down opposite him, her chin in her hands. Her sleeves slid back, exposing her fine arms. He watched her with pleasure and respect.

'You hadn't packed?'

'I didn't bother. Frans was going to send it by plane – what I wanted, which wasn't much.'

'Is, and want. Nobody stops you.'

'No. I'll wait for Erik now. You've seen that he loves me, and that is handy for you; he'll be more manageable. But you see – you will laugh, it is comic – I love him, too. Most ridiculous, the tart with the gold heart. A woman like me, imagine. Thinking as I do, living as I do. The whore – the old whore; I am thirty-six – in love with the boy of eighteen. There've been fine funny songs made about that. Most sentimental and pathetic; I think it can be a good joke. How can it last? Oh, I am not stupid, whatever else; it won't. How could it? But I can educate him. That's what Frans wanted, after all. I can do that at least without making a fool of myself. I owe him that, hey? But I hope that no one will grudge me a year or two of happiness, as a sort of casual by-product, isn't that the word? If he still wants me, after a year – two? – three? – in prison.'

'Look, Fé. It's better for the boy, for Frans, for you especially – and yes, for me too – that you go to Spain. I apologise for the conspiracy; I was ready to take advantage of the boy's being attracted by you; I was sure it would loosen his mouth, which was and is important. But I did not foresee love. Frans was taking you away when?'

'Tomorrow morning – this morning.'

'I want you to go. There is going to be a scandal, and inevitably publicity. I should prefer – I owe you things too – to spare you that, but I can't risk any tricks. If I heard, officially, that you knew part of this story, I'd have to hold you, as a witness. I want you out of here, before I can find out that you exist even. As for Erik, if he tells now what he knows, freely, openly, it will make a great deal of difference. It shouldn't be too long before he joins you. And . . . ? Have you and I been right about all this?'

'Yes. Jansen. I shan't tell you. You and Frans with your tape recorder. I did not use it. Ignoble. When you want proof, look at the books in Jansen's flat. I think that Erik will tell you. He knew that he could not go to Spain. But if he will not tell you' – suddenly – 'neither will I.'

'Erik will tell me. He's like his father; sees things through.'

Very extraordinary thing, he thought; look at me all emotional here. He understood, perhaps, why Frans Mierle thought a lot of this woman. 'I'd better ring Frans, I think; tell him to put his head on the pillow.'

He dialled, yawning a little.

'Frans? Van der Valk. Yes, I'm here, you understand? I only wished to tell you to have no real worries. . . Yes. . . Good, come if you like, but I'm not the Emperor Napoleon, I need sleep. . . . I'm waiting for one of my men. . . . Yes. . . . Yes, if you like.' He yawned again. It would suit him to fall on Fé's bed, just for the sleep necessary to bring him back into the human race. Bart could take the car back to Amsterdam. . . . It would not do, of course, for several reasons.

She read his thoughts. 'Sleep here if you like.' Her charming wicked smile. 'I shan't be using the business bed. In my own bed, you understand, I sleep alone.' He understood. Erik was the first, in years certainly, who had slept in her bed. Was it in a book of Colette's? – the prostitute who had never allowed anyone in her room. 'Paris is big enough for my business.'

The front door sounded a brief blip, and Frans Mierle was in the room, still in his dark business suit, and his starched white collar. He bent and kissed Feodora as though he were her father.

'I came for company as much as for anything.' He nodded abruptly to Van der Valk. 'I hadn't realised how nervous I was, till I got your message. Scratching like a dog with fleas; no, no coffee, Fé. Boy give any trouble?'

'None whatever, thanks to his good sense, and to Fé here. Looked a bit as though mounting the steps of the guillotine, but we all tend to dramatise these occasions. He realised that he wouldn't go to Spain yet awhile. What had you told him?'

'Simply that the police were after him, to go and stay here in Fé's flat, and that I'd take steps to get them both out of the country this morning.'

'Tell me about the steps.'

'Tell you like hell. I assure you that it can be done, and under the noses of a lorry-load of police. Can be done and has been done.'

'Oh yes,' unemotionally. 'Can be done and has been done. But it costs a lot of money. And people with a lot of money disappear easily, but they always reappear, generally in Switzerland, where they've parked it. They have to cash cheques, sell diamonds, pass the word, whoever they are. That's when we get them, if we want them.'

'Don't get excited; nobody's gone yet. You going to put the boys over the jumps tomorrow?'

'Unless Erik makes it all quite clear. He feels brave right now; I'm hoping he'll stay that way. I've known people, all ready to tell, to dig their heels in suddenly; refuse to say a word.'

'He'll tell you,' said Feodora quietly.

'I'm waiting to hear this story,' said Mierle, 'with some anxiety.

There is one thing which I admit candidly has got right under my skin. You told me that they'd raped a woman. Five of them. Remember?'

'That's right.'

'Why not six? There are after all six of them.'

'We'll find, likely, that one always stayed on guard. To pinch a car, too, probably.'

'It's just that I'd be happy to kid myself that on that occasion at least Erik was the odd one out.' He slouched in his chair and stuck his hands in the pockets of his suit, dragging it out of shape. 'I'm staying here with you,' he shot at Feodora. She stood up and came behind him, feeling with strong hands for the nerves running along the spine, below the heavy muscles. 'What are you doing about this louse Jansen?'

'Whatever I judge to be right. When I've heard the stories. In the morning, when I've slept. When everybody's got a quieter head. Answered?'

The buzzer popped twice cheerfully.

'There's Bart at last. Good night,' he said abruptly, and walked out.

'Holy mackerel, what took you so long. Now, let's get a ripple on.' It was precisely two-ten in the morning.

*

Late the next day, when he was in Boersma's office making his final report, he accused himself angrily of having been very stupid.

'My mind was concentrated on having it fool-proof. I didn't mind an extra day's work provided I made sure. Messy business, and will lap up the front pages; I was nervous, scared if you like, of putting a foot wrong. Jansen was responsible for the whole thing: good. I'd always been sure of that anyhow, but I had to have proof in black and white; the thing taped, no loopholes; no chance for some slimy bastard later on to create legal quibbles. Nothing was complicated once the boy stuck to his resolve to come clean. I was sure of him; he had the feeling he was over the watershed, and that cutting loose from the gang showed that he was more adult than they were. Fake maturity, of course. Induced by discovering what a real woman could be like, instead of a snotty little girl. She fell in love with him too, which I had not counted on. Perhaps it tipped the balance decisively; I don't know.

'As for Jansen, I felt sure of him too, nobody more. I took ordinary precautions – man outside with instructions to keep him tagged if he started wandering about. But I didn't doubt I'd find him when I wanted him. So inflated, you know; convinced that he could twist everyone in the town – and me – round his finger when he wished. Characteristic criminal mind; despises everybody. Not the type to bunk or lose his nerve; secure in his certainty that whatever we suspected or guessed or even knew – we'd never be able to make it stick. I knew he'd be there, calm and dignified as a wedding cake – and then this bloody fellow goes and balls it all up.'

Boersma got up and walked about, puffing furiously at his pipe. It wheezed in a repulsive way. He bent lovingly over his precious begonia rex on the window-sill – a gigantic and lurid specimen; Van der Valk loathed the thing.

'Oh ja ja ja; all you say is quite right. Don't fuss now; there's no real harm done. A few chips out of the furniture, nothing anybody will notice. Looks like a hell of a nonsense all right; that's largely your fault, certainly. You incline always to be too goddam clever; think you're Maigret or something. I'm not trying to crab your credit; you thought all this out in theory and then you broke it very neatly. But get out of the habit of decorating everything, will you. Simplify, simplify: cardinal rule of police procedure.

'All right, I've given you a rocket; let that be the end of my criticisms. Just don't worry always about having everything perfect. As you remarked yourself, that's the Officer of Justice's worry, not yours. Don't get the notion that I'm shouting at you for being intelligent; we get quite enough of that mentality here. But it's unreasonable to expect everything to fall neatly into place, like the last page of some piddling detective story. These things are never tidy – always a mass of loose ends. Another time, when you see the faintest chink of light, grab it; don't sit waiting for it to get bigger. I see that you were in a tricky situation, nominally under Marcousis' orders as well as in his territory, so I'm not going to labour the point.

'However, I may as well say that I was annoyed with you. Your brilliant performance nearly didn't come off, and when, incidentally, will you learn some discretion? Still, as far as everybody else is concerned you did a damn' good job. Marcousis is as pleased as a cow with six tits. And we'll get no kicks from higher up; quite the contrary, you're commended. I've had Sailer on the phone; yes, Procureur Général, taking an interest. The Officer of Justice in Bloemendaal is biting into the sweetest hunk of publicity he's ever had – got everything; horrible disclosures, parental neglect – all the holy burghers of Bloemendaal are ready to get under the bed.

'As for this Russian woman, there'd be an outcry of course if anyone knew; since nobody does, kicking up a furore would do no good at all. Everybody knows anyway that it's perfectly possible to leave any country without a rubber stamp if you want to hard enough.'

*

It had been nearly three when Van der Valk finally got home and into bed, yawning and scratching bitterly. But he had fallen asleep at once, and was only dragged back to consciousness by the brutal telephone. Visser, in Bloemendaal. Half-drowned, still, he had rested the speaker against his jaw, squinting blearily at the ceiling. 'Van der Valk. ... Yes yes yes; don't explain so much; just tell me briefly what has happened. ... Huh? ... Christ upon a bicycle, weren't those fools awake? ... I take it you've notified the Commissaris? ... Well, lock them both up. Start locking up the whole of bloody Bloemendaal, will you? ... What did the doctor say? ... and the other? ... I see. Nice fools we'd have looked if they'd both been dead. ... Yes, yes, of course I'm coming. I haven't wings. An hour won't make any difference.' His watch told him it was twenty to seven.

Muttering to himself he started to dress wearily, and was half ready before he decided to take a shower and began to undress again. Arlette was already out of bed and in a housecoat.

'You've got to go at once?'

'Yes; trouble; I've no idea exactly how it will affect everything. Case is broken, but all the wrong way round; always happens to me. How I hate the name of Bloemendaal; never-ending pest this has turned out to be.'

'Take your shower; by the time you're down I'll have coffee ready.' He cleaned his teeth – 'Here's a clean shirt for you and the shower's running' – and turned the water on full. Arlette had dosed the coffee with brandy; his stomach stopped slipping its clutch, and she made him eat two soft-boiled eggs.

He was out in the chill, sharp morning light at ten past seven, smelling rather of brandy; he gunned the motor of the Mercedes hard through the waking city and out over the North Sea Kanal. In the office at Bloemendaal Marcousis was smoking furiously. Van der Valk felt alert; he had driven with the window right down, feeling the sea air blow the dust off his brains.

'Morning, Commissaris.'

'Morning, Van der Valk. I don't think there's great cause for concern; in fact I think we may have got what we want, indirectly. He asked for you especially, however, which is really why Visser telephoned so early. The doctor says he's perfectly fit to talk; it's not nearly as bad a wound as we first thought from the look, so you can relax. He's lost a lot of blood, that's all.'

'Can he stand, or sit, or whatever?'

'Yes; he's not even really badly hurt, apparently. But it looked nasty. Long flesh wound; went right through him and broke a rib, but it came within three centimetres of missing him altogether.'

'What sort of a gun?'

'Lüger nine millimetre.'

'Oh my Carmen, my little Carmen. He was lucky, wasn't he?' Well, if he's still here . . . ?'

'Yes. The doctor strapped him up.'

'Then I suppose we'd better get him in, huh, and give him the works.'

Frans Mierle looked pale and tired. His body, especially the upper half, moved stiffly and painfully. But his eyes were calm and steady; he looked neither abashed nor worried. His suit was heavily bloodstained, and he wore no shirt; as he sat he winced at the tight strapping round his chest. Van der Valk watched him with a bleak eye that lacked sympathy.

'You asked for trouble and it appears you've got it. You're lucky to be alive at all, which should teach you not to interfere in police business. Not every day one walks away from being shot with a Lüger. Lucky, but not clever. I've no pity to waste on you.

I gave you some small confidence, which I thought you had the discretion to respect, and you go too far with some little conspiracy and play the fool. Well, you asked to see me, and I'm here, so make it fast and make it good; it had better be both.'

Mierle looked calmly back into the furious blue eyes; he put his hand laboriously into his side pocket, took out a piece of paper, leaned forward with a grunt, and gave it to the policeman. Van der Valk unfolded it, glanced at it, and tossed it contemptuously down upon the desk.

'A confession.'

'Yes.'

'Which you forced out of him. At gun point. Or something of the sort.' The tone was as contemptuous as the action.

'Something of the sort,' equably.

'It's not worth a halfpenny stamp. You're a business man; if someone made you write anything under a threat you'd repudiate it, the moment you got the chance.'

'He'll repeat it.'

'He'd better, if you're going to stay out of big trouble. Now what, Mr Mierle, led you to go and pick a quarrel with this man Jansen?'

'I came to the conclusion, shall we say, that this man Jansen was responsible for the crimes and offences that six boys stand accused of, including my son.'

'Your son confided in you?'

'To some extent.'

Cute enough anyway to make no mention of Feodora. Just as well, thought Van der Valk; I'd be in trouble, then.

'I conclude that you got information relevant to this enquiry, and you withheld it from the police. Instead, you acted on your own initiative. You are able to realise that this sort of obstruction is serious. Why did you do it?'

'I had reason to believe that my son, out of some misguided sense of loyalty, might refuse to tell the police the story, getting himself into worse trouble, possibly.'

'Reason to believe, mm.' Thin ice over which Van der Valk chose to skate rapidly. 'I don't follow your process of thought too clearly.' He was not worried; Marcousis would not be inclined to bear down on a business man as well known as Mierle. Provided he got his sacrifice.

'At four in the morning then, or thereabouts, you went to the Ange Gabriel. Why at that time?'

'I knew that he would be closing the bar, and that his staff would be in a hurry to get home. We would be alone, and would not be interrupted. He would be tired, and his resistance at low ebb. I judged the time opportune.'

'He did not refuse to see you?'

'No. He was curious. I think he flattered himself that I wished to enlist his help in defending my son. It pleased him to think that.'

'What did you say to him?'

'I asked him to lend me a book.'

Oops: ice bending. 'A book. And why did you take a gun to borrow a book?'

'He would realise that I possessed his secret. I hoped that I would have no occasion to use a gun. I was confident that my character would prove stronger than his. I was right.'

'Very well. We establish the situation. You went, taking your gun – in case it was needed, mm – what exactly did you need it for, in view of your confidence?'

'I proposed to arrest him.'

'Very melodramatic. You went, then, with the purpose of forcing a confession from this man, to provide evidence that would, allegedly, exonerate your son to some degree. I still do not understand why you did not wait until morning and turn your evidence over to me. You knew that I was in charge of this enquiry. You had spoken to me, and you had gathered that I was myself not satisfied that your son and his friends were altogether responsible for the misdeeds that drew our attention to them. Occasionally,' with irritable sarcasm, 'I carry a gun myself. With or without it, I would have been quite capable of arresting Jansen, whenever I judged that necessary. You have a reputation, Mr Mierle, for good judgement. Why the melodrama? Why the big act?'

'I will give you a reason, Inspector; you may not be disposed to accept it, but you will, since, as you say, my judgement is good. I did this because I had lost my son's confidence. I got what information I did by means of a trick, more or less. What I did, I decided to do, firstly, to show him that I did not regard myself as belonging to a different, superior world to his. Secondly, to regain some of the confidence I had lost, for which I reproach myself.'

'Hm.' Van der Valk thought for a moment, his chin on his hand, heavily. 'He shot you, and you shot him, then. Is that it?'

'That is so.'

'He may very likely say that you shot him first, mayn't he? How are we to know?'

'Character, Inspector, character. He has not the courage, you know. Think about it. I had no reason whatever to shoot him. I wanted him here, to bring him here myself, and if possible hear him snivelling out his miserable little tale to your ears.'

'Mm.' Van der Valk was thinking about the night before, when he too had concluded that Jansen, in the long run, would not have the courage to stand up against him. He had determined to win a battle of nerves. Was he annoyed that Mierle had frustrated him?

'Where are the guns?'

Marcousis, as loaded down with artillery as Philip Marlowe, produced them; two dull clanks on the desk.

'Been printed and checked,' he said. 'Story fits, so far.'

Van der Valk poked at them distastefully with his ballpoint. The Lüger was an old model, rather. Number, surely, was a familiar one. Yes, he knew about this gun. And a short, shiny Smith and Wesson revolver, a nasty brute with a trigger action as sensitive as a rattlesnake. Unusual gun; American. Heard about them; never seen one before. Same calibre as the other. Well-balanced shooting match. Mierle was right. The man with more courage had won.

Both guns carried marks of the powder used to check them. Of course the story fitted. Why had that damned fool of a policeman allowed Mierle to go into the Ange Gabriel at all, at four in the morning?

'You shot him deliberately?'

'Yes. He tried to kill me. Ask him why.'

'So you tried to kill him. No? Tell me why I shouldn't think so.'

'All right, Inspector,' peacefully. 'I understand that you have to test my story. I'll tell you why. I'm an excellent shot; I'm good at most things. Give me that gun and I'll shoot anything you like. I shot him in the place which would hurt him most without any risk of killing him. His knee-cap.'

'That right?' To Marcousis. The Commissaris nodded. Why, he was thinking, did that idiot let him in at the door? (This was an excellent instance of parallel thought; nothing telepathic about it – all police minds tend the same way.)

'What started all this shooting?'

'We were in his flat; he was sitting at his desk. I told him what to write; he didn't want to. I compelled him, shall we say? He was nervous and excitable. He wrote it and signed it. He said then that he would repudiate it. I put it in my pocket, and told him that he would now come to the police bureau with me, and repeat it, without any nonsense about repudiation. On a nervous impulse, I should guess, he produced that gun suddenly, and shot me. I had my hand on my gun, in my pocket. I had not expected' – almost impishly – 'to be shot, but I had been prepared for him to try something. The bullet knocked me on the floor, but I had not let go. He dropped his; I think he imagined he had killed me, and it frightened him. I shot him – he wasn't expecting that. It gave me considerable pleasure,' finished Mierle, deliberately.

Van der Valk had been writing rapidly.

'We'll expect you to sign a statement to this effect.'

'Yes.'

'You got up off the floor, after, we can take it, a little rest, and went out to get a policeman, who, as luck would have it, was outside the door. A clot who had heard and noticed absolutely nothing. You are not required to confirm the last remark,' pleasantly.

'What you say is correct,' wooden-faced.

'Very well. Let's get Erik in.' Van der Valk scribbled on a piece of paper. 'This fool performance has at least given us one concrete piece of evidence, needed to pour it on Jansen. The Lüger is the identical one stolen from Schubertstraat.' Jansen must, certainly, have been in a deplorable state of nerves to have been tempted to use it on Mierle. Which was a very damaging fact.

Marcousis nodded, and drew a little picture under the scribble. It might have been a cartoon of a missionary in the cannibal pot, or, with the imagination stretched a little further, Joan of Arc. But it was, unmistakably, a fire lit under Hjalmar Jansen.

A policeman brought in Erik Mierle.

The boy looked around him curiously, and stared when he saw his father, in a stained suit, with bare throat. The lack of a shirt gave the big man a poverty-stricken, naked appearance, but he was equal to it; he looked neither disconcerted nor woe-begone.

He sat peacefully in the uncomfortable wooden chair, meditative and withdrawn.

'Sit down, Erik. You know me. This is the Commissaire, Mr Marcousis, who is in charge here. I have to begin by making you a speech, partly explanatory, partly, in a sense, an apology. Take a cigarette, if you want one.'

'There's no need to worry about your father; he's not seriously hurt. Hjalmar Jansen shot him, luckily without grave result. Your father shot him back; he's in hospital, feeling sorry for himself, with a policeman by his bed. You know that the ravens and the cats have been arrested. For what they have done, Jansen is in some sense responsible. To shut everyone's mouth, presumably, Kees van Sonneveld was killed by the girls. It looked at first as if this had been cleverly done. We concluded, though, that it was no accident, nor suicide; the girls have admitted as much, but we still find the reasons obscure. It became plain that Jansen engineered it. Your father did not wish to see you or your friends sit in jail while the real author sat thinking himself immune.He went to see Jansen, discomposed him by showing that he knew things Jansen had supposed would remain secret, and exerted enough pressure on him to make him admit his responsibility. This written confession is in itself largely worthless, but Jansen shot your father in an effort to recover it. He shot, moreover, with a pistol reported stolen from a flat in the Schubertstraat in Amsterdam. Here's the note: read it.

'I may as well say that Jansen will contest this paper; he will claim that he wrote it under duress and attempted to recover it in order to prevent prospective blackmail. That he showed a pistol in an effort to meet a threat by an equal threat, and that the shooting was simple self-defence. He will try and dramatise his wound, and will even provide excuses for his possession of this pistol. A clever lawyer, and a cool head, could help a lot to clear him. You can sink him. We want you to tell us about him, to show us how he persuaded others into doing unlikely and sinister things, and in the end even got a human being killed. There is another point, too, that depends largely upon you.

'We have to arrest your father. Anyone who shoots anyone else, even though he may have excellent reasons, is held automatically till the affair is cleared up. Unless we get proof – my judgements of character are not enough – that what your father tells us is true, he may be prosecuted for unlawful wounding. You see that we rely on you, in all this, very considerably. What about you, Commissaris? You wish to qualify what I have said?'

Marcousis used the same unemphatic, unemotional voice. 'Only to say, I think, that, as Chief Inspector Van der Valk remarks, papers with written confessions are untrustworthy when forced. Suppose I said to you, "Talk or you'll get hammered," or, equally, "Talk and you'll go free," your statements would, in law, be forced, as much as though I had hit you, or held a gun on you. We want you to feel that you are speaking for your own reasons, rather than for ours. I might say, too, that you need not feel nervous of speaking in the fear that it will become publicised. All these statements are confidential. Nobody reads them but the Officer of Justice. You will have understood that you will be pursued by the law, eventually, for any misdemeanours – even crimes – that you yourself may be guilty of. But quite certainly, when you come before the Assize Court, the prosecutor as well as your defending lawyer will make it quite clear that you, and your friends, are not answerable in the whole for whatever you may have done. That's all, I think.'

There was an uncertain sort of silence, as though everyone were waiting for the other to begin speaking. This silence became portentous. Van der Valk snapped the tension.

'I could do with a beer,' he said plaintively.

## *Chapter Ten*

'Can I speak to my father?'

'Sure.'

'Did – you know – was it all right?'

'No worry. All went off as planned.'

The policemen disregarded this dialogue.

'I've thought it out,' said Erik abruptly. 'I wasn't going to tell you anything, because I wasn't going to be the one to give away his friends. But I think I'd better tell you, especially now my father's got himself into this. I think it's very stupid of him. He may not mind going to jail; I do. I mean' – hastily – 'I don't mind going myself.'

Van der Valk wondered whether Frans Mierle's lunatic notion had not after all proved a good one. 'I accept this account; I'll pay it.' The boy had noticed; oh yes.

'Well,' embarrassedly. 'I've decided. I'll tell you anything you want.'

'Suppose you start by telling how it began, in the first place.'

Marcousis had pressed his buzzer, and sent someone for beer. A police stenographer sat down in the corner and flipped his shorthand pad open. Van der Valk offered a cheap cigar to Frans Mierle, who accepted, and examined it with raised eyebrows; Van der Valk lit his with every appearance of enjoyment. He scribbled on the back of a file with his Bic to see if it was running properly, and puffed happily.

The boy started to talk hesitantly, self-conscious. But as he warmed up he forgot the twin spectres in the room, of examining magistrate and assize court. Van der Valk wrote steadily in neat longhand; the inspector with the pad scribbled Arabic, strokes and dots, with a hand deft as an ant-eater's tongue. Marcousis drew sailing-ships on his scratch pad, head a little on one side.

Frans Mierle did nothing; he listened. Beer arrived, and punctuated the uneven, boy's voice with a gentle hissing.

'More, you silly bastard,' said Van der Valk crossly to the waiter, wiping an unshaven lip.

'Well: we used to get into the Engeltje quite often, all of us. We started going there because he had all the new records as they came out, and it was nice in there as well: you know, good atmosphere. And on the boulevard, near where most of us lived, and not too big; less scruffy than those places down the town. About eighteen months ago he extended it with this place on the first floor. That was terrific then; the noisier kids were kept out right from the start, because Hjalmar said it was to be kept quiet. Because it was his flat; I mean it had been his flat but he said it was too big and just the top floor was enough for him, but that was immediately above still, of course.

'We'd never seen him much before, but then we got to know him more. He came into the place often, and he might stay an hour talking, and we liked him, because he didn't talk down. You know; a bit heavy, and sarcastic, like a schoolmaster who thinks you mustn't forget that he's the teacher, boys. He might buy us a beer, and he might talk or not, but either way he wouldn't shove his nose in.

'Then he told us that he would put us in charge in a way, and that if we thought any of the kids were no good for upstairs because they were stupid or rowdy, well, that we could fire them out and he'd back us up. To get the place like his club next door a bit; fewer people but better, see? Pretty good business for him really, because we came regularly, pretty well every night, and we spent quite a bit of money, except old Wim of course, and he's always broke, but nobody minds. And because there were fewer there the service was better: I mean the beer cold and the coffee hot – you know. And his prices were fair.

'But it had got too crowded and we did throw a lot out. We made sort of rules and got it down to maybe thirty or forty all told, and as many girls perhaps. About a year ago, I reckon, we were the regulars and the originals, as well as the oldest. A shower of us used to knock about everywhere together; me and Wim Brinkman, and Mich Carnavalet, and Gerrit Wouters – he moved though – his father went to work in Pernis. We used to do some pretty daft things.

'I suppose we really began to get thick with Hjalmar after we found what good records he had. We were all pretty hot on jazz, and he has dangerous good stuff, hundreds of old records you can't get any more; some from way before the war, been off the catalogue for years. His stuff on Eddie Lang – and Dajngo –formidable! We called ourselves the Hot Club, and just the few of us he would let sometimes go up to his flat to play records.

'Outside we were about together too; like I said, we did some pretty rare things about that time; we used to knock stuff off out of shops and offices, not to steal them – often they weren't even valuable, or else no earthly use, but just for the hell of it. Sometimes we even brought things in here. Awkward things, the queerer the better, like adding machines or concrete-mixers. We never got pinched.'

Van der Valk looked sideways at Marcousis, lip pushed out naughtily, but that gentleman was shading an elaborate figurehead, and refused to be drawn.

'Hjalmar found out, of course, because we didn't bother particularly to keep it dark, and we used to plan these gags up in the Engeltje. He told us we were plain stupid, and that though he wouldn't give us away, we'd get pinched and be in trouble, just for nothing. Then there'd be a record, and we'd be known about, and whenever anything at all happened they'd drop on us. And he wouldn't allow it, anyway, he said; he'd throw us out for getting his place a bad name.

'That was all sensible enough. We didn't accept it straight off just because he'd said it was so, of course. But then that mad bastard Wim almost did get pinched, driving off a big lorry that had been left outside a garage. He had to jump out and run like smoke, with two police agents after him. And that choked us off for a bit; we didn't know if he'd been recognised and we'd been rumbled.

'Hjalmar just laughed at us. We saw he was right, then. Wim said after that we had to be organised, like a commando. It sounds a kid's game now, of course, but this was a year ago, remember. Wim had a lot of fights with his family, I think; his father's a nice fellow, but very respectable and sort of conventional. Wim got a lot of stuff from the library about the Foreign Legion, and he went on about the paras all the while. We practised the things he thought of, like jumping off moving cars. We hadn't a car but we did it with our autocycles; get up on the carrier and when you have a good lick on go off on the sand at the verge. It's easy if you can ski. We did a lot of shooting, but we got bored with those baby rifles at the Engeltje. Frank got a pistol in Belgium, and we let him in with us for bringing it. It's only a six-thirty-five, but it's accurate enough to about ten metres.

'We did a lot of stunts with knives too, and swimming. We used to play "the law" up in the club. We had a good time round about then, because we all left school, and started going to classes in Amsterdam. It's good at first, when you leave school. That was last summer.

'We were all knocking around with girls of course, and they were in the club too; we had a good crowd. They used to come and listen to music as well, in the flat sometimes. Ja, I don't say I'm a saint myself, but that silly sod Michel really is a lecher, and Hjalmar came into the flat one night, and Mich was there with Lies alone – they had a craze on for Artie Shaw – and he had her pants down, of course.

'He had the wind up because he thought we'd all get chucked out, of the flat at least. But Hjalmar never batted an eye, apparently; he just said next day that the club wasn't complete or properly organised without girls, but that he wasn't having a whole mob of them in the flat, so we each had to pick a regular girl, and those we could take in the flat, any of them, but no others because there'd be gossip, and good ideas always came to nothing because of somebody's big mouth.

'We used to talk a lot, up there. You see we went to a lot of different classes,because we weren't all in the same course. The lecturers were always chucking stuff at us that we had to take home – you know the sort of thing: make a précis of this in three hundred words; discuss such a proposition with reference to. We used to help each other of course, and the Engeltje was handiest for that; we did a lot of serious work up there, and often we'd get started on some subject ourselves – discussing it, I mean. Hjalmar was interested in any serious talk; he used to sit with us often. He's an educated man, you know; brainy geyser, as well. Political economy – oh jé, he's full of it. He's not exactly a communist, or anything, really, but he has a whole system. Governments are all tripe, according to him; democracy a farce and communists or dictators no better, he says, because you still have to fill in forms to keep a lot of parasites on the pay-roll, and the pickings get shared out among the top politicoes just the same. Paternalism; he's great on that.

'Anyway, this was how he saw it – you interested in all this? Sure? Because I mean it's all guff, I can see that, but at the time we all went for it. Over the last three hundred years – that's the way it went –there'd got to be less and less personal liberty, until now it had got so bad, with restrictions, and permits, and the Government handing out sweeties, that the only way to ensure your own liberty was simply to take it. And one person was not strong enough ordinarily; you had to form a gang, or a cell, he called it. We had the right instincts, he said. The communists were formed like that in enemy territory, and all the private armies; I mean the Union Corse, and the Mafia and the Freemasons, and everybody.

'Then, that it was just sentimental to think about freedom; the world never could be free, and anyway people didn't even want liberty because they didn't know how to use it. They just wanted to be looked after and get free handouts – pensions and football pools and stuff. For every one that really wanted liberty there were a hundred that asked nothing better than to sink to the bottom and stay there, and draw the dole from the kind Government. But six well-trained and really determined activists – that's another of his words – could do anything, and he could prove it to us if we were interested, and would do what he said. He had a lot of stories.

'Secret societies that got really big were in concentric circles, and at the centre you got a hard core that was the one per cent that could put real leverage on their whole surroundings. Not even one per cent; one in ten thousand. But for that you had to be really tough. That was one thing the communists did understand, he said; they weren't afraid of police or jail or anything else. If you were disciplined you could get on top of any jail.

'Then he said that this para stuff that Wim was keen on was all right in itself, but the wrong angle of approach. He said even the paras got beaten by guerilla warfare, and that that was the one type of warfare that nobody ever found the answer to. Armies were tripe, and just for decoration, because they couldn't fight the bomb, whereas ten well-trained and equipped guerillas could tie up a whole regiment. Look at Algeria, he said; they tied the best army in the world completely into knots. And Napoleon was beaten less in Russia than by a guerilla war in Spain.

'I guess you think that all this sounds real eyewash, but I can't tell it like him. When he talked this way it didn't sound silly, but convincing, believe me.'

'It's not stupid,' said Van der Valk, lighting a fresh cigar. 'Sound fact, for a good way along. Would be fine if it didn't disregard the whole of civilisation and ten centuries of Christianity. He's one of these semi-educated nihilists; I see it all now. They're wonderful but nuts. Want some more beer?'

'Well yes, if I may; it's all this gabbing. We used to discuss all these things all night, sometimes; the girls too. They asked where they fitted into this scheme. Marta wanted to be like the militia in Israel or Cuba – you know, the film star with the sub-machine-gun. Hjalmar said no, that women had to be activists too, but on the moral front, and that a bed was a better weapon than a machine-gun. In a decadent society, he says, the women have all the real power; in America they run everything. A courtesan had absolute power because she left the men the responsibility.

'We got impatient, though, with all this talk, so he said he would be pragmatic and show us a working example. We would gain control of this whole town, he said, the girls as much as the men. In ten years the twelve of us would be able to do exactly as we pleased here. But that meant a lot of lessons to be learned quickly because training should begin in childhood. The first and most important was discipline; you couldn't control others unless you had perfect command over yourself, and that was why there was only one penalty for disobedience or treachery, and that was death. You couldn't afford, ever, to give anyone a second chance.

'So we would have to realise that if ever we got into difficulties, and one of the cell gave in or gave anything away, it was not only a duty but a bare necessity for the others to kill him at once, and they had to do it themselves. He said that was dead easy; under ten per cent of murders, he says, are even suspected. And in any case the girls would infiltrate the police.

'One of the girls – Carmen – said all this was all very well, and interesting, but she didn't want to be a female Jesuit – made us all laugh. Hjalmar had an answer all right, though. It's funny. I mean that I can see now how all this fancy stuff doesn't work, because human beings, somehow – well, they just aren't like that are they? But he could convince us, because ja, that's not the stuff you get taught at school, is it?

'He said she was dead right, and that people could not do things cold-bloodedly unless they were very unusual, and that most people needed an ideal. Not only that but a religion. Even communism was a religion, he said, but a failure like the others because too puritan. That you needed romance in life, and you couldn't abolish that, and there wasn't enough in the world any more. I'm explaining this bloody badly.

'He used to illustrate points, you see, with stories. Not just Hollywood crap but real. Like a gang in Sicily, and he – the leader – was always afraid of betrayal, and he had written on his gun, "I can look after my enemies: God protect me from my friends." Hjalmar wouldn't let us have any chief, because he might get betrayed out of jealousy. Just a political commissar, and that was him. And the girls would fight for a leader. We had to share all the girls. I mean, Wim was the top kick among us, because he's very tough, and he's daring. He's got a big imagination; he's often scared but he won't let that stop him.

'Of course, I can see as well now that Hjalmar was all theory and no practice. But he can talk anyone over. That's how the raids started. To learn warfare, he said. But sorry, I was telling about the religion. He said boredom was the danger to power, but he had the answer worked out, he reckoned.

'He said that only the strong emotions were worth having. "Les émotions fortes" – he had a thing about that. To learn to appreciate them you had to be tough. Fear was the strongest.

'He got his idea from some book; it's in the flat there; he showed it us. A sort of ghost story – more a fear story really because there isn't a ghost. This chap is a sort of wandering tourist, who decides to go to some little French village, very primitive and off the map, and in the train an old man asks where he's going, and the fellow says, and the old man makes a face; he'd never go there, he says. Why? the geyser asks, and the old man tells him, "Because of the silence, and because of the cats."

'Well, the fellow thinks the old man potty of course, and he goes on, and after a good hike gets to the village and stays in the pub. There's a nice girl serving at the bar there, whom he takes a fancy to, and at night he goes after her and finds that she does turn into a cat, and so do all the other women. It's a good story – it does grip you.

'Hjalmar thought up his scheme from that, roughly. He went on about this goddess, Artemis or Astarte. I never did work out quite which was which or what the difference was, but she was the Phoenician goddess, and more or less the same as Demeter the Earth Mother and Diana of the Ephesians too, I think, though I'm none too tidy about any of them. Anyway, goddess of love and power and life.

'The girls went and read it all up, and got steamed up about her, but to be honest I never altogether took it all in. But the idea was similar to this witch stuff in the French village. The girls would turn into cats, figuratively, and there would be a bond which we could never break, because Astarte would take vengeance. The cats would hunt us down.'

Van der Valk listened, blowing fans of smoke and making careful notes. Balance in all things, he thought. This wretched Jansen, with his explosive rag-tag of power philosophy, had been, as the boy realised, a sufficiently poor adept. He had not been able to contain this rubbish in his own rather immature character; in the wish to corrupt he had himself become corrupted. Romance indeed! Where had he got it from? Elements of National Socialist stuff there, of course. And this lurid stuff, now, about the goddess Astarte – wasn't that from Frazer? He didn't really know, but vaguely remembered Frazer from his own philosophy classes. It had eaten up the man, and left the boys not really deeply touched, he thought.

He wondered what Jansen was thinking now. All that about discipline; resist pain and the police. He could put in a bit of practice there, now, lying with a smashed knee-cap. Let him try, now, to marshal his horrid little ideas against an adult for once, and a professional.

But he had had his moment of success. The cats had killed Kees van Sonneveld to shut his mouth and all the others' mouths, yes, but they had killed him, too, in the sacrifice to Astarte.

He was not too sure whether Marcousis had really taken all this in. He sat there impassive, drawing his ruddy ships, while in the corner the shorthand expert ticked away like a teleprinter, but did he understand how it all worked? Van der Valk remembered that he had not seen any significance in the flat, and it had been that, after all, which had first clearly shown him the basic, fundamental immaturity of Jansen's character.

Erik was well launched, now. Repetitive, and confused, often enough, but lucid. This statement, when typed up, would really light a bomb under the Officer of Justice. He could see a neat little thesis for a doctorate now. 'Primitive religions and fascist elements as contributing to delinquency.' Lovely.

Had the boy gone into such details in telling Feodora? Clearly not, but she had not missed these salient points either. He felt convinced that having once told her the bones, at least, of this tale, and heard her thoughts, the spell, such as it was, cast by Jansen had been broken. The boy had had a night to think it over, and had got a little distance away from the emotional upheaval, and now he was calm and detached.

'Crap it all does sound, huh? I think, really, that I knew all this was fantasy, but at the same time I believed it. I mean I didn't really believe that the girls would turn into cats, but the fear – like he said – a strong emotion. If you defied the goddess a curse would fall. It had a queer effect. Even last night I felt I'd never be able to tell. You knew it wasn't true, and you were scared just in case it was.

'We all laughed at it at first. Hjalmar got mad at that, and said we were ignorant and would never be any good. There were more things in heaven and earth than we dreamt, and so on. When we had lived as long as he had we would know how many things had no materialist explanation. Old Wim upset him: got on that he was going to be an engineer and didn't believe in anything that hadn't a chemical origin, but Hjalmar shut him up. The girls were enthusiastic; they carried us along a good deal.

'And it really was eerie, I can tell you. I would never be able to talk about it. I think I only can, now, because – well, I knew a woman, and she screwed it out of me, and when I least expected she just burst out laughing, and that sort of broke the ice. It's easier to tell things to a woman; Hjalmar was right, there.'

Van der Valk grinned.

'Easier to tell a woman in bed than policemen round a table, sure. Since the woman laughed you can see the ridiculous side. We don't laugh because there's a second side, concerning us sharply. You said it was all crap. Why, so it is, but because of it a boy got killed, and we all sit here.

'Listen, the boy was killed for no reason, except to increase this man's feeling that he possessed power. He translated power – that's the fallacy behind all this – as a moral ascendency over other people. He kidded you that you would have power over others, when really he simply acquired power over you. The man is just a common blackmailer. Blackmail is a common crime enough, but it never loses its power to disgust ordinary people. That's because it's a moral perversion, breeds fear and disgust. Just as this does. Go on telling.'

'Ja, this is the difficult part. I suppose, then, that Hjalmar planned it carefully. He said, just casually, that we should stay after he shut up shop, and he'd show us strong emotions. There were only four of us then, and four girls.

'When we got up to the flat after the place was cleared, about twelve, he said it could only be one of each of us, so we pulled shortest straw, and it was Michel and Lies. It was like a party; he had good stuff to eat and drink, and South American cigarettes. He put on a long-player, not jazz but something like; he said it was from Haiti. He had juju cigarettes too; like Russians, with a big mouth piece, and pretty loose, but bigger, coarser, you know? He said they were the best anyway; honey-cured, from Curaçao.

'The jujus are – you feel you're very clever. That you understand everything. You can do what you want because you can work it all out; you don't care about anything stopping you. This music, for instance – it wasn't dance music, not for us anyway – the rhythm was wrong, but we were all dancing to it. I'd heard about tea, but I thought it would stupefy you perhaps; you'd go into some sort of coma and have weird dreams. It wasn't like that at all. You feel immensely sharpened up; there's nothing you're afraid of or can't do.

'Lies danced by herself then, and took her clothes off. There again, we weren't surprised or bothered a bit; it just seemed ordinary that she should. Time goes a bit funny; you're never quite sure how long anything's taken, with jujus. She was dancing by herself, and she had a knife that Hjalmar gave her, and she had a cat on her shoulders, a live one, but it lay like a collar. I suppose he'd doped it, maybe with some sleeping pill.

'Hjalmar had a sort of poem on the gramophone. It's in Greek, but I understood it; at least I thought I understood it. I can't have, because each time I thought I'd remember it next morning – it seemed so familiar. But I never did. It has something to do with Ariadne in Naxos, and I think it's Euripides.

'He made Lies lie on the floor, and he told Michel to make love to her; the cat lay across her throat. Just as he was – ja, just at the point, Hjalmar killed the cat with the knife; the blood went all over them. Horrible, I suppose, but you see it seemed logical then. We all made love then, in a kind of ring, and Hjalmar took Lies too himself. He put another record on; it's called the poem of ecstasy. I'm a bit vague; I think I went to sleep for a bit.

'Anyway I felt all right when I woke, not dopy or anything. A bit hung over; Hjalmar made us drink Fernet Branca, and the girls made coffee, and we all went home; it was about six.

'Next morning after that first time I remember the edges were gone off it all. I thought that it might be queer to see the others, but we met as usual and they were just ordinary; Lies and Mich were as they always were. What had happened seemed disconnected from the other days; I couldn't make much sense of it all. I mean Lies, for instance; she's fairly quiet, not like Marta, who's a wild bitch, or Carmen; she's not especially noticeable.

'Pretty, of course, and she has a wonderful figure, but – well, that's all ordinary enough, isn't it? Nothing exotic, I mean. Looking at her there drinking beer with the others, it didn't seem very likely, somehow, that I'd seen her the night before, dancing naked with that cat, and a knife. So improbable. I think the others felt the same.

'Hjalmar was just wandering about, the way he had, and he was perfectly ordinary too. It was a day or so later, I suppose, when he said quite suddenly that Lies and Michel had offered a sacrifice together, and the goddess possessed them, and Lies would kill Michel if he betrayed us.

'We believed that. Not straight off. But inside three months all four of us had been in the ring the same way, and Hjalmar said we were blood brothers. We could exchange girls still – I've been with all of them in the flat alone – but this goddess thing was around all of us, see?'

The boy was silent; obviously tired. Van der Valk scratched his jaw.

'You told that well, very well. Go off and have a sleep, if you like, or I'll find someone who can lend you a paper. One tiny question only. Why did Jansen take in Kees van Sonneveld?'

'We all wondered that. We had enough with six of us, and we didn't go for him that much at all. I think if anything Jansen was keen on Troost; she's a good-looker and he fancied her, maybe.'

'Perfect. That's all.'

Marcousis pressed his buzzer. 'Let this boy keep his bedclothes, and skip the morning exercise, will you? The others in twos only, with a guard, right?'

Erik looked over at his father. 'Thanks, Pa,' a bit diffidently. Frans grinned and said nothing.

Marcousis looked at Mierle thoughtfully.

'I'm afraid I'll have to lock you up, Mr Mierle.'

'I understand.'

'I'm going to ask you to be patient until we have this extraordinary story in some sort of order. That won't be at all long; a day or so maybe, until we get the necessary steps taken. This has become exceedingly complex – and fourteen persons under arrest, that is a lot of responsibility. As soon as I possibly can I'll see about getting you released provisionally. I must thank you for your cooperative manner, and the frankness you showed in questioning. I'll speak to the examining magistrate.'

Alone, the two policemen exchanged looks.

'Well,' said Marcousis, 'better get the Officer of Justice on the ball, huh? How to handle these girls is a thing he'll have a job to decide. And what's the degree of responsibility with all this Artemis stuff? Frankly, I don't understand all that too well.'

He tapped his fingers on the table and glanced at the shorthand man, who was flexing his hand and staring blankly.

'Get this typed up, Schuiten, will you, and when we have some sort of systematic presentation I'll go up, I think, with it to the Palais.'

He looked at his watch and made a solemn face; like a parson, thought Van der Valk, making a joke to show that he's one of the boys. Now that the part he didn't understand is over pomposity seeps back into him. Only really human when he didn't know what to do. Back with the paper work now; red-hot administrator can show his paces.

'Well, talk about a bomb. Can't let the Press anywhere near that story. What will the parents say?'

'Serve the bastards right. Children come in at six in the morning, full of drink and marijuana, after a nice dance and a royal tumble, and nobody notices a damn' thing. Shift the paper work off to the Palais, and the bodies off to the House of Keeping, or we'll drown. Press'll be here like a column of driver ants.' Portentous nods. 'I think I'll have a little word with Frans Mierle, and then I'd better get back to Amsterdam and turn in a report on this.'

'See Mierle here if you like; I'll have to get up to the Palais. Magistrate will release him, for sure, but we'll have to charge him with something, for appearance' sake.'

Left to himself Van der Valk yawned enormously. He wanted food, sleep, and a shave, in that order. It was over; his part, at least. Thanks to his ideas about aqualungs, thanks to Boersma's idea about marijuana, thanks – most of all – to Feodora. That had been luck; he had needed that. This Astarte thing was all nonsense. Voodoo stuff; the Press would have it a Black Mass before they could turn round if nobody stopped them. The magistrate would suppress all that, he guessed. The private army things, and the marijuana, would cook friend Jansen's goose. He woke from a long reverie, got up and scratched and walked about. He heard the whine of a car starting, and saw Marcousis' Taunus glide past the window.

Bah! he thought: as a police operation it reflects no credit on any of us. And it will certainly give pleasure to nobody. Poor old Marcousis. Paper everywhere, tangled up in self-importance and magistrates; he won't be able to sit still a second. What a mess, Christ. And Feodora, the only reasonable person in the whole story from beginning to end, gone. Frans Mierle was not a negligible person, certainly, but had he exactly made things easier? He walked out and spoke to the brigadier on duty.

'Bring me in Mr Mierle, would you? I'm in the Commissaire's office.'

The brigadier was a handsome man, in a starched shirt and spotless uniform: Van der Valk disliked him, unreasonably. I'm in a bad way, he thought; I hate everybody. He sat down again in the room that still smelt of the sweat and fear Jansen had brought into the lives of spoilt but harmless children. Poor old Drinkman, he would be upset. Could anything be done to get these boys off light, he wondered. He thought of his own home, his own children. He sighed; he was most heartily sick of Bloemendaal.

## *Chapter Eleven*

'Now that we won't be interrupted, because our good friend the Commissaris has gone off to conspire at the Palais de Justice, a few brief words will do us no harm, I thought.'

'I have no appointments.'

'Just so. I haven't been exactly delighted, you know, with your role in this affair. I appreciate that you wanted to regain the boy's confidence, but the fact remains that your intervention was ill-advised, badly timed, and, for you, surprisingly hysterical. Out of character, huh? I think that you may have good reasons for acting out of character. I should guess, if it were any of my business, that you had come to feel deeper about Feodora than perhaps you realised – and your family affairs had become suddenly more important than you had tended to keep them. I am able to accept your story. We won't go into it, and above all, let's have no explanations; I've had all of them I can stand.'

Mierle stayed silent; face smooth, nothing written upon it.

'I hope now, maybe, that we'll be able to tidy the boys' side of this up, without too many policemen, or other imbeciles scribbling in little books. These people and their Officers of Justice have to have their pound of flesh, you understand? The thing's got completely out of hand; over-heated, over-dramatised. I should have preferred to play down all the drama and emotion. Balloons, blown up with fantasy. In my office, in a calm atmosphere, I might have done so; here, I hadn't a chance. You messed that up. Now, they've got hold of this ritual rubbish; goddesses and naked girls, yah. I hope and believe that the magistrate will suppress all that. I'm telling you in order that you may realise that you've behaved, for once, like a foolish virgin.

'Marcousis is pleased. Your shooting Jansen at least gets him out from under foot. He can't even walk; he can sit there, nice and convenient, while they have time to decide what to do.'

'Lot of bullshit?' asked Mierle gently.

'Correct. I can get out of that; this is not my district, and I can concern myself with the boys only. They aren't so deeply involved: to them it was all just a ghost story. But there will be law-books here, yes, and speeches. Enormously.'

'Which you hate.'

'Yes, which I hate. I also called you here to ask if you wanted me to see your wife. You want clothes, cigars, all that stuff?'

'I'd be grateful, yes. She'll know what I need.'

'What about your office?'

'Look after itself; Miss Pons will run it. My being in the ice-box won't worry her for a moment. Are you really letting Feodora off, or was that a gag?'

'No gag. Her name needn't appear, now. I am grateful to her; she gave me this affair on a plate when she rumbled Jansen.'

'You know he wanted to sleep with her? She refused.'

'Yes. Things like that had perhaps more effect on Jansen than we would imagine. But I'm no longer interested in him. How did you get Fé off?'

'I have a private plane. Also a chauffeur who is an ex-Luftwaffe pilot. She'll be in Barcelona this afternoon. I owe her a lot.'

'Save it; I'm sick of it all. When this is over I hope I may get a holiday: I'm due for one. You and your private plane. Best day I spent here was playing with that aqualung; that thing caught my fancy. Spanish coast, mm; I could do with some of that under-water stuff. Now – I'm leaving; tell me what you want your wife to bring; I'll write it down.'

He rang his home to say that it was over, and that he would be home for lunch. That did him good, already. When he had to face Boersma, back in the office, he felt more fortified, though he knew he would get told off. All he said was – 'Had lunch?' He had his own ways of getting to things.

'Yes. Went home. Good lunch.'

'What did you have? Longer I sit in this office the more I get interested in food.'

'Cassoulet. Beans, with goose.'

'Goose, by God. You've a French wife, lucky bugger. I had fish. Mullet. Was good too; I like fish – know a chap in Ijmuiden gets it for me. Well, I suppose I have to hear a long boring story.

You got Jansen, then?'

'Yes; by accident. I'd have got him anyway, but it went sideways on me.'

'Don't they all. Your wife put garlic with this goose?'

'Yes. And red wine; good.'

'I'm learning to like garlic; annoys my family. Apple sauce?'

'Lots and lots of apple sauce.'

'Once I was in England. Went in a restaurant; there was roast pork. Good; waiter comes. Apple sauce, sir? Yes, I say, of course. But you know what he gave me? Two teaspoonfuls. Teaspoonfuls. Thought it was mustard or something.' Reluctantly, the head of the juvenile-and-morals police abandoned apple sauce. 'Tell then about Jansen. Try to make it brief.'

'He looks smart – is smart – quick with the clever stuff. But he's a kid. Childish mentality. One saw it in his flat; looked like a boy of eighteen lived there. Keep fit stuff, model ships, weapons, jazz records, a fancy picture of naked women. Romance; he's great on romance. I don't think women liked him much, and that might be the spring of this affair, somewhere. But he was a riot with the girls in the ice-cream shop. They loved him. So he loved them. Paraded them round his flat with no clothes on. You were right too about the marijuana. And the boys liked him because he was a real little pal. Then he got too fancy.

'He filled them with Hitler Youth stuff; a gang of superboys. Then he saw that if he got a real ascendancy over these kids - the top families of the town – wouldn't that be something, now? So he developed the gang instinct, and the feeling of revolt at that age, all he could. They were doing the usual things – pinching silly things out of shops, joy-riding in cars – all ordinary. He started working them up with the old power-philosophy stunt – the communist cell, the secret army. Played madam with these jazz records of his to get them in the flat and in bed with the girls. Probably watched them making love through the keyhole. Tumbled the girls himself; they thought him a hell of a fellow. Over the boys he never got the same ascendancy, but they were plastic. He invented the raids here to satisfy their urge for danger and excitement; guerilla warfare, he called it. They were not altogether happy, we may guess; think of all that wanton damage, and then the rape. They didn't tell him about that, we may suppose. He wouldn't have liked it. He never realised that it was that put us really on the warpath.

'He took precautions. When they turned up with that Lüger he confiscated it. But he couldn't resist keeping it himself; he has a passion for toys. Adolescent, like them; pistols are a treat to him. Wonder what he did with the other, the little six-thirty-five? It'll turn up somewhere.

'Rage for sensation, would you agree? He thought up a magic game, then, with spells and rituals. When they got back from the raids there'd be a party, smoking tea, and rape the girls in a ring. And an initiation rite. Strip a girl and kill a cat; blood goes all over her.

'Very immature; all this nonsense with the acquisition of power, and the bedroom scenes – cheap pornography; arrested development. But a clever blackmail trick too; it bound them fast to him. They believed they were irreconcilably committed to this anarchist slosh. I wondered how they came to swallow all that cheese, but one mustn't underestimate him; his mind was like theirs under that sophisticated successful exterior.'

Boersma was getting interested. His horrible pipe waggled up and down with his jowl.

'Not bad. Go on; let's hear how you thought it out.'

'He genuinely didn't realise, I think, that his plan for dominating this town through this gang was nonsense. He saw them as the children of rich business men; right, they'd grow up the same, and become important local figures. But he didn't take into account that their minds would mature. They would cease to believe in this Mafia of his. His mind hadn't developed beyond that stage, and I think this simply never occurred to him. He saw them as a vein of gold, better than any money to him. Because at the age of eighteen they sat at his feet, and thought of his piddling jazz-and-coffee bar as the centre of existence, it would always remain so to them, he seems to have thought. Hadn't he the other club for adults, next door, and hadn't he had plenty of opportunity for studying the big business men off duty? Childish also, uncontrolled, vicious in little petty ways. I guess he really thought he'd discovered the secret power over people. Huh? How d'you like my reasoning?'

'Like you, daft but with grains of sense. But that's not all. What about this death on the beach?'

'I still don't know, to be honest. But I deduce that with this basic flaw in his judgement, thinking all men were the same, all childish and all corrupt, he got an immense conceit of himself. Judged everyone by his night-club crowd, all whisky and call-girls, and judged us by Marcousis. Trouble with him is he's a good man in times of peace. Come war he was scared; scared of getting an answer that the burgomaster wouldn't like. When that boy was found drowned he was ready to write it off as an accident. He was quite aggrieved that I wasn't. You see that it would have been easy for Jansen.

'Admitted, he was well covered up; it took me some time and luck to get on to him.

'Sending his commando here to Amsterdam for their games was cute too; why should we ever think of Bloemendaal? I only went there on the vaguest guess, and I got my first thread by what I suppose was a genuine coincidence. I ran into this Russian whore, no slouch about men's characters, and she knew something about Jansen.

'Then the boys – they were pretty well organised – weren't going to get caught by some bum policeman on a bike. Active, resourceful, one always on guard in a stolen car – quite formidable. And who was going to connect that with these virtuous children, so quiet, so well brought up?

'He got a severe shock, must have, when that first solid camouflage failed. There I was, all friendly, sitting in his bar, letting him see openly that I smelt hanky-panky. How had I known? His security couldn't be that good. This pain of death stunt – the boys would never be absolutely safe, because they never took it altogether seriously. The first thing that Michel Carnavalet – the most intelligent and the most nervous – blurts out, when I shook him up a scrap with a few trick questions, is a totally unnecessary remark about cats; made me curious, naturally.

'But Jansen thought them safe as houses. His suspicions, like the others', fell at once on the new recruit, Kees van Sonneveld. The ironic thing was that it was precisely him that took the pain-of-death stuff the most seriously. The kiddo never told me anything much, as you know, but they thought he did.

'Then the unhappy Kees, who hadn't understood why I had questioned the others and not him – which was just tactics of course – knew the others didn't quite trust him, and was probably a bit hysterical at his recent introduction to naked goddesses, runs away. Blew the can't-imagine-what-you're-talking-about line apart.

'I suppose it's reasonable to say Jansen lost his head too, there. Anyway his cockiness led him by the nose. He thought the police would be too stupid and frightened ever to guess the truth, and would never be a real threat. He couldn't resist the temptation to try out his power in a final, terrible way. And by God it worked. I had my eye on the boys, but he'd use the girls, the cats; they'd do the trick. That's how I read it; don't think it can be far out.

'I haven't read up this Astarte stuff, this ritual he'd thought up with goddesses. But the boy this morning mentioned Euripides. Isn't that the *Bacchae?* And *Ariadne in Naxos*. Vague in my mind; something to do with maenads. What do you know about them?'

'Heer jé, I've forgotten my Greek. Didn't the maenads tear a human sacrifice to pieces? I think this Bacchus lark meant the next year's crop; wine and oil, huh, and corn, I suppose. Propitiate the Earth Mother. They fought to make love with him. Maddened with wine and religion. Would the Earth Mother be the same as this Astarte mare of yours?'

'Parallel's there, anyway; pretty sinister. Jansen filled the girls up with stories too. Through sex they would control things too. And infiltrate the police, if you please. Then the wine and religion. He used to give them drinks in the flat, and make them dance, and sticks of tea too. You think that if you made these girls pretty drunk on fancy liqueurs, and then marijuana, and this sexy religious talk, you could produce maenads?'

'I don't like this story too well; I rather think you could. It would get out of hand.'

'It did. They drowned him neat as a zip-fastener. The little Troost girl was the only one to break a bit. They took the boy on the beach – the aqualung was a good bit of camouflage – they were all naked; they got him to make love to Troost, and just held him under. Was Jansen frightened then, I wonder? But his conceit didn't fail even if his courage did; he was sure that I would never reach the truth.

'I blame myself. I let the boy go as bait, to catch a bit of evidence. Boy, I got it. Say that otherwise we might never have hung anything on the girls. But it cost the boy his life.'

Boersma tapped the ashes out of his pipe; clink clink on the big Woolworth ashtray.

'I did exactly the same once, back in forty-eight. I let a fellow go, after questioning him, thinking he'd drop off the tree if I let him ripen a while longer. Two days later I found him with a knife inside the collar-bone. One can't always guess right. I got a rocket with stars and stripes from the boss – that was old Theo; you never knew him, did you? – and that's why I'm not shouting at you. Marcousis hasn't kicked – can't, without you he'd have been in the shit. He has Jansen and the girl friends, for this homicide; we get the boys, for the Beatrix Park and the Schubertstraat. What I'd like now would be to get it linked up a little. Have some documentation for the Officer of Justice here, to show how the homicide was master-minded, say, by Jansen. I want to establish a clear picture of his influence over the boys. You could get that, please.'

'Marcousis will have it laid on. He's arsing about now, deep in paper.'

'Him – he'll still be busy with the procès-verbal against Jansen a month come Tuesday. I want quick action, so that these boys can get it over. I think we only need a statement, say, from one of the girls, giving her mental slant, to complement what you got from this Mierle boy. We'll need no further presentation; facts talk loud. Listen, Van der Valk. I'll get an order through to Bloemendaal, to bring one of the girls over here – where are they, Huis van Bewaring? – and you get a nice smooth story from her, you hear, and that will complete our file. Without, I think these boys might still get hammered more, maybe, than they deserve. Right?'

'Right, Commissaris.' He was not enthusiastic. But he realised that, having heard it all and understood, Boersma was now letting him down gently. Very gently, even.

*

Van der Valk had a beer first. It was good; covered in condensation but not too cold. This girl ought to be the same, he told himself, grinning. He wiped his mouth and hid the bottle; picked up the telephone. 'Get me in the girl Wijsman, will you?' One good push, he thought, and then maybe this lousy affair will be over. He was not really proud of the role he had played. Till the girl came in, he thought mostly about Feodora.

'Nice to see you again.' Lina looked at him coolly.

'You aren't hoping to get me to talk by saying it's nice to see me?'

'No. Talk or not, as you please. I have some things to tell you; I hope you'll have some things to tell me, but I'm indifferent. Today I have plenty of time, and it's a pleasant change for you, from the House of Keeping. They got you separate over there, or together?'

'We're together; two threes. We know why, of course; they're hoping one three will tell a different story to the other. Divide and conquer – that's the police system, we've learned. Troost is by herself, little bitch. I don't care either way; a day or so – they'll have to let us go.'

'You've seen nobody, yet?'

'Not yet. When they called me out, this morning, I thought things were going to happen. Only you again.'

'Oh, things have been happening. Not to you, perhaps, but you've had your share for a while. Let's see; since yesterday morning, as we can't count the night before. Here, have a cigarette. Hjalmar's in hospital. Erik Mierle's father shot him,' casually.

Eyes widened.

'Yes. He'd found out, you see. Made a rather neat job; poor old Hjalmar, you should see him, immobilised with a busted kneecap and a policeman sitting knitting by the bedside. Why? Well, they had words. Started as a little chat, about girls and cats and juju cigarettes. Goddesses, curses, dances, ancient religions – most interesting, and unexpectedly relevant. Our friend Hjalmar signed a confession that he was the author of all these literary ideas. Author as well, incidentally, of a boy's death. You get me?'

Narrow look; girl had a funny expression; well she might.

'Hjalmar got an idea – bad idea, like a lot of his. Pulled a gun – a gun we've been looking for, incidentally. Lost his head. Mr Mierle's not a jelly-baby, and he had a gun too. Must have been like a cowboy picture. Smashed his knee as I say. Hjalmar's a gone goose. Mr Marcousis had a look round his flat; found all sorts of exciting things. We know it all.

'Well, they're going to be on at you. Not me, I have nothing further to do with it; I was only concerned in the first place with what happened right here in Amsterdam. The boys will be on the carpet for that, but I suspect that the president of the court will be inclined to blame Hjalmar for a good deal of what happened, even here.'

'Look,' savagely. 'Stop this kidding, all the joky joky stuff, and this sarcastic baby-talk. Talk sense and I'll listen. What exactly do you want? What did you bring me here for? Just to gloat?'

'For just what you mention, to talk sense. Now you're doing just that, and so will I. You want it straight; here it is. This is between us, by the way; I'm taking no notes, and we don't have any hidden microphones or anything exciting at all here. Just you and me. Will you listen for a little?'

'Yes.'

'Good. I pulled a gag on you with that biology lesson. Not now. No tricks. Now there's no law against dancing naked on a hearthrug in a private house. All that, I think, will be kept quiet, even though it's known. But you will get hammered about the beach. Maybe I will agree with your lawyer, who'll say that Jansen is entirely responsible. But the court will make you bite on the bullet. They know about the parties, the sticks of tea, the dead cats. All about Astarte. That will not, probably, come into court, but the episode on the beach will, and will be, likewise, in the papers. You might tell the others to take a deep breath and be ready to face that. Will you get mad, now, if I give you a piece of advice?'

'I won't get mad. Just don't snow me with any sob-sister business.'

'Not me. There's going to be some weeping about fallen women, yes. Not from me. I don't care about cats or knives, and I don't care if you've been turned upside-down by every sailor from here to Hamburg.'

He looked at the girl; couldn't tell what she might be thinking.

'Why did Jansen take such a risk, of letting Kees van Sonneveld get into the act, do you think?'

She weighed the words for a moment, but she answered:

'He wanted Hannie Troost. She's a sexy little piece.'

'Uh. You can see now, then, that he's a fake.'

'Look, be honest. I said don't snow me. I'm not covering up for Jansen. So don't pretend. Don't tell me what a stinker he is to make me talk. If you just want me to tell you about Jansen, then I will. But don't expect me to say a damn' thing about what I'm supposed to have said or done. If he's been fool enough to get himself over a barrel, that's his look-out.'

'Did Jansen seduce you?'

'Yes.'

'He give you tea to smoke?'

'Yes.'

'He suggest that you dance in the flat, naked?'

'Yes. That what you want?'

'Did you enjoy it?'

The girl looked at him sourly. 'A real policeman, aren't you? Sentimental. Bothered about whether I enjoyed it. What's it to you? Does it make me worse if I say yes?'

'No.'

'Answer is no, I did not enjoy it, and if you ask me I've never seen anything particular to enjoy. You have found out that Jansen was just a great mouth, and you think that's news to me. He thought himself very tough, but he was just as easy to handle as any of the boys. Always running after us with his tongue hanging out like a dog.

'I didn't learn all at once, that's true. When I was fifteen I thought it pretty exciting to get my knickers pulled down by one of the boys – but I've come a long way since. I hate being tumbled if you must know. Why do men think a woman enjoys being degraded like that?

'I suppose some women do like it; Marta does, if you're curious. But, mister, all I learned from Hjalmar Jansen was how to get a man on the hook and keep him there, and if being tumbled is what it takes then I don't care whether I enjoy it or not. Answered?'

'Sure,' said Van der Valk unexcitedly. 'Familiar answer; I've heard it many times sitting in this chair. I'm not surprised. If you'll allow me to say so, I could even carry your argument a bit further for you. But it's two-edged; you'll have to realise that. You want me to treat you as an adult. Very well, so I will. I'll warn you first – you'll understand this – that if you persuade a court to treat you so too you'll get a rougher passage than if you accept the idea

– even though it is uncongenial – that legally you're still half a child. The law is out of date, certainly, but be advised not to kick at that.

'Listen to me now quietly, like an adult. You've told me your viewpoint; I understand it. Others might not. Keep your mouth shut in front of the Officer and the court. You're determined as it is to keep quiet about the beach. Keep quiet as gold, by all means; you have the right to defend yourself. But keep on doing so. Right now you don't mind whoring for what you get out of it. I won't argue. I'm not bothered; not even interested. I'm a policeman; whores are my bread and butter. But when you meet a man – remember this at least – who doesn't know this, who loves you – then, then – don't throw it all in his face. Don't spit out things you aren't really in the least proud of. You're proud of having no illusions; good. Everybody says that, but you will find that all people have illusions, dislike losing them and will not thank you for destroying them.

'Now; I'm just a dumb cop; I'll say no more. I won't try to screw you over anything that you've done. What I want from you now is a short statement, saying that Jansen did and said so-and-so, and proposed such-and-such. Simple questions and answers. Anything you refuse to answer, you've only to tell me; I just write down unanswered – it's understood that you refuse to say anything you consider might prejudice you. Then when I've got it typed you read it over and sign it. It will not affect you later at all – it is part of our case here regarding the boys, which we have to verbalise for the magistrate. Do you agree to that?'

'All right. That is fair enough.'

## *Chapter Twelve*

Van der Valk opened his bottle of beer and watched it hiss in the glass. These girls! He had to laugh; Jansen was supposed to have corrupted them. Believe half what they said and you came out concluding that they had corrupted him. Oh well, so they had. Look at it so; he never had, say, a satisfactory relationship with a woman – a proper woman. Feodora, a public whore, had flatly refused to go to bed with him. Wasn't that the start? Mightn't he then have decided really to go to town on this youthful flesh? Hadn't he maddened himself with it, thinking up new and exciting tricks to do with it? Wasn't that, really, how the maenads had been created? These girls: ha.

He drowned a resounding snort in his beer. The innocent and sentimental policeman – why yes, he was, too – who knew nothing about girls. He waved a hand affectionately at memories, from Hamburg to Rimini. Ending with Feodora; now she was a queen bee. Look at her, and then at this pathetic little slut. Emmerdeuse, la gonzesse. He could do nothing about her; her goose was truly cooked.

Jansen would quite likely get away fairly easily in the end. There would never be any convincingly legal proof that he had incited the girls to murder. Nor that the girls had committed any murder. It would be watered down to manslaughter. The Officer of Justice, prosecuting, would hitch at his gown and get red in the face, and bang everyone's ears with the flushed words beloved by prosecutors – degeneracy, perversion, evil deliberately sought and deliberately enjoyed – what a theologian – Saint Jerome was nothing to a prosecutor in full flight. The President of the Assize Court would keep blowing his nose, and writing down wisdom on his paper – probably a memo to complain about a frayed shirt to the laundry – and the assessors would sit wise as owls as they always did, and a long expensive row of suave defending talent would interject soft-spoken, sly comments.

After a lot of wrangling the girls would be found – what was that lovely moral phrase the English had? – 'In need of care and protection' – that was it. They would be sent to some barrack of a 'Rijks Opvoedings Gesticht' – oh we have phrases here, too. Along with the delinquent children who were prostitutes at thirteen, muscular toughs who had terrorised their wretched parents. Street-corner athletes, Lesbian where there was nothing else handy – he wondered which of the cats were already Lesbian. The bulging busts and pear-shaped calves, the low lurching pelvis and simian features of girls who, one felt when watching them, were female more through absentmindedness than anything else. Those who forced authority to employ physical restraint: left-right, one-two; make-up forbidden and the locks taken off the lavatory doors: whom one could not reach by any method save through the strong hand.

He himself had had to study these subjects – only name for them – for his diploma in juvenile police work. He had seen the patient efforts made to reach them through love and understanding, the carefully simple schools for the overwhelming proportion of backward, near-illiterate, fringe-mentally-deficients. In his days on the streets in uniform he had been one of three tough agents held at bay by two of these girls with broken beer-bottles. Against his own judgement he had used the rubber stick, to stun the biceps muscle – as developed as a butcher's.

He thought of the girls who defaced library books with the painfully scored obscene graffiti of the obstinately illiterate; who if allowed to use a swimming pool promptly urinated in it. Would we have to send Hannie Troost in with that? She could not help being blonde, pretty, spoilt and oversexed; those poor little devils could no more help what they were. One was the product of a modern society, which we have created to replace the other – now obsolete, mercifully. But was this really better than the other had been?

And what would the Government do, timid, old-fashioned, parsimonious? We have as good a government here as anywhere in the world, caring deeply about education, social care, enlightenment. But how long has it taken to reduce, to the minimum intake of the feeble-minded and physically abnormal, our prisons for women? Now, we are going to refill them, with girls like Lina. And would they be kept apart, the Linas and Carmens and Paulas – and Marta, who liked sex – and wretched little Troost, from the toughs milling round the pig-trough?

He rocked what was left of the beer round in the glass to try and freshen it up. It stayed flat but he drank it off, shrugging. Beer was like life. The spark went quickly out of it.

There is an inevitable price to pay, perhaps, for the highest birth-rate in Europe and the wonderful children we are so proud of. Here in Holland we never used to have much trouble; we believed always in large families and a very strong, tight life within that pattern; but now we are getting progressive, hm? Mothers who have only one child and go out to work themselves to buy their clothes, because Pa's wage will only barely cover the car payments. This blasted Bloemendaal might be a microcosm of what Holland will become – unless we watch out.

What was that English law? Parkinson, that was it. The more bureaucrats there were, the more work became available to occupy them – heer jé, that Parkinson must have Dutch blood. Now was there a Van-der-Valk law too? The fewer children and the more leisure for parents, the less time there is for caring for them. Both laws operated on the same principle, and both, he thought, are true of Holland. And yet we have so much to hope for. When I am not a policeman I am father of two boys. How do I think about them?

These children are what we look to, to make a revolution, huh? – to refuse to repeat the imbecilities of their elders. One hopes that of every new generation. Is one always disappointed? Are they only good when young? – say, below twenty-three. Is there any sign of progress from the boys in 1848, who went to the barricades to sweep Louis Philippe from Paris, to those in Hungary, in 1954? It's the same old world. Once they grow up they find good reasons for perpetuating the old infamies.

Yes, but the best are killed, always; the best never survive to become the judges, the law-makers. Were they? Was the best of France killed on the Chemin des Dames and in front of Verdun? Was the best of Germany bleached bones in Russia? And we have not that excuse, he thought; in Holland we had no such holocausts.

I wonder whether we are in consequence doomed, so to speak, genetically, to a higher proportion of monkeys like Jansen?

We will have headlines on this story soon, he thought, proclaiming the misdeeds of these dozen children to a shocked, but lip-licking country. But who would notice, really notice? And a week, a month later, when there would be little paragraphs in weeklies in France and Switzerland, in Argentina and in Russia (of course; their Press attaché would be entranced), full of holy sorrow for the sins of others? Who would notice there, either?

And Feodora. Lucky that she was out and could be kept out. Just the type of person bureaucracy does not approve of. A foreigner – damning, that. Disorderly too, without proper papers, without solid reassuring ways and proper respects, with altogether too much liking for independence. A common public prostitute too, who certainly brought grave disrepute to fair townships like Bloemendaal aan Zee. Van der Valk spat, viciously, into his waste-paper basket.

Undesirable aliens; deport them. Oh, so this one has seen the light, and taken herself off, has she? Good riddance. Feodora had been well pestered by that devoted defender of civic virtue, Commissaris Marcousis; she herself had been able to laugh at the hypocrisy of life, but not always easily. Now was there a sneaky truth buried here? One of those inconvenient thoughts that come in the middle of the night? Was it perhaps barely possible that Spain, fascist Spain, was after all a more civilised country than Holland the champion of liberty, where the first principle of the constitution is that no man shall be preferred or rejected on the grounds of his beliefs? Than Her Majesty's most holy Kingdom of the Netherlands?

Frans Mierle had said that of course it was true. He had said that in Spain independence and individuality were still prized, and that bureaucrats were even sometimes defeated. In other countries – like here, he had said – we have got very rich, and nobody ever laughs any more. He had said that Spain was the country for Feodora. I hope, thought Van der Valk, that this is true.

*

There was no great difficulty in disposing of the ravens. Within two days they had all given way at the knees; twenty-four hours after that they had all passed under the carnivorous eye of the Officer of Justice and taken up residence in the House of Keeping. Till the paper work got done. Most of this, despite Boersma's hopes, had to be done in Bloemendaal, and it was taking a very long time. The examining magistrate there had gone into a perfect paroxysm of outrage, and all that Van der Valk had feared was coming to pass – noisy, pompous and sententious as a bad German orchestra. Poor old Marcousis.

Frans Mierle, who knew so many people personally, had been kept under arrest three days, charged with illegal possession of an offensive weapon – but not with unlawful wounding – prosecuted in front of the kantonrechter, or local police court, with notable lack of fire, sentenced to a month in prison (suspended) and promptly released. His lawyer turned his considerable abilities to representing the ravens, and the pot containing Jansen started to get warm with all the crackling of thorns that went on. He was in hospital all this time; his knee had been very thoroughly smashed.

Marcousis had tried questioning him, had not come terribly well out of it, and had sent two different inspectors of the recherche to try again, with no better result. Rather a humiliation for the Bloemendaal bureau; the goddam fellow not only refused to admit anything; he refused to say any word at all. Boersma found out about this discomfiture of the police, and laughed rather spitefully. The Officer of Justice had not seen him at all yet, though the sharpened knives lay ready. He was kept strictly 'au secret' by that functionary's orders; in a private room of the local hospital, with a police officer on twenty-four-hour watch by the bedside – a most unpopular tour of duty. He had not even been properly charged yet. No lawyer, no talk; silence; occasional contemptuous or sarcastic remarks. This, and the stupid fellow's damned leg, was holding everybody up and getting greatly on everybody's nerves. Without Jansen, nobody quite knew what to prosecute anyone else for, exactly. Marcousis came over to Amsterdam for a conference about this with Mr Boersma.

'These boys must be tried. It must be finished and done with, dammit; there's been too much hawing and hanging about already, by half. I've talked about it to the examining magistrate here. Now he takes quite a reasonable view; you'll notice we're civilised here, Marcousis. That so-called Officer of so-called Justice you have over there is not a lawyer; he's a sport, a goddam throwback; ought to be in a museum along with his antediluvian ideas. Old Johannes here went into a huddle with the Procureur Général, and the result is that he's prepared to prosecute from quite a liberal angle, and accept that there is a strict limit of responsibility even before the point is argued on the parquet. But Sailer won't have all the blame just shoved on to Jansen as a handy scapegoat. The fellow must of course be given the opportunity of defending himself, and without knowing at least what he proposes to say and do we can't get on here; can't even start. The defence lawyers have been bombarding Sailer with demands that Jansen should actually be tried before what they call 'his victims'. You'll have to get the bugger out on a crutch or something.'

Marcousis' voice was jagged with grievance.

'The doctor says he'll be fit to move in a day or so, and he told me privately that he'd consider discharging him from hospital in another week, if all goes well, of course.' Don't blame me, the voice said; I didn't shoot him. 'He was badly smashed, you know; nerves and ligaments and so on; he wasn't to move. You can't just drag a man in that condition up the steps of the Palais.'

'Quite, quite,' Boersma's voice disregarded the grievance. 'We know that you don't get a nine-millimetre bullet smack through you at ten feet with no more than a curse and a good scratch. It's the handling that seems to me negative; he's getting an idea that we are helpless to shake him up as long as he lies there comfortably talking about his poor sad knee.'

'What is to be done? I'm perfectly open to suggestion. He won't talk. The procès-verbal is complete; once we have him on his feet he can go before the Officer, be charged, get his precious lawyer, and we can go to town, or the prosecutor can; it'll be out of my hands then, thank heaven.'

'Yes, certainly. I should like, however, to have less waiting on Mr Jansen's convenience. Put on some pressure; puncture his self-esteem a little. Any objection to my office having a little go at him?'

'None whatever. If you can make any headway no doubt the prosecutor will be pleased; he's fairly foaming at the mouth.'

'What I have in mind is sending Van der Valk over there. You know how he is – talk your trousers back to front while you're sitting still. Jansen knows him, knows that he's a dangerous man. Pushed him off balance before; that's what I want to happen now. Shake him loose, and perhaps we can get something done to break this deadlock. Van der Valk won't like it, of course. He was unhappy; felt he'd boobed over there in Bloemendaal. Maybe I did have criticisms of the way he handled things; I generally do. He doesn't exactly go to work by the book, and he's a sensitive cop, heaven preserve us. But he gets results. Got a good record of doing the wrong thing and coming up with the right answer. And between you and me, Marcousis, he got you out of the cart there.'

'Don't think I have any criticisms of your chief inspector, Commissaris,' said Marcousis hastily. 'I'm the first, believe, to appreciate his help. And recall that I pitched in a strong official commendation of his handling of the whole affair, to show my thanks for his co-operation and to forestall any possible query or complaint from the magistrate.'

'Good, then, it's understood. He won't like it perhaps, but when it's pointed out to him that he can get away on holiday when this business with the boys is finished with, he won't be naughty.'

*

A typical hospital room. Small and severe, but sunny and airy. A bed with its bottom end wound up; a cradle under aseptic bedclothes; distempered walls and a Van Gogh print, carefully labelled 'Farmhouse near Arles'. No radio, no newspapers. Pity we can't bring over the sugar-candy nudes, thought Van der Valk; make him feel at home. No flowers, no visitors, no conversations with nurses. A curt police doctor accompanying the surgeon when he inspected the wound, which was done in a deep-freeze of hygiene and silence.

Van der Valk took his coat off leisurely. The showery, windy weather smelt good through the open window, of earth and fresh leaves and liberty; the hospital garden was a riot of flowers. In defiance of a strict order on a large printed notice, Van der Valk had picked an early rosebud, and stuck it in his buttonhole, feeling like Mr Nehru come to visit the aged and infirm. Flashing false smiles. I've brought you some narcissus, Sissi.

Jansen lay flat like a malevolent sick bird, quite ready to bite the hand that fed it, with moulting feathers. A horribly bored policeman in uniform, from the Bloemendaalse bureau, was doing a crossword puzzle. The Officer of Justice had ordered that he should be allowed no writing materials, no contact with anybody except functionaries. Library books and nothing else. Any remarks he made were to be taken down. The police guard had offered to play chess with him, but had been snubbed. Van der Valk walked up to the bed, radiating health and hateful bonhomie, and looked down at his adversary.

'Good morning.' Silence. 'I see. Silent as gold, excellent. But you know me. We're old friends. No need of that.' Silence.

'Why?' The vicious yellow eye rolled over towards the policeman, who had dropped his crossword on the entry of his superior officer, and was trying to look alert and intelligent, with his shorthand pad on his knee.

'You can skip off out for a walk,' said Van der Valk pleasantly.

'Yes, but my orders, Chief Inspector . . .'

'Your orders are to take down what he says, right?'

'That's right, Chief, and – '

'And as long as you're here he doesn't say anything for you to take down. I'll ring for you when I'm ready; I can write too. Piss off.'

The policeman retreated, clutching his notebook with a dignified air of affront. 'Idiots,' said Van der Valk to the closed door.

He walked round the room, looked out of the window a long while without speaking, studied the charts pinned on the board, like a man with time to kill.

'You'll talk to me, if I want you to,' he said, uninterestedly, at last. 'I don't think you have anything to say, of any great value. Temperature normal all this last week, bowels nicely open; you're doing fine. No need to sit there like a hen on an egg. Tomorrow you'll be up. A week from today you'll be on parade at the Palace of Justice. Knee-joint immobilised – it'll feel a bit odd at first but you'll soon accustom yourself. It'll be the same all your life after all; souvenir of happy days in Bloemendaal.'

His voice got stronger as he warmed up. Talkative bugger, as all his superior officers throughout his career had never failed to remind him.

'Perhaps you'll be able to kid people you got it from the Russians, like the disabled veterans in German post offices. The bloom of eternal youth is gone, I'm afraid. Exit Dorian Gray, reappear as Veteran Jansen. You've found out at last that guns are naughty things; they shoot you. Of course you're going to find Holland a little small for you. No more night clubs, of course. Even the post office would shake their head. You might manage to get to South America – until some policeman takes it into his head to ring us up. This time, it's going to stick. I'm looking a bit far ahead, I know. You'll have plenty of time to make plans, because you're going to be out of circulation a good while. The silence hasn't improved the prosecutor's temper, and it hasn't improved Mr Sailer's opinion of you either. You know the name? – yes, the Procureur Général, in Amsterdam: he takes an interest. Big operation ahead on Mr Jansen, without benefit of anaesthetic this time. Do more to you than just your poor knee.

'We realise that you're training yourself, just as you tried to train the boys. Tough nut, huh? They can kill me but they can't eat me. We like that; we don't have to feel delicate at being a bit rough. It looks bad; as though it's going to be pretty tough on you.

'While we were polishing the parquet ready for you, I thought I'd take a stroll over, and see how your vanity, that remarkable conceit of yours, would react to a bit of tea and sympathy. Not everybody will be as direct about this as Frans Mierle was – though you'll find the court quite direct enough. Of course, putting a bullet in you was hardly fair, and we've rapped his fingers for that; told him that respectable people in this town don't carry guns. So many respectable people in this town – you'd hardly credit it.

'All those, now, who used to come to the Ange Gabriel to drink with you – friendly lot, weren't they? – all tut-tutting now over the papers, sweating at the idea that it might have been *their* dirty little vices made public. And naturally, to show how unstained they are, they're particularly censorious towards you. Can't altogether blame them. Their private lives are not exactly Persil-fresh, of course, but they're dewy virgin violets compared to yours.

'It's the way people react to different things – seems haphazard but with experience like mine, for instance, one gets to know what they will turn against. You'll remember a few years ago, the man who put a new phrase into the language. 'Het goede Heertje' – the kind gentleman – the whole country called him that, remember? Sensational crime – nation-wide publicity – very like your instance here. There wasn't a man or a woman anywhere that didn't laugh and wish him luck. He got hundreds of letters of encouragement and sympathy. What had he done? – what everyone would like to do. Lived like a prince and been generous to the poor. The fact that he'd embezzled a tidy few thousand bothered nobody, outside the walls of the Palais.

'Pity you can't see the letters you're getting. Bloodthirsty – poor you. They'd lynch you. It is their daughters you seduced, you clever fellow, their sons you corrupted.

'I'd like to take you for a day to Amsterdam, just to ride through the streets. You know how the boys there take up any character that strikes their fancy. The harbour workers – or the bus-conductors, best of all. They'd fix you so you wouldn't enjoy a girl again, my boy. Or the girls, say, from any of the factories. I could hardly find myself being sorry for you, but in their hands I almost think I might. The master gangster. Discipline, ruthlessness, and of course romance – the public image of you is different, somehow.

'The Press coverage, too. Getting a little acid, and tending now to jokes. Little rhymes by Clinge, sayings by Alexander Pola. The jokes are harder to bear than the abuse, aren't they? You never intended to finish as a joke. Or a term of insult among butchers' boys. The bird-fancier, the white-slave angel. "Got any cat-food?" they shout. You remember the Congo, and how the lorry-drivers used to yell, "Get out of it, Lumumba"? New one now: "Come on, Jansen, buy a barge." Popular celebrity, you are. I thought it would do your vanity good to tell you. Cheer you up.

'This silence of yours – a clever tactic, you've thought, doubtless. It hasn't been altogether well received. A reporter asked the Officer of Justice "whether perhaps a cat had got your tongue?" The magistrate was not greatly amused, but pretty well every paper in the country picked that one up. Or you know how the bus-conductors have their own language? These days it's all kattekop, kattekwaad, kattetongen. And the gutter urchins – they've got a naughty song. Vulgar – they are inclined to be vulgar, not civilised like you and me. All about greasing the cat's arse. You see, I don't want you to lie here deceiving yourself thinking it's going to work, your big plan.

'Have you realised yet that there's no longer anything left of your fantasy world? When I got the story it didn't surprise me at all. The goddess Astarte – out of a child's story-book. Black magic stuff – always has a great appeal to the immature mind. A schoolboy with toys – ships and swords and cannons, and a bit of romantic sentimentalised pornography. That picture on your bedroom wall – a poor substitute for a real woman.

'You've never had much luck with women, have you? They aren't very satisfactory when they prefer the schoolboy type. But of course you went over well with the girls; the little Troost one was just your cup of tea – oh yes, I noticed the resemblance between her and the lollipop on your bedroom wall. All that blonde hair, and a bottom like a boy's – sensational. The others had given you a real schoolboy appetite for green fruit; you couldn't keep away from that.

'So having played with all these kids, who shared your tastes for romance, you decided to play with adults. With professionals. With me. Look where it's got you.

'You've already had your knee busted by one adult – the game here's a bit rough, you find? You've had a nice lie in bed, and this babyish refusal to talk has made you feel that you're not beaten yet, that you still have a chance. Ha. Won't talk indeed. You've seen that without opening your mouth I can read your immature little mind like print.

'It's the grand gesture, that's what we're waiting for from you. A romantic gesture. For you to get up and say, "It's a far far better thing." Just a day or two now, and you'll be ripe for the far-flung far-far stuff. Wait till you're in that romantic prison cell, and the boys walk in, in their romantic big boots. You know why you haven't been charged yet? Because the police want a go at you first. Whatever you do have to say, you'll tell us, before we turn you over to the Officer of Justice. And if necessary, we'll kick it out of you, my bird-taming cat-fancier. The doctor says you're all well again. We'll see each other soon, sonny.' Without waiting for an answer or even looking at the glaring yellow eye in the bed, Van der Valk picked up his coat and walked out.

*

It was the following day; he was busy in his office, with one of the perennial nuisances in parks, which the police classify as 'old men offering sweeties'. Burrr went his phone; he picked it up without a thought.

'Van der Valk. . . . No, Mr Boersma's not in. Put him on. . . . Hallo, Commissaris, how are you? . . . You don't say. . . . What with? . . . The same one? . . . Where did he have it hidden? . . . Yes, yes, I know; makes a nonsense of the guard though, doesn't it? . . . What did the magistrate say? . . . Yes, I can well believe that . . . but the lawyers will be happy, huh? Tacit admission of guilt, can be written in to the record. . . .' Boersma was putting his nose round the door; Van der Valk covered the receiver and hissed 'Marcousis.' The voice in the earphone quacked. . . .

'Why not? It's the trouble of a trial saved. Naughty for your end, I realise, but there are consolations though, aren't there? . . . Thanks. . . . Details on the telex, right. . . . Yes, yes, of course. . . . No, no, naturally. . . . Quite understand. . . . Yes, I'll tell Mr Boersma. . . . Yes. . . . 'Bye.'

He grinned at his chief, with a disgusted face.

'That Marcousis. I don't know what's wrong with him and his half-baked staff, but this time there'll be an enquiry for sure. Jansen has shot himself; I'm by God glad that there were no witnesses to what I said to him. I more or less told him to, thinking of course that they'd be watching out for just that. Stupid bastards. All I wanted was to puncture his conceit; I was rough with him.'

Boersma's reaction was typical. 'Lot of paper work saved.'

But Van der Valk was troubled. 'Jesus, Chief, how was I to know? That little gun, the silver-plated thing, the six-thirty-five that was taken with the Lüger. They didn't turn it up in Jansen's flat, so assumed he'd ditched it. Now I ask you. He had it, as far as they can see, tucked into one of those leather cases that hold shaving kits. Admitted, it's both small and flat, but how they missed it . . .'

'Not for you to worry. Sloppy security. I understand – you're upset at the thought of another death as the result of your interference, put it like that. I take full responsibility – the death was called for – direct result of the other. And nobody knows – and only I guess – what you said to the fellow. Don't get emotional. Wait till you've been forty years in the police force, like me. You can afford emotions, then.'

'Their excuse is that a bagful of things was brought to the hospital with the ambulance, when they first brought him in. The first-aid johnny just chucked pyjamas and stuff in a bag. In the excitement it was not minutely checked – oh, just washing things; that stuff. They started letting him go to the lavatory at the end of the corridor because they wanted him to exercise the leg a little, and tac. . . . It looks bad for them; au secret, under twenty-four-hour watch, and he shoots himself. Marcousis wet his trousers.'

Boersma broke into a slow grin.

'I'd be ready to bet,' he said craftily, 'that you may be upset, but you aren't really unhappy.'

Van der Valk thought about that. At last one side of his mouth curled unwillingly.

'Well; it can after all be said that it's the best possible solution for everybody, I suppose. And speaking purely selfishly, it might also mean that I get away on holiday a month earlier, mightn't it? And I know that it's not very kind, but I do get a kind of horrible satisfaction watching Marcousis talk his way out of it.'

*

By a day or so later he was nearly happy, and going home a week or so afterwards, after the boys had been brought to trial, he had performed a familiar conjuring trick, and put police business out of his head.

'What's to eat?'

'Larded liver,' said Arlette, 'and I know you're fond of that. And there's a parcel for you; messenger service. I haven't undone it. Big and heavy – here; do you know anything about it?'

'I've no idea what it can be.' He was kneeling down immediately, opening his knife, full of curiosity. Under the lid of a sturdy cardboard carton was a large printed card.

'With the compliments of Mierle N.V.' There was no personal message, which was just as well. Policemen are not allowed to accept presents. . . .

Inside the carton, neatly packed, was a brand new aqualung.